Copyright 2011 Patricia Lynne
Cover art and Design by Keary Taylor

This book is licensed for your personal enjoyment only and is a work of fiction. Any names, characters, places or incidents are products of the author's imagination, and used fictitiously. Any resemblance to actual persons, living or dead, businesses, events or locales is entirely coincidental.

Acknowledgements:

A huge thanks goes to Erin Bachand, for reading through each draft and helping me figure out the best way to tell this story. Thanks to my cheerleader and writing partner in crime, CJ Cook, to all my beta readers, Mary Beth, Marni, Dan, Brad, and Cynthia. Without you, this story wouldn't have shined as brightly. Thanks to Keary Taylor for the beautiful cover. I get giddy every time I look at it. Thanks to Cassie Robertson for editing it. I am utterly hopeless when it comes to punctuation. Lastly, thanks to all my readers, the ones who read my ramblings on my blog and the ones who read this story.

Thanks for reading
Paula
Patricia

Part One: Brothers

It is said vampires forget their human lives. As soon as they are turned, the memories start fading. One theory is because of need. The need to sate the hunger and thirst overtakes their senses. It consumes their thoughts and washes every little bit of humanity away until they no longer remember their human life. Another theory is that their mind changes too much. They no longer know how to think, move, talk or feel like a human. The final theory is that they simply let it go. They aren't human anymore, so what's the point of remembering?

Maybe it's a combination of the three.

What I do know is that vampires forget being human. *I* forgot being human. Can't even remember the biggest details. Did I get along with my parents or was I a bad seed? Was I good in school? Did I enjoy sports? Did I have lots of friends? Or maybe even a girlfriend?

I don't know any more or care. Why should I? That human life is behind me, forgotten with the first taste of blood.

Guess the first theory is accurate. Wake up in the evening with thirst burning in my throat and lay down at dawn with it simmering in my stomach. Sometimes I feel like a junkie, always looking for my next hit, my next meal – a victim, according to humans.

There are some things from my human life that matter a lot. Events, places and one human in particular I can't forget. I know these things because they happened *after* I was turned.

The first thing that came to me, when I woke in a small clearing in the woods, was the darkness. It was dark, but at the same time... not. I could see everything, every tiny detail was clear as if illuminated by light. But there was no light, not even moonlight. I stumbled around the small clearing, disoriented as the world bombarded me with sensations.

A gentle breeze howled in my ears and felt like talons ripping across my cheeks. The world beneath me felt unstable, as if it slowly rotated. When I reached to touch the ground, the grass beneath my fingers felt uneven and sharp, biting into my skin. I jerked my hand away, drawing a breath, and the smells hit me like a hammer. Dirt, grass, rocks, trees and animals that were no longer there. Hundreds of scents hung in the air; my nose twitching as it took every scent in and my mind distinguished everything.

As I stood in this familiar – yet alien – world, I felt my memories start to fade away. What had happened in the clearing was the first to disappear. I didn't try to hold onto it. *Just a dream*, I told myself. That couldn't have happened to me. I needed to get home before I was grounded.

Maybe I had been a bad seed.

The journey home felt like it took forever, but in reality, took a matter of minutes. I stopped often. First because my new sight had me stumbling, but, as I grew accustomed to it, my stops became ones of confusion. Where was I going? The answer was home, but I grasped for a reason why. Did I need something there? A drink? Could it be that simple? After all, my throat burned as if I had swallowed a mouthful of hot coals. A need to quench that fire burned in my mind, driving me forward.

When I reached home, only a sliver of human denial persisted. *It's a bad dream, get a glass of water and go to bed*, it whispered. But a much more insistent part of me screamed, *Get inside and satisfy your thirst!*

Welcomed home, my parents fussed over me. My mother sighed I needed to get to bed and my father scowled and scolded me for being irresponsible. Why had I disappeared without telling them where I was going? Didn't I know vampires were waiting in the shadows to feed on the unsuspecting?

Humans knew that vampires existed. It had been an accident, an unintentional slip on the old vampire's part. Tired of existing, she sat outside to wait for the sun. The rays washed over her and her body burst into flame while a tourist bus witnessed the event. The tourist company called the news stations, a few reporters investigated and found all that remained of the vampire – a pile of ashes. The ashes were sent to some scientists for testing. The scientists discovered the ashes used to be human, but there was something not quite right – not quite human – about them. Then a video taken by one of tourists surfaced on the Internet, next national news and it became open season on vampires.

After that, any vampire discovered was caught, bound and left to greet the morning sun. Or set on fire. Anything to make the vampire burn until nothing remained but a pile of ash. Scientists gathered the ashes to study and figure out how to best destroy a vampire. It was, of course, an *approved* genocide. Who would protest the killing of a creature so evil?

Now comes the part in the story where I'm expected to say everything turned out okay. My family was horrified I had been turned, but accepted me as a vampire and we hid it well.

That's not what happened. What happened was I hid in my room, huddled in the corner, as the overwhelming vampiric instinct washed away the last remnants of my human life. There was only one thought and it consumed me: Hunger.

The hunger devoured every thought, dominating my mind with its heat. It drove me out of my room and into the dark hallway. Rhythms echoed in my ears, sounding like a drum set that beat just for me. Maybe the rhythm was instinct, telling me what to do and where to go. At the time, all that mattered was the overwhelming hunger and how I knew exactly what would quench it.

When I opened the door to the room that contained the loudest rhythms, it didn't make a sound.

The next few moments were the best of my new vampire life. Blood and heat, life slipping into death, all flowing into me like a river I couldn't get enough of. I wasn't aware of who I was feeding on, only that I was quenching the hunger and need. It was the most blissful thing I could do. No longer did I care about the humans who had been my parents. They meant only one thing to me now: sustenance.

With my fangs deep in the human's neck, something came to me. A warm hand touched my shoulder and a rhythm behind me beckoned. I abandoned the dead woman in my arms, letting her fall to the beige carpet next to the lifeless male. Both were already forgotten as I turned to face the human behind me.

The rhythm halted and the noises stopped. Not a single creak or chirp was heard. Every breath stopped as the world paused. This human…

He looked just like me!

I wasn't sure how I knew that. The human memory of what I looked like had faded away, but I felt deep down, where my heart lay, I looked like him. Dark brown hair, fair skin, rosy cheeks and eyes as blue as the sky. He was skinny too, sinewy and lanky. His voice would be mine as well; we were identical. Or used to be.

He looked like a healthy human boy and I knew that I didn't. My skin had to be pale with a permanent sheen of death on it. Where my eyes still that blue?

A tormented look shone in his blue eyes. His fingers grazed my cheek like he was afraid I wasn't real. Then he whispered one word and everything changed.

My brother said my name.

A weight slammed into me, crushing me with ugly realization. The humans behind me were more than blood. They had been my parents and I had murdered them. Worse than that, I had been planning murdering my brother as well. The thought ripped through me like a tornado. My eyes twitched and my throat tightened like I was going to cry.

Tears never came; my eyes stayed dry and I whispered, "Danny, what have I done?"

"It's okay," he said, instead of answering. He knelt in front of me, his eyes locked on mine and his hands on my shoulders. "It's okay," he said my name again. "You're going to be okay. Just relax."

"How?" I asked, unable to grasp the concept of relaxing. The idea of emotions felt foreign, like they no longer applied to me. My voice must have sounded void of emotions because my brother's face wavered and I heard whispers of his thoughts.

They say vampires stop caring. Has he already stopped caring about me?

I considered answering his thought, but said something else. "I can't stay here."

"Why not?"

His eyes were still locked on mine. Humans should never look into a vampire's eyes. Thoughts whisper from behind the eyes, telling the vampire what the human is thinking, enabling the vampire to take control of those thoughts and bend the human's will.

"You can't be seen with me," I said, but I thought to myself, *I'm terrified I'll kill you.* I didn't want to scare him. He was acting so reserved; his voice didn't tremble, his face was calm and there was no fear in his scent. Any other human would have panicked, started screaming, and the smell of their fear would have been like a drug I couldn't resist.

Maybe he knew it was vital to stay calm. He knew that, as my twin, I wouldn't want to kill him, that I couldn't – which was why I stopped when he touched me. The horror I had felt about murdering my parents was fading. There would be no guilt over their deaths or for any of my victims to come. It is the reason that humans believe vampires have no feelings. They say we are cold and emotionless monsters.

That's a lie.

Love, hate or sorrow; a vampire still feels them. Our reactions are simply different, faster and often missed by humans. If I had harmed my brother that night, I knew I would have felt the emotions. Guilt and anger would have torn at me, demanding to know why I had hurt him.

"I don't care who sees," he said. "You can't leave me. We have to stick together."

I shoved him away, my strength sending him flying across the room. He landed against a wooden dresser with a cry of pain. The sound tore at me, but I didn't dare turn back. I dove out the window, landing on my feet and sprinting away. Behind me, I heard him yell my name, his voice filled with anguish.

"I have to leave," I said as I ran, knowing he wouldn't be able to hear me. "Your brother is dead and there's only me now."

****

I ended up in the woods outside the town I was certain I had lived in as a human. I wandered among the trees until the sky started to lighten. Digging with my bare hands, I dug deep into the ground where it was cool and quiet. I drifted through the day in half awareness, but never really asleep. You don't need to sleep when you're dead. You only need to lay still and rest.

As the day passed, I wondered. Not about the vampire who turned me – that no longer mattered. Vampires aren't loving parents who stay by your side to watch over you and make sure you get everything right. No, they bite and drain you, leaving you to turn and wake alone and confused and to figure everything out for yourself. I guess instinct is enough to keep any vampire *alive*.

My mind wondered again and again about my brother. I couldn't help myself; my thoughts returned to him unbidden.

There were no memories other than the ones from the night before. Anything else about him I felt. Love and caring, concern over his wellbeing. I felt connected to him; I didn't want to be away from him. I knew he felt the same for me; I had seen it in his eyes in our parents' room. Even in death, the twin bond was strong.

When the sun began to set, my body vibrated with energy. Eagerly, I dug myself up and shook the dirt off. My first thought was to feed. Hunger lay curled inside me like a beast and I remembered how good it had felt to feed. Heat had coursed through me, giving me a surge of energy that strengthened me and made me feel more than alive.

Then I remembered my brother.

Somehow, like I knew who he was when I saw him, I knew he wouldn't want me to kill and that mattered to me. What he wanted shouldn't matter, I knew, but it did. He was important to me and the urge to not disappoint him gnawed at me.

"I want to feed!" I told the night sky. Pacing back and forth, I tried to figure out how to get the blood I needed. No, it wasn't need fueling me, it was want.

How?

How could I feed and not sadden my brother?

I felt it was impossible; I couldn't feed without hurting him. Frustrated and confused, I slammed my fist into a tree and sent bark flying as the dry wood splintered. With a growl, I shoved the tree, sending it crashing to the ground.

"Why do you have to matter?" I shouted. "Why can't I forget you like I've forgotten everything else? I'm not human! I don't want to be!"

The words froze me. Already I didn't want to be human? That was how fast vampire instinct worked? Washing everything human away in a matter of hours until there was left nothing but a lethal predator? I couldn't even grasp the concept I was once human.

I sank to the forest floor, ignoring the urge to hunt and drink blood, and letting the night slip by. Bats flew above, crickets chirped, the stars sparkled and the moon shone. I ignored it all, lost in thought over the puzzle of my brother and my hunger.

Eventually I rose. Enough musing and agonizing over my brother; it was time to satisfy myself. No destination or plan in mind, I headed out of the woods and into the town. I knew what I was going to do and how to do it. There was no rush.

Well, maybe a little rush. With only so many hours in the night, I couldn't afford to waste too much time. There were more hours during the day, but I would be useless then.

The streets were deserted, all humans inside their homes, so I moved outward, hanging along the roads. Cars sped by and I raced to catch one. Above the drone of the engine, the rhythm of four hearts beat. Tempting, but I wanted to take it easy. I dropped back to wait for another car. The next one had a single human in it, one rhythm beating. I picked up my pace, pushing to match the speed of the car, and jumped.

I landed silently on the roof of the little sedan. The wind whipped around me, wild and chaotic. I paused for a moment, enjoying the feeling. It felt pure. Nothing could corrupt the wind or stop it. Unlike the rhythm beating below me.

Music muffled through the roof, the rhythm of the human's heart almost keeping beat to the tune. *Is it not enough/Is it not enough/Everything that was said/Everything that was done/In the end I gave all I had/Sacrificing all I loved for you/And I forgave you for it all.*

The last line stuck in my head, a truth ringing in the words.

I had murdered my parents and thought about killing my brother and yet he didn't hate me. I wasn't necessarily sure that was right. How would I have felt if it had been my brother who was turned and murder our parents?

With no memories to indicate how I should feel, I turned my attention to the human below me. Quickly, I smashed the passenger side window and the human inside screamed. The car swerved, out of control, and into the other lane. Moving quickly, I slid through the shattered window, instinct directing me. My gaze connected with the human's and I pushed my will against hers. The car slowed to a stop, pulling to the side. The human didn't move, her gaze locked on me and her thoughts blank from the force of my will. I did not want her thinking about dying. That would only make her struggle.

Maybe it was because my first kill had been my sleeping parents. They hadn't been conscious, there was no struggling or screaming, and that had imprinted on me. Or maybe I liked the idea that if the human submitted to my will and stayed calm, I could enjoy the blood more. Savor the taste instead of trying to contain a frightened human.

The fear never left her eyes as I moved closer. I thought about reassuring her, saying it that was all right and it would be over quickly. But it felt like it'd be in vain. My words would be a lie. She would disagree that killing her was *all right*.

I had to say something though. I felt like my brother would want me to. He'd rather me say, *I'm sorry* or *Nothing personal*. A small reassurance instead of nothing.

But those words wouldn't help, my mind reasoned as my lips touched her neck.

I should say something though, I argued.

Then it didn't matter.

It didn't matter what my brother thought or how scared this human felt. Didn't matter if a torch-baring mob surrounded me. My teeth were buried in her neck, the crimson blood pulsing onto my tongue and flowing down my throat. My want and yearning was satisfied. That was all that mattered as I fell further and further into the rhythm of blood.

****

I left the dead human in her car on the side of the road. It was fine where it was, where it would be found. That's how it should be, I mused. Vampires fed on humans and leave the bodies so the other humans could bury them.

Why did humans bury their dead?

The question took me aback and I knew I should know the answer. I must have known the answer when I was human.

"It doesn't matter!" I yelled at the world around me.

Why was I talking to nature? I should be in a good mood. I just fed and the human had delicious blood. What would humans compare it to? What foods were considered a luxurious treat? More answers forgotten.

Why couldn't I forget my brother?

As if on cue, a faint breeze carried a scent. It drifted to me, surrounding me and tickling my nose. I turned and followed it like a sailor would a beacon to safety. As I ran, the scent intensified, growing more pungent in the dark air. It seeped into my surroundings, embedding itself in the trees and the ground. The scent said it belonged here; my brother belonged here. Why?

Was it because I was here?

The sound of water gently lapping broke the silence as I ran. I changed direction slightly and moved toward the water, knowing he would be near it. The trees around me thinned, opening up to a large field. No, it wasn't a field, it was a yard.

A few hundred feet ahead, on the edge of a lake, a cabin stood bathed in the light of a half moon. The sides were rough-hewn wood with windows cut into them, a chimney nestled against one side of the peaked roof, and a porch stretched across the length of the front of the cabin, uneven steps leading to it. Nothing adorned the porch, no chairs, tables or mats.

"I knew you'd remember this."

I turned to find my brother standing at the edge of the lake. His shoes were off, pants rolled up as the water lapped at his toes. Across the lake were more cabins, a few with twinkling lights. If I listened closely, I could make out the rhythms beating inside them.

"I don't remember. I only caught your scent and followed," I replied.

"Oh." His shoulders slumped. He perked up a little. "You still came."

"I didn't want another to find you."

"Another what?"

"Vampire. Because if one's going to kill you, it should be me."

His eyes widened, his mouth opened in shock and he croaked one word, "Oh."

I looked at him, seeing and smelling his fear. "I wouldn't do that though."

"Oh," he repeated, not so horrified.

"I don't want you dead."

"Oh?"

"No," I confirmed and paused, considering my next words. "You're my brother. I don't remember being your brother, but I feel it. It's why I stopped when you touched me. I saw you and knew who you were." I looked at him, catching his gaze. "I won't let anyone hurt you. If they do, I'll kill them."

The Adam's apple in his neck bobbed as he swallowed. "You don't have to do that."

I tilted my head. "Why not?"

Another bob of his Adam's apple was accompanied with a step backward. "You look creepy when you tilt your head. It looks like you're thinking about eating me."

I untilted my head. "It's crossed my mind."

"But you said you didn't want me dead." His voice was slow and uncertain.

"I don't," I assured him. "I can bite and not kill. I choose not to."

For a long moment he was silent. Emotion flashed across his face: confusion, fear and anger. His words seemed carefully chosen when he finally spoke. "You *choose* not to... So you don't *have* to kill, but you do because you *want* to?"

Before I could answer, he turned away from me and headed back to the cabin. I followed him, wondering why he didn't want to hear my answer. Should I have lied to him? There was no reason to lie to him. Lying was pointless.

He tugged his shoes on, unrolled his pants and lay on the grass. He spread his arms above his head, eyes staring at the dark sky. I lay next to him, looking at the sparkling stars and the half moon glowing. The scene felt peaceful, full of serenity that was missing here on the ground. I wondered what it'd be like to be up there, surrounded by peace.

"Are you mad at me?"

My brother looked at me and I realized that the question had come from *me*.

"No," he said. "I'm trying to understand you. It's unnerving, seeing you this way. So emotionless and void. You say everything in a matter-of-fact tone, like it's the truth and there's nothing I can do about it."

"I feel emotions."

"You don't sound like it."

I sat up, looking at him. He stared back up at me, waiting. I smiled and still he remained silent.

"Well?" I asked.

"What?"

"I smiled."

"I didn't see you smile," he replied. "Your lips twitched. Were you smiling again?"

"I was frowning," I corrected and lay back down.

"Guess you do it too fast for me to see," he sighed.

We lapsed back into silence. The only sounds I could hear were the water lapping at the lake's edge and my brother's breathing and heartbeat. All three were steady and soothing noises. I felt like the world around us didn't matter. It was me and him and I didn't want it to end.

"Tomm–"

In a flash, I sat up, silencing him with the sudden movement. I stared at him, a feeling of unease welling in me. "Don't," I whispered, "ever say my name. Don't say mine and I won't say yours. Understand?"

"Okay." He raised an eyebrow at me. "Guess it's true what they say, vampires fear names."

"Names have power. Power to make you see what you don't want to see."

"What don't you want to see?"

I leaned closer and he shifted uncomfortably. He kept his eyes on mine, trying not to let his fear overpower him. Was that human instinct? To naturally fear vampires? Had I? It made sense. Vampires hunted humans. I hunted humans, but he was more than just blood to me. He was my brother and that was so important it trumped every vampire instinct in me.

My voice was a whisper, just loud enough for him to hear. "We don't want to see you."

****

The next night I returned to the cabin. As I wandered around the dark building, my mind shifted between my brother and my hunger. I had no intention of hunting. Last night I hadn't needed to; that was me being a glutton. The reality of vampires is that the hunger is always there, but the need – the driving force behind the hunger – isn't. Need arises once or twice a week, maybe less; it depends on the vampire.

While I waited for my brother, I peeked in the windows of the cabin, looking past the curtains. White sheets covered the furniture and the fireplace was cleaned of soot. I turned and looked at the cabins across the lake, glowing with twinkling lights. Why did this one feel abandoned?

Time ticked by as I waited, pacing across the length of the porch. The moon moved across the sky, disappearing behind the trees. Still, my brother didn't appear. I figured he'd come back. Okay, so I hadn't said anything to him about meeting at the cabin again, but I figured it was a given.

I jumped off the porch and stalked around the cabin, smelling and listening. The smell of grass, water and wood was thick in the air, but my brother's scent was fading. I headed down the gravel driveway, his fading trail leading me that way.

There was still no sign of him when the gravel turned to pavement. I kept walking, moving into the ditch in case a car passed. I could have a snack, I mused. I shook my head. No time for snacks. Not until I found my brother.

At the edge of the town, I melted into the shadows and headed to the only other place I figured he could be: our home. Yellow police tape was strung across the front door. The curtains on the first floor windows pulled tight. I climbed to the second story, finding open curtains. The room where I had murdered my parents was covered in more yellow tape, white chalk outlines and little numbered markers. The smell of blood hung in the air, reminding me of my only memory of them. That memory no longer mattered, so I pushed it back and moved to the next window. That window revealed a small and tidy bathroom. The next window showed another bedroom.

A bed was nestled against the window, the blankets dark red and pulled back. Shoes and clothes were scattered across the floor. A dresser held a small TV and a video game console. This room was obviously my brother's, I concluded. But he wasn't in it. Maybe he was downstairs? I hadn't seen any lights shining behind the downstairs curtains though.

I glanced down the side of the house and saw one more window. I climbed to it, maybe this was it. My brother was in this room.

But who did the other room belong to?

I peered through the curtains in the last room. The bed was in a different position and it looked like the contents had been hastily removed and anything unimportant discarded. To my dismay, he wasn't in this room either.

I dropped to the ground, frowning. With an irritated growl, it hit me. There was no rhythm coming from the house. No steady heartbeat indicating my brother was inside. I had been so preoccupied with finding him that I completely ignored my senses and overlooked that fact.

I marched to the nearest house and pounded on the door. An outside light flared to life, a lock clicked and the door inched open. I shoved it, snapping the security chain. The elderly human on the other side cried out in shock. I grabbed her before she fell out of reach, her arm frail in my grip.

"Where is he?"

Her mouth soundlessly opened and closed, fear filling her scent with its alluring odor.

I sighed in annoyance. Humans scared too easily. Wiping the irritation from my face, I tried again. "Where is my brother?"

"I-I-I don't know who your brother is."

"Bullshit! He looks just like me." I pointed at my face. "His skin's a little pinker and he smiles more. He's alive. He wasn't at the cabin and he's not at our house. I want to know where he is."

"Maybe if you tell me his name," she stuttered.

"Not on your life. You're not holding any power over him!" Anger out of control again, I bit it back and made my voice as pleasant as possible. "His parents just died. They were murdered–"

"You mean Da–"

"Don't say his name!" I snapped. "Just tell me where he is."

"His aunt and uncle took him," she gasped, her breathing labored. "They live in New York City, but I heard he's still attending school here since it's only a few miles away." Her eyes were abnormally large and spit dribbled down her chin.

"Are you going to die?" I demanded. "How can humans tell?"

"I don't know. My knees feel weak and my chest hurts. Why?" The last word was whispered.

"If you're dying, I'm going to kill you because that would be a waste of blood."

She did the oddest thing then. Her eyes rolled back until all I saw was white. Her knees buckled under her and she collapsed in my arms.

I shook her, trying to wake her. "Wake up, you need to tell me if you're going to die."

When she didn't stir, I propped her against the doorway, where she slumped over, and headed down the steps. At the bottom, I paused. Maybe I should push her inside. Humans did enjoy staying in their houses. Every human I had seen tonight was in their home; the ones at the lake were in their cabins, my parents and brother had been inside when I came home.

I stood at the foot of the steps, torn by indecision. The human looked like a discarded doll, sprawled in the doorway. I supposed if it was me, I'd want someone to push me back inside.

Crackling energy filled the doorway, reminding me I wasn't welcomed in, as I pushed the her inside. Once she was inside, I came across another problem. The door swung into the house. I pushed on the energy, trying to reach inside and grab the doorknob, but jolts shot up my arm, slicing my skin open.

"Whatever. I don't know why I'm bothering," I grumbled and darted down the steps.

****

New York City. The last light from the sun had dissipated into blackness and humans filled the city streets. They scurried down the sidewalks, looking unconcerned, yet in a hurry. Cars packed the streets, honking at one another. Businesses glowed with lights, signs flashing in the windows.

"Best not to linger."

I whirled around at the voice behind me, stumbling out of the shadows I was hidden in and into the light. An uncontrolled growl escaped me and I clamped my hand over my mouth to stifle it. The humans around me halted, their eyes locking on me.

"Easy." The vampire stepped into the light and the human's eyes shifted to him.

Another growl rumbled, instincts fighting to decide who the bigger threat was: the many humans surrounding me or the single, older vampire before me?

"Easy," the vampire repeated. "If you ignore them, they'll leave you alone. They figure if there's a lot of them, then they're safe. True, a lone human is an easier meal than a single human in a crowd."

"They're not afraid?"

"They are, but you'd be wise to hunt elsewhere." He shrugged. "Humans here carry these little torches. It doesn't produce a lot, a foot long flame, but we're sensitive to fire and it spreads quickly."

I looked back at the thinning crowd, now noticing little black devices clutched in the remaining humans' hands. Even with those little devices, they had cleared out quickly. "That's weird."

His head tilted slightly. "How old?"

"Three days," I said, continuing to watch the humans.

"That means your instincts aren't fully developed and it's dangerous for you to be here," he replied. "Not until you have everything figured out. There are too many humans. A new one like yourself should stick with small towns or the roads."

He was right. My instincts warned of the dangers pressing on me from all sides. The sheer number of humans had me on edge, a desire urging me to escape to safety.

"I can't. I have to find my brother."

The look the vampire gave me was uncertain. Like he thought I was crazy or going crazy. "What brother?"

"He's my twin. An old human told me our aunt and uncle took him here. I have to find him and take him home."

"Are you saying your brother is human?"

"Yeah." My eyes narrowed at the vampire. "I'll kill anyone who tries to harm him!"

"Your human brother?"

"Yeah."

"Your brother... is human?"

"Yes," I snapped. "I don't remember being human or his brother, but I know it. I *feel* it. After I woke up, I returned home and murdered our parents and he was there. Now he's not and I'm told he's here somewhere and I *need* to find him."

"So, he's your brother, but you don't remember anything else about your human life?"

"Yes," I sighed. "I don't care about my human life. I care about my brother."

"Now *that* is weird."

I glowered at him, annoyed the vampire wasn't getting it. He was my brother. That didn't mean he had to be a vampire too.

"Well, good luck on your search. Remember, as long as you don't bother them, they won't bother you." The vampire sank back into the shadows and flitted up a wall. I watched his silhouette glide across the rooftops.

The vampire's words in mind, I started searching. When possible, I stayed in the shadows, trying to be invisible to human eyes. When I couldn't, I moved as fast as possible. The vampire had been right though. As long as I ignored the humans, they mostly ignored me.

As the night wore on, there was no trace of my brother. I didn't see him among any of the many human faces I passed, didn't catch a whiff of his scent either. Desperation curled in my stomach. Maybe if I made my approach look harmless, I could ask the humans if they had seen him.

The first one shrieked when I approached, brandishing the mini flame-thrower. As human eyes bore into me and a hostile feeling filled the air, I darted back into the shadows. I ran as fast as I could, finally halting blocks away.

With the next human, I tried calling out. That human took off running while the rest stared at me in confusion. I tried approaching a few more, all with the same results.

Frustration welled in me as I stood on the street corner, humans hurrying past. I stomped into the middle of the crosswalk, planting myself in front of a taxi. The driver's eyes widened at me and I saw the locks on his doors click down.

"Hey!" I kept my voice loud and calm. "I'm looking for my brother. He looks just like me, but he's alive. Has anyone seen him?"

Every human froze in their spots, the cars motionless in the street. They watched me, their mouths hanging stupidly open. It was like I stopped the world and it couldn't restart.

"Well? Has anyone seen a human like me?" I repeated after a long moment of silence.

Something clicked in the humans. Eyes blinked, mouths closed and the humans came back to life. Heads shook and they continued on their way. A driver timidly honked his horn at me and motioned me to move. I moved back onto the sidewalk, defeated.

Not one of them had seen him.

I took a deep, calming breath. I'd try the next intersection. I'd try until I found someone who had seen him, knew where our aunt and uncle took him.

"Excuse me?" a timid voice trembled.

Hope rose in me and I dashed to the human.

Almost as fast, she thrust the mini flame-thrower in my face. Her hand shook as she held it, fear oozing from her. She gulped down a breath and spoke. "Are you sure you didn't kill him?"

"No, I wouldn't kill him or do anything to hurt him! I just want to find him so we can go home. I've decided I'll live in our house with him. I don't care what the humans back home think. They're not separating us," I snapped.

"Okay," she squeaked. "Maybe you should file a missing person's report."

"He's not missing; he is here in this city." This human wasn't being nearly as helpful as I wanted.

"Did you get the address?"

"No!" I snarled.

"Sorry," she squeaked and stepped back. Her eyes darted around, seeking safety.

I followed her gaze, noticing a group forming. Mini flame-throwers were out and one human even had a tire iron. The group watched me, waiting for me to make a move. I quickly wiped the anger off my face and took a step back. "Not your fault. Thank you for helping. No, I didn't get the address. The old human fell asleep and I couldn't wake her." I paused. "I'll go back and maybe she won't fall asleep so I can ask."

"She probably fainted."

"Why would she do that?"

The human looked at me curiously, some of her fear melting. She was careful to avert her gaze from mine when I looked back. "You really have no idea?"

"No," I said. "I wasn't going to kill her. I told her I'd only do it if she was going to die because that would be a waste of blood."

She laughed nervously. "Wouldn't that make you faint?"

"No." I glanced up at the sky, then the mob and back to the human. "Thank you for trying to help... have a good day?"

I wasn't sure about the last part, but I threw it in to make sure I sounded harmless. If I wanted to harm her, I wouldn't say that, right?

"You too... I guess," she replied.

The mob surrounded her as I walked away, asking her if she was okay, if she wanted to sit or needed something to drink. I rolled my eyes. Humans were paranoid. If I wanted her blood, I wouldn't have wasted time talking to her; I would have bit her neck and enjoyed myself. Who wants to talk while they eat anyways?

****

I couldn't find my brother all week. All week! I rested close to the cabin and as soon as the sun set, I rushed to it. When I didn't find him there, I went to our home. I had to be careful when I did that. The old human I apparently scared had raised the alarm. The humans were looking for me, looking to destroy me before I killed again.

How else was I going to get fresh blood?

Not that I hunted while looking for my brother. He was more important than the hunger gnawing at me. I knew I'd have to take time off from the search one night to sate myself. I kept pushing it back, hoping each night would be the night I found him.

I knocked on the door, feeling the wood buckle with each blow. "I just want to know where my brother is. I won't kill you. Promise. You don't even have to open the door."

"Demon be gone!" the voice on the other side commanded.

"What? I just want to know where–"

"We know what you want, monster," the voice interrupted. "And we're not telling you. We will not let you condemn poor Da–"

"If you say his name, I will rip the door off and then rip your tongue out!" I interrupted this time.

A pause on the other side. "We won't let you condemn his soul. God will not be denied another child."

"Who's God?" I asked. "Does he have my brother? Where is he? How do I find him? I thought our aunt and uncle had my brother."

"The only one interested in you is the Devil. You will burn in hell, monster."

This human wasn't making any sense. My brother was God's child? And where was Hell? Did he even know who I was looking for?

The wail of a siren pierced the night. Red and blue lights flashed and a bright light washed over me. A silver and black car squealed to a halt, *Vampire Forces* gleaming on the side, and two humans jumped out. They stationed themselves on each side of the car, guns aimed at me. The one on the left was calm, his gun steady. His eyes held determination, a level of control that showed he knew what he was doing. The other was nervous. The gun in his hand wavered and sweat covered his brow.

I gazed between the two, mind and instincts racing. I knew the threats these two humans were to me, understood who they were. Vampire Forces, humans who hunted and destroyed vampires. They combed the darkness, searching for the hunters and turning them into prey.

The one to the right yelped when I lunged at him, knocking him into the car. A cracked echoed, the other human shooting as I raced away. I ran until I reached the city, immersing myself in humans that didn't care I was a vampire.

There, I resumed the search for my brother, pushing my close call with Vampire Forces to the back of my mind. I moved from street to street, approaching each human with extra caution. My first approaches had been too fast. To the human, I had simply appeared. The reactions were the same though, silence and stares.

I asked other vampires about my brother as well. They shook their heads like the humans and hurried on their way. One warned me what streets Vampire Forces staked out in hopes of destroying vampires. *If you value your survival, young one, avoid those streets*, she warned.

The restrictions made it hard; I wanted to search the streets I had to avoid. Often I abandoned my search, diving into the shadows as I caught sight of a silver and black car. Staying calm when talking to humans was becoming a chore. I sank a fang into my tongue more than once when biting my anger back.

All to no avail. My brother had vanished into thin air. I desperately missed him, searching my mind for memories, sometimes hoping to stumble across a human memory that hadn't vanished. There were none and I replayed the few I had of him over and over.

I knew I shouldn't use his name, but I didn't care. I wanted to find him. "Danny, where are you?"

The only answer I heard was the city. It pulsed around me, thousands of rhythms beating out life. I trudged through it, feeling weak and fatigued, unable to focus or concentrate.

I needed blood.

I melted back into the shadows, pushing every thought but one away. My stance turned predatory, instincts whispering what to do. Each step became more careful, every sound taken into consideration as I hunted. I scanned the city streets, a sliver of nervousness tickling my mind.

This was my third time hunting, but the first time in the city. What if something went wrong? What if the human fought? What if Vampire Forces caught me and destroyed me?

Down a dark alley, a rhythm called to me. A human was curled on a pile of discarded newspapers, his snores bouncing off the alley walls. I moved closer, scanning the darkness. Why was he alone? Humans in the city knew to stay in groups.

I stalked around the alley, checking and double checking for signs of other humans hiding, but there were no others hidden in the darkness. I turned to the human, rolling him over and exposing a dirty neck. A stale odor was thick on his breath, his body reeking of sweat and waste. Was this why this human was alone? The other humans were repelled by his filth?

I rubbed at the dirt, trying to clear a spot. I licked my fingers, spit on the skin and cleaned until there was a sizable spot. Need warred with a nauseous feeling, the odor turning my stomach. My fangs refused to cooperate. Finally, I forced them out and bit.

The stale smell of his breath was also in his blood. I gulped it down, choking as I struggled to finish. The stale taste coated my mouth and I licked at my lips, smacking them. Now I understood why this human was safe alone. I was tempted to find another human, wash the bad taste away. But I didn't. The weakness was gone and I was ready to begin my search for my brother anew.

The air around me begged to differ, growing warmer as the sky lightened. It wouldn't be long before for the first rays appeared. Minutes maybe. I fled the city, heading for the cabin. A tingle crawled over my skin, the start of a burn as I rushed through the trees. I slammed to a halt and started digging, immersing myself in the ground.

I waited in half awareness, trying to be patient. The stale blood had revitalized me and I was eager to resume my search. My mind mused on places to look, each spot revealing my brother. By the time the sun disappeared, I could barely stand it. I clawed my way out of the ground, racing towards the city.

A scent drifting on the night air stopped me and I fell forward, my sudden halt throwing me off balance. I scrambled to my feet, turning in circles and catching the scent again. I raced back the way I came, the scent leading me straight to the cabin. Of course, the one night I opted to go straight to the city was when I should have checked the cabin first.

I dashed around the car parked next to the cabin, smelling my brother's scent. It led me to the front and I raced up the steps, stopped only by the energy surrounding the building.

"Danny?"

"I thought you said not to use each other's names?" He was relaxed in one of the sheet covered chairs, feet kicked up and a grin on his face. The smile faded as I remained in the doorway. "Can't you come in?"

I lifted my hand, pressing against the energy. A snap cracked through the air, blue lightning spidering from where I touched it. My hand was thrown back, a jolt of pain running up my arm. "You have to welcome me in."

"Damn." He jumped up and stopped on the other side. His hand was unaffected as he waved it through the doorway. "I wonder why it does that."

I tilted my head at him, then remembered he didn't like that. "Wouldn't it be bad if vampires could enter homes? There'd be no humans left. We'd kill you and then starve."

"Disturbingly, you have a point," he sighed. "Well, come in." He gasped as I lifted him off the floor in an embrace. He squirmed and struggled, face turning a little red. "Tommy, let go!"

It was like I had no choice, my arms released him and he thudded to the floor. He grunted and winced in pain, then yelped in shock when I pulled him to his feet.

"I've been looking for you," I informed him. "All week. You weren't here or home, then an old human told me our aunt and uncle took you to the city and then she fell asleep on me. I've been half mad with worry. I thought maybe God took you to Heaven!"

"What?" The question was accompanied with a burst of laughter.

"I was looking for you, trying to find where our aunt and uncle took you, and this stupid human started rambling to me about God and Heaven and the Devil. Who are they and what do they have to do with us?"

Tears were in my brother's eyes. He slumped back into the chair, beating on the arm with his fist as he roared with laughter. "You thought God was a person and heaven a place on earth? I can't breathe I'm laughing so hard!"

"So this human was lying to me?" Fury boiled in me. I was going to find that human later and kill him! "Why are you laughing? I thought I wasn't going to find you." My voice turned timid, the anger fading into fear. "I thought I'd never see you again."

His laughter died and regret filled his eyes. "I'm sorry, To-"

"When I said your name and you mine, that was an exception."

"Oh," he mumbled. He looked at me, curiosity shimmering in his eyes. "Have you really been looking for me all week?"

"Yes. Why didn't you come back here? How come you were never home?" I demanded, releasing my pent up worry.

"I was getting settled in at Aunt Dee and Uncle Dick's. Do you remember them?"

"No, who are they?"

"Mom's sister and brother-in-law. We'd always go visit and you and I would sit bored out of our minds the whole time. No games or TV or anything," he explained. "I spent the whole week moving stuff from home to there. Next week I go back to school."

"You're not going to live at home?" I asked, crestfallen. "I thought we'd be together, in our home."

His eyes widened in shock. "You want to stay with me?"

"Yes, I figured if I behaved, the humans wouldn't bother me. That's how it was in the city."

"Aunt Dee said there were a bunch of vampires in the city. She said they're like bees, let them be and you won't get stung. Uncle Dick said people should call VF and every vampire be destroyed. I reminded him you were one now." His smile turned into a frown.

"What's wrong?" I asked. If my brother was staying with our relatives, then so was I.

"Everyone expects me to believe the same, that I should hate you." He looked away, voice hollow and sad. "Maybe I should, but I can't. When you got home, you went straight to your room without a word to me. I sat in the hallway trying to figure out what was wrong. I stayed there until Mom made me go to bed."

"That other room is mine?"

"Yeah, we used to share a room, then Dad separated us. We spent all our time in yours because you had the TV." He fondly smiled and I felt slightly envious he remembered and I couldn't. "Anyways, I don't know what woke me. Don't even know why I got out of bed. Something pulled me down the hall and there you were; Dad already dead and Mom dying. I was horrified." He looked up at me. "But it was you and I... You had been missing almost two days. You never left without telling me before."

"So you don't know how the vampire found me?"

He shook his head. "There have been rumors of vampires staring in windows and willing people to open them. Nobody said it, but I knew that's what Mom and Dad thought happened to you."

"But if they thought a vampire got me, why did they let me in?"

"Probably didn't think about it, they were too happy to have you home to even notice how you looked," he sighed.

"Are you still upset I murdered our parents?"

"I'm not upset."

"Good."

"I'm sad."

"Oh."

He shook his head. "Your apathy is going to take some getting used to. I'm always gonna be sad about Mom and Dad and if you were human, you'd be too."

"They'd be alive if I were human," I pointed out.

He grumbled. "I'll be sad for the both of us. I'm sure there are support groups or something. Anyways, I saw you killing our parents but I dunno, I can't hate you. You're all I've got now."

"You're all I've got too," I replied. "What do we do now? I'll go where you go."

He averted his eyes. "You can't, Uncle Dick wouldn't hesitate to try to kill you himself."

"I'll kill him first," I replied darkly.

"No," he sighed again. "You're not going to kill any more of our family."

It didn't miss my attention that he didn't use my name. He could have used my name and I'd be more likely to listen – would listen. Maybe not using my name was his faith in me. He hoped deep down there was something human left.

I tilted my head at him, staring until he shifted uncomfortably. "I'm not human. Don't treat me like one in hopes I'll change. I kill whoever I want and anyone that tries to keep us apart."

"Will you?" he challenged.

"Yes!" I insisted, then remembered my internal struggle on my second night. "No," I amended. "I wouldn't kill someone if it hurt you."

A faint trace of a smile filled his face. "Guess I can settle with that for now." He kicked back, lacing his fingers behind his head. "I'll just have to work on training you again. Took me fifteen years to get you to listen to me when you were human. Should take no time this time around."

I laughed despite myself.

"Creepy," he informed me. Sadness crossed his face, along with guilt. "I better go. I kinda took the car without permission. Aunt Dee would crap kittens if she found out I took it out of the city after dark – with no license."

"But when will I see you again? Are you sure I can't come?"

"You know, your voice almost sounded like it had emotions," he replied. "You can't and I dunno when I'll get the chance to visit."

I exaggerated every emotion so he wouldn't miss them. I scowled and frowned; irritated, I told him I wouldn't kill someone because of him. If I could kill my uncle, then this problem would be solved. Our aunt sounded like, as long as I didn't bother her, she wouldn't mind me there.

"You're acting like a baby," he chuckled.

I bit back a growl, annoyed I didn't have a retort.

"You were always bad at comebacks too." He shrugged, trying to act casual despite the hitch in his heartbeat my glare caused. "Fine, you big, fanged baby. How about this: I'll show you where I'm living now and you can visit whenever you want." He jabbed a finger at me. "But you can't come inside."

"Not your home to welcome me in to," I smugly retorted.

He waved his hand dismissively. "The roof of the back porch is right under my window. You can sit outside and we can play video games until the sun comes up. Just like we used to. Come on, I'm driving."

****

"Do you dream?"

I sat outside the window to my brother's room in our aunt and uncle's house. He was almost opposite of me, sitting on his bed, and leaning against the window frame. A curious look filled his face, waiting for me to answer.

"I don't sleep. I close my eyes and relax and when the sun sets, I open them."

"Relax?" he asked after a curious silence.

"I rest," I clarified. "My mind is still active, still thinking, but at the same time I'm relaxed."

"You think?" he teased with a smile.

I frowned long enough for him to see. "Didn't I as a human?"

"I'm joking," he replied in a sour voice. He turned his back to me, a succession of clicks sounded as he grumbled at the video game. Once he finished assaulting the buttons, he turned back to me. "Are you sure you don't want to play?"

"No," I said, staring across the rooftops.

Lights glimmered in windows, most only thin lines of light that escaped through closed curtains. In the distance, tall, dark buildings rose into the night sky. At the end of the street, twin lights appeared and a familiar drone grew in the night, one I learned to recognize as a Vampire Forces car.

I froze, pressing against the side of the house. "Turn the light off and shut the curtains."

"Why?"

"Just do it!"

The light died and fabric slid along metal. As quickly as it came, the car disappeared around the corner, the drone fading.

"Okay, you can turn the light back on."

"What was that about?"

"Another vampire told me to watch out for Vampire Forces. She said they'd follow until sunrise, finding where I rest," I explained.

"You know other vampires?"

I shook my head. "I saw her on the street while looking for you. She said to avoid certain areas because of Vampire Forces."

"So you aren't freaked out because you decided cops looked tasty?"

I looked at my brother. "Humans look tasty?"

He shrugged. "I dunno, do they?"

"I go on smell."

He nodded, looking thoughtful. "Did you see many vampires in the city?"

"Too many. This one was shocked I wanted to find you. He was no help either."

"You told another vampire about me?" He chewed on his bottom lip – gnawing almost – the video game forgotten.

"Was that wrong?"

He was silent for a moment, then he forced a smile, meeting my gaze. "Naw, it's fine. You sure you don't want to play? It was our favorite."

It'd make him happy, so I slowly nodded. He popped the screen out, setting it aside and handed me a controller, the cord stretched tight. I leaned my elbows on the window sill, feeling energy crackle at me.

"What do I do?"

"Try to defeat my character. B is punch, A is kick and joystick moves you around. And don't push the buttons too hard or fast either. I'll kick your ass if you break it with your vampire strength," he teased and started the game. It took him only a moment to send my character flying out of the ring. The next round ended with the same results. He laughed the third time my character flew out of the ring. "You used to be good at this. Played it non-stop. Mom always said she regretted getting it for your birthday."

"Don't you mean our birthday?"

He chuckled. "No, I was born at 11:57 and you 12:32 the next day. We gotta be the only twins in history born on different days."

He started another round and I watched him out of the corner of my eye. He smiled, laughed and poked fun each time my character was knocked out.

"What?" he asked when he saw me watching.

"What's the point of this?"

His cheer died. "What do you mean?"

"I don't get why we're doing this. What's the point of playing a game?"

"You're kidding, right? To have fun. Get together with friends and kick each other's ass," he replied awkwardly.

"Why would I want friends when I have you?"

"You serious?" he asked and I nodded. "But aren't you curious about our other friends? What we used to do? Where we hung out after school?"

"No."

He slumped back against the window frame with the same look he gave me after I murdered our parents. Like what he saw before him was something he didn't know, something strange and unfamiliar. Something that was horrifying. I was horrifying.

"What's wrong?" I asked. "What did I say?"

"Everything," he sighed. "You're so empty. Your eyes, your voice. It's like there's nothing in you. Even when you show emotions, it's like a ghost of who you were. And I wonder, do I even know you? Are you still my brother?"

Panic flashed through me. "Of course I'm your brother. Don't you feel it?"

He crawled through the window and sat next to me. "I know you're my brother. Kinda hard not to notice we look exactly alike. Well, you look like a dead person. It's just, you say these things and they sound so empty."

"Am I that different?"

"Yeah." He nodded. "Before... well, you know how I am?"

"You smile a lot."

"That's not what I meant."

"You're overly emotional?"

"Not what I meant either."

"You're smarter than most humans." I was sure I figured what he meant.

He laughed. "I imagine most people would think I was completely insane. Normal people don't have deep conversations with their vampire siblings." He adjusted his position.

"You move a lot."

"You don't move enough."

"Why are you worried about how I act?" I asked. "You know I'm not human, you accept it. Why does it matter if it makes me act different?"

"It doesn't. It shouldn't," he replied with a sigh. "Maybe it's something I need to get used to. You're matter-of-fact. This is what you eat and this is what you need to do to eat."

"It's survival," I supplied and paused. "But I can learn. You can teach me."

"You want me to teach you to be human?"

I shook my head. "That's impossible. You can teach me to have fun. Tell me how I used to be. I'm curious about it. I do want to know."

"You do?"

"Sometimes you smile and it says you're thinking about something we did together when I was human, but I no longer have the memories. I wonder what you're thinking. I want to know everything about you and to do that I have to learn about me," I explained.

He considered my words a moment. When he spoke, he made no sense. "There are these soldiers and they receive a new tank. They're discussing the tank and the Sergeant says he wants to call it the warthog. The soldiers ask, *Why warthog?* Sergeant says, *It looks like a warthog. It's got tusks.* One of the soldiers disagrees and says it looks like a puma. Know what the Sergeant says?"

I shook my head.

"Stop making up animals!"

I busted out laughing.

****

My brother told me amazing stories. Stories about birthday parties, going to school, family vacations and other activities we did together when I was human. Every night I'd go to his window and he'd pop in a video game and we'd play for hours while he talked. He'd talk until he couldn't talk anymore or fell asleep, chin on his chest, controller in hand.

I wouldn't say I learned about myself. I felt like I was listening to him talk about someone else. I couldn't see myself saying or doing any of the things he told me I did. I felt nothing when he talked about a crush on a girl we both had, had no feeling of friendship when he mentioned our friends and no feeling of pride when he said we were both on a basketball team and won lots of games. There was no connection between the vampire I was and the human I used to be.

We did discover my sense of humor hadn't changed. I laughed at every joke he told. One time so loud, he had to pull the curtains, shut the light off and pretend to sleep while I hid as our uncle peeked in the door.

"Hey? Are you awake?" My hand hovered, millimeters from the energy. It hummed at me, a faint crackle echoing. I pulled my hand away, accepting I couldn't reach through.

On the other side, my brother was fast asleep. He looked peaceful, mouth slightly open. It made me wonder. Was *he* dreaming? And what did he dream about? What went through a human's mind when they slept?

I'd have to ask tomorrow night.

Silently, I slid down the roof, landing on the ground. A feeling churned in me, one that had been growing all week. Need. I needed to hunt and feed. Once again, I had been putting it off because of my brother. We didn't talk about my hunger. I think he feared what I would say. I didn't hold back according to him, just blurted the truth out without considering how he'd take it. I didn't see what was wrong about that.

Still, I felt I should explain how a vampire's hunger worked. I caught thoughts about my hunger when I looked in his eyes. How many humans died because of me? I wanted to let him know I didn't have to feed every night.

Tonight, I was going to find a human to kill. Anticipation, need and hunger welled in me, fueling me forward. I licked my lips, almost tasting the blood. No homeless human either. They were easy to find alone, but smelled bad and their blood tasted stale.

I headed out of the city, following the roads of my preferred hunting grounds. I had to catch the car and stop it, but there were always cars on the highways.

The vehicle I picked was a heavy-duty truck. Huge tires lifted the body off the ground, the engine roaring as it barreled down the road. I couldn't imagine what had this human in such a rush, but I was enjoying myself.

That was something I learned on my own. I loved feeling like I was flying as the car drove down the road. The wind blowing around me, watching the ground blur, sent thrills through me. I'd prolong my hunt to enjoy the feeling a little longer.

In the end, I'd have to come back to reality. It was vital I paid attention. If I was going to kill a human, then I had to do it well out of city limits and while no other cars were around or risk a human calling Vampire Forces.

Opening my eyes and ignoring the wind around me, I took note of my surroundings. Trees were thick on each side, ditches dry and filled with soft grass. The truck was still a few miles out of the city and heading farther out. Ahead, headlights appeared and I lay low as a car flashed by. Once the car was gone, it was the human in the truck and me.

I reached down and smashed the driver's side window. Digging my fingers into the metal, I groped through the broken window and yanked on the steering wheel. A voice yelled, hands grabbing at me and trying to break my grip as the truck careened through the ditch and into the trees.

Metal twisted and crunched, wood cracked and splintered, sending shards of both into the air as the truck collided with a tree. The momentum of the crash threw me from the roof and into the trees. I stalked back to the truck, circling around to the driver's side. The human was bent over the steering wheel, causing the horn to wail into the calm night. The smell of blood filled the air, sweet and fresh. My jaw tightened and my fangs slid out as I crawled into the truck and grabbed the human. Veins twitched and I felt the warmth of the blood as it pulsed and followed the rhythm of his heart.

Without warning, the human moved. He screamed unintelligibly, swinging his arm wildly. The blow caught me in the chest, throwing me back. An annoyed growl ripped out of me as I scrambled back up. Only to jump back when a foot long flame burst from the truck.

The human vaulted away, escaping through the other door. Instinct had me pursuing, catching up in a matter of seconds. I grabbed the back of his shirt and yanked him off his feet. He cried out as he collided with the ground, feet kicking and pedaling in the air. He fumbled for his mini flame-thrower and I knocked it from his hand and into the bushes. Weaponless, he tried to shield his neck, eyes bulging in terror.

I slapped his hands away, grabbing his head and slamming it into the ground with all the fury I had. The chase and struggle had woken something in me and the fear from the human fueled it, propelling it forward. Ferociously I bit down, severing the jugular. I buried my face against the human's neck, gorging myself on the blood that poured out. I heard his gasps of pain, felt his skull cracking and breaking under the pressure of my grip.

When the blood gone and the feeling faded, I sat back. The world around me was eerily silent, as if everything was dead. My gaze fell on the human. His neck was ripped to shreds, head split open and only one eye remained. His blood stuck to my face and chin, thick in my fingernails, plastering my shirt to my chest.

My full stomach churned and a sick feeling rose in my throat. I darted to my feet, feeling like the world around me was closing in. It was like the trees were looking down, seeing what I had done and were appalled.

I wiped at the blood covering me, feeling dirty and filthy like a homeless human. Only I wasn't covered in dirt, but blood and that was much worse. What had come over me?

The desire had been like nothing I had ever felt. Nothing like the feeling of need. Need was simple, my energy was low, my body weak from lack of blood. I needed to feed to survive. Desire had nothing to do with survival and everything to do with want. I had wanted to rip into the human, wanted to make him feel fear.

I dragged the human back to his truck, slinging him inside and raced to escape, seeking something familiar. I ended up at the cabin, kneeling at the water's edge. The water lapped at the shore, soothing and calm as I washed the blood away.

Never again, I told myself. Never again would I let myself feel desire. Not if it made me an out-of-control monster. What would have happened if another human had come along?

I shuddered to think of the possibilities; each one soaked in blood.

Once the disturbing blood was washed away, I headed back to the city and perched outside my brother's window. He moved on his bed, sprawled under the blankets. Guilt churned in me as I watched him sleep.

"Danny." My voice was a whisper and he didn't wake. I continued anyways, I wanted to say this now. "I hunted tonight and something happened to me when the human tried to escape. I felt like a monster and it was horrible... and intoxicating. I never want to kill like that again. I only want kill when I need to – for survival." I turned to leave, but paused and turned back. "Have good dreams." I added, then disappeared into the night.

****

"Hey... hey? Hey, Tommy!"

"What?" I snapped my head around.

My brother half leaned out his window, staring at me. "You okay? You look a little lost."

"I'm good."

"Talk slower, my poor human ears didn't catch that."

"I'm good," I repeated slower.

I hadn't said anything to him about hunting. Hadn't even mentioned the little speech I gave while he slept. I didn't want to think about it because if I thought about it, I'd think about the desire and the rush it had been.

"You're distracted tonight." His voice cut into my thoughts. "Maybe we should do this another night."

"No!" I protested. "I'm fine, I was just thinking of..." Desire "...something."

He raised an eyebrow. "What sort of something? Secret vampire something?"

I couldn't think of anything to say so I snapped my mouth shut and stared until he shifted uncomfortably.

"You know, all the old stories, the ones about vampires before we knew they existed, said vampires didn't blink," he said. "I kinda wish it were true because the way you blink... you do it real slow and it's creepy."

"You say that a lot."

"Yeah, you creep the hell out of me now. My skin crawls looking at you. Even now. You're sitting still as a statue, barely moving. *Except* when you blink. I swear that's gotta be the only slow thing about you. You hardly ever show any emotions and when you do, it's weird, like you can't get it right. Stop that."

I untilted my head. "What do you mean?"

"Well, when you laugh. The way it sounds, it's not quite right. Like you're trying to exaggerate or something. If I had to describe it, besides creepy, I'd say it's intense. Everything about you is intense," he explained.

My mind drifted to the desire again. That had been intense. And terrifying. It horrified me with how it made me act, but at the same time I felt intoxicated. It was like sitting on the roof of a car, only better. Every part of me had reveled in the feeling as I fed and despite my resolve never to feel desire again, I found myself wanting to experience it again and again...

"What... was that?"

I tilted my head. "What was what?"

He looked warily at me. "You have this creepier than usual look on your face and you just licked your lips. Just when I think I can't be any more creeped out, you raise the bar."

"What bar?"

"Wha... nevermind. We need to get going if we're going to do this." He climbed through the window, sliding it almost shut and inched down the roof until he reached the edge. Grunting, he slid over, clinging by his fingertips before letting go. He crawled to his feet, brushing at his jeans.

I stepped off the edge, landing next to him.

"Show off," he grumbled. He darted to the side of the house, falling into its shadow. There, he crept along the side, peering around the front, and then motioned me to follow.

I joined him by the car in the driveway, amused at his attempt at stealth. "You're lucky humans have bad hearing because you're being very loud."

"Shut up and help me push," he replied. "This is a lot easier with you," he added as we rolled the vehicle down the street.

"Why are we doing this?"

"Might wake someone if we start it in the driveway." He threw me a sideways glance. "Our hearing isn't that bad."

"If you say so."

"Becoming a vampire has made you an ass. This should be good, come on." He scrambled into the car, starting the engine.

As we left the city behind, the locks on the doors clicked down. I tilted my head, looking at him.

"Aunt Dee says to keep the doors locked when driving at night because vampires have been attacking cars, especially on this road," he explained.

"I don't bother opening the door, I break the window," I replied, staring out the window at the road and longing to feel like I was flying.

Or desire.

Don't think that, I thought.

"You what?"

I turned to him, seizing the distraction. "I don't bother opening the door; I break the window and make the human crash. I want to sit on the roof. I like how it feels."

"Hold up," he said. "*You* are the vampire attacking cars?"

"Yes."

Silence filled the car. I felt it pushing my brother away from me, a great divide between us. He refused to look at me, focused on the road instead. I leaned against the window, staring at the dark world, deep in thought. I thought he understood and learned to accept I killed humans.

Did he know about the other night and the desire?

The silence continued as we pulled into an empty parking lot. He climbed out of the car, walking ahead. I followed, unsure of what to say, wanting to break the terrible silence.

"I killed someone the other night. On the highway we were just on. I thought he was unconscious, but he wasn't. He ran, but it didn't take long to catch him… I'm sorry."

"Killed them too." He knelt in front of a plaque, brushing his fingers across it and wiping debris away. "You killed our parents, but you sound more distraught over some stranger's death."

I knelt next to him, glancing at the plaque before us. I traced my fingers over the names and dates, memorizing them. "You want to know why I'm more upset?"

"Yeah."

I picked my words carefully. "When I murdered... Mom and Dad, it was peaceful. They were asleep. They didn't feel anything, didn't know."

My words propelled my brother to his feet. He stood over me and glared down. "That's supposed to make it better? I'm supposed say, *It's okay, at least they died peacefully?* How can you expect that of me?" He paused, trembling as he searched my face for something. "Did you think the fact they were asleep meant it was a blessing? They were spared the knowledge it was you?"

"I didn't think murdering our parents in their sleep was a blessing," I stammered.

"What did you think?"

For once I avoided his gaze. I stared at the plaque, hating my answer. "I didn't think anything."

"Of course," he replied bitterly.

"I thought you weren't mad at me. You said you'd be sad for both of us. Why isn't that enough?" I pleaded.

"Why do you think it has to be enough?" he yelled. "What exactly makes you think I'm okay with what you are?"

"You said you were okay with it, you accepted me," I countered.

"*I lied!*" Moisture filled his eyes and rolled down his cheeks. "I lied about accepting you as a vampire. I've been pretending and faking, acting like you're still you when you're not! I want my brother back! The twin I knew so well I knew what you were thinking!"

My heart ached where it lay in my chest, mirroring my brother's pain. I hurt him, badly. It was a terrible concept and reality. One I desperately wanted – needed – to fix. I rose to face him, giving him the only thing I could: the truth. "I know I hurt you and I don't like it, but I can't... I don't feel anything about our parent's deaths. That human I killed was the first time I felt something when I hunted."

"Keep going." His lifeless voice grated against my ears and I hated it.

"I got this feeling... I didn't like it."

He scowled when I fell silent. "Didn't like what? You're not being specific." Some of his anger faded when I refused to answer or meet his gaze. "Tommy, what happened?"

I sank back down, tracing the lines of the plaque. I was almost grateful he was forcing me to speak. "I only hunt when I need to, a couple times a week. The humans are subdued, unconscious or I force my will so they don't struggle. But this one I chased and when I did, I felt desire and I wanted more, desired more. More blood and fear. It made me feel like a monster and I don't want to feel that. I don't want to be a monster. I don't want you to hate me."

My brother sat back down, his voice soft. "I was lying about not accepting you. It's hard to deal with you sometimes; you make me feel like I'm the only one who feels anything about losing Mom and Dad. And I need to know that's not true, I need to know that you still feel something."

"So you don't hate me?"

"No, I'll never hate you."

A weight lifted off me with those words. I had been certain he'd tell me to leave, force me to leave. I was positive without him the desire would consume and control me until I turned into the monster humans feared.

"Please don't make me leave," I whispered.

"I'm not gonna tell you to leave."

"I'm sorry I hurt you by murdering our parents."

"I know."

"Are you scared of me?"

"Naw, never gonna be scared of my little brother."

"I'm scared. Scared I'll turn into a monster."

"I won't let you, Tommy. Promise."

****

The house was bare. Outlines on the carpet showed where furniture once sat, while lighter squares on the wall showed where paintings and photos had hung. Boxes were piled around doorways, waiting to be moved. Moonlight shone through the bare windows, making what remained look sad and forgotten.

The emptiness felt weird as I wandered around what had been the living room. This house shouldn't be this empty. It should be full of furniture, the walls covered in photos and paintings. The kitchen should hold a table and chairs, dishes should be stacked in the cupboards. The windows should be draped in colorful curtains, pulled back by ribbons. The rooms upstairs should have beds and dressers. I clearly saw how this house should be; remembered how it looked when I came home after my turning.

"Where is everything?"

"Packed up or donated," my brother replied. He opened a box and dug through the contents. "Except for Mom and Dad's bed, we took that to the dump. Uncle Dick has a storage unit and we've been moving everything there. Then when I get my own place after college, I can take what I need." He laughed, shaking his head. "Can you believe that? *When I get my own place.* Before, college felt like a million years away, something that didn't matter because I could always come back here, but now I don't know where I can go."

"Why can't you come back here?" I asked. "This is home."

He paused his quest, his head bowed and shoulders slumped. "It's not the same. It's been... tainted."

"Tainted?" I waited for him to explain. Instead, he kept digging through boxes, ignoring me. "I don't understand,"

"Of course you don't."

"Then explain it to me."

"It's tainted because of what happened," he replied, a hint of fear in his voice. He refused to look at me, keeping his attention on the boxes. "People died here and while that may not affect you, it affects me. Memories haunt me and I'm afraid I'll lose myself to them."

"We should go then."

"Just a second..." His voice was muffled as he leaned over a box. "Aha! Got it!" He straightened up, holding a book.

I wandered over, peering at the book. Photos lined the pages, dates written in a quick hand under each one. I instantly recognized my brother in the photos. The two older humans were our parents, but I barely recognized them.

"Is that?" I pointed at the last human.

"You."

I touched the image, amazed. A wide, happy smile filled my face, life in my eyes and cheeks. I was alive in this picture! That concept fascinated me. I was curious to know what had been going through my human mind at that moment. What had made me so happy?

"I was human, a happy human?"

"Mostly. You were a stubborn jerk sometimes, but then again I was too." My brother watched me, a hopeful look on his face. "Does this spark anything? Any memories?"

I shook my head and he looked away, sadness replacing the hope. He had been hoping the pictures would jar my memories. That maybe a human memory survived, buried deep beneath the vampire instincts.

"Please," I asked. "Don't ask me to be someone I'm not anymore. I can't be him. I don't remember or know how and–"

"And you don't want to be," he finished.

"Yes," I replied, staring at him.

"What?" he sullenly asked.

"What am I thinking?"

"I dunno, that I finished your thought?" He looked at me, a light shining in his eyes.

I smiled slowly so he wouldn't miss the action. "I'm not human, but I'm still your brother."

"Unfortunately," he teased.

We looked up as lights illuminated the empty living room. A car engine cut off and footsteps crunched on dirt. A loud knock echoed through the empty house.

"Tom-" my brother started, but I was already hidden. From my perch, I watched him answer the door. "Hello, Officer William."

The human strode in and looked around. "Hello, Danny. Received a call there was a car parked outside and movement inside."

"Just me," my brother answered.

"What are you doing here so late? Don't you have school in the morning?" The human's voice was scolding.

My brother clutched the photo book to his chest. "I wanted to get something and couldn't sleep until I got it. Sorry."

The human looked at the book, his stern look softening. He placed a hand on my brother and I twitched at the contact, unsure what it meant. "We'll find the vampire, don't you worry, Danny. We'll find it and it'll be destroyed for killing your parents. They were good people. They didn't deserve that death."

"Yeah, I better get going," my brother awkwardly replied.

"I take it that means you didn't tell your aunt and uncle about this nighttime trip?" the human asked with a slight smile.

"No, sir."

"I'll give you an escort back to the city then. Can't have you driving alone at night."

My brother cringed. "You don't have to. I'm sure-"

"Nonsense, it's part of my job." The human led the way out, head turning as he scanned the night. He stopped, hand going to the gun on his hip.

"What?" my brother asked, panic raising his voice.

"Thought I saw something move," the human replied. "Come on, in you go."

I stayed in the shadows as I watched the two cars disappear down the road. With a sigh, I headed back into the empty house. The photo book lay on top of a box and I picked it up, wondering if my brother knew he forgot it.

Maybe he left it on purpose so I could take it with me. Even though I felt no connection between my human and vampire life, it had been the truth when I told him I was curious. Tucking the book under my arm, I took off into the night.

****

"In other news," the human on the TV announced, "Vampire Forces was called to a torching on the outskirts of the city. Complaints from neighbors summoned VF where they found ten men, slightly intoxicated, had bound a vampire with silver chain and were dragging it behind their truck while waiting for the sun to rise. VF sent the men on their way and took the vampire into custody where it was later destroyed and the ashes sent to local scientists."

I glanced at my brother and he quickly looked away. His shoulders were stiff, a wary look in his eyes. I kept staring, knowing if I gave him my *creepy vampire stare* long enough he'd cough up what was bugging him.

"Didn't that bother you?" he finally asked.

"No."

"The newscaster talked about destroying that vampire like they were putting a rabid dog down. The men that caught it were half drunk and were just *sent on their way*? Shouldn't they have been taken to jail to sit overnight? Something to condemn what they did? How did they even restrain a vampire with silver chain? That doesn't work. None of the old myths work. Wood stakes? Ha! That quickly killed the vampire slayer movement," he ranted.

"Old myths?"

"We've known about vampires our whole lives – I mean when you were human too, you knew. Anyways, before people knew vampires were real, there were stories, fictional stories that told all sorts of absurd things. Wooden stakes, garlic, crosses and coffins; the only thing that was right was sunlight."

"Why do vampires die in sunlight?"

He shrugged. "Dunno, still haven't figured it out. There's like a million scientists working on studying vampires. Well, they claim to only be studying the ashes collected, but there are rumors they have live specimens. It's never been confirmed or denied, but everyone figures that has to be how they've disproved most myths." He turned the TV off, leaning against the windowsill. "I don't even know why they bother. If you see a vampire, you're supposed to call VF."

"You don't like this subject," I noted.

He looked away. "We went to one once, a torching. You, me and a few friends. It was on the outskirts of the city. Most vampires are caught in big cities, never in small towns like ours. Everyone was gathered around this pyre, the vampire tied to a post in the middle. It was starved, you could tell. Vampires look like chemo patients when they don't get blood, thin and sickly... sicker looking. Probably the only way they caught it. Everyone cheered and clapped when they lit the pyre. It screamed the whole time, this awful banshee wail. On the drive home we joked about it, but truthfully, we were freaked out."

"And now you feel different because of me."

He picked up the photo album and opened it, flipping through the pages. "I thought I knew everything, had life figured out. Then you became a vampire and everything changed."

I took the book back, staring at my human self. The human me smiled, a sparkle of life in his eyes. "Everything changed because I turned." I turned to him. "I didn't want to. I remember thinking, *Not me*."

"Denial, they say every vampire gets it," he sighed, propping his chin on his palm. "It's why they go back and kill their entire family."

"That's not by choice," I replied. "When I came home, why do you think I hid in my room? I still had memories; they were fading, but I tried to hold onto them and ignore the need I felt. I didn't want to hurt my family."

"You remember that?" he asked, hope in his voice again.

"I remember the feeling," I said. "The memories disappeared, but I still had this terrible fear of hurting someone, but I no longer remembered who. I understand now it was my family I hadn't wanted to hurt. You." I looked at him, tilting my head. "I don't miss being human though."

"Hard to miss something you don't remember," he agreed.

"I'm better off now," I assured him.

He frowned at me, but a yawn stopped whatever he planned on saying. "Sorry," he murmured. "I do not want to get up for school tomorrow." He paused, looking at his clock. "This morning."

"What is the point of going to school?"

"To bore the crap out of me." He yawned again, and then glanced at me. "You're serious? To learn."

"Learn what?"

He sighed in frustration. "You're always asking questions. Why this, why that. You don't get anything about humans, do ya?"

"I get you need to eat to live. And sleep."

"You understand survival. Or maybe it's deeper than that. It's the only thing left in you, everything else disappeared." He nodded thoughtfully.

I tilted my head, mulling his words. "My caring for you didn't disappear. Somehow it survived."

He looked at me, a tired look in his eyes as he smiled. "Yeah, some things never change… or die."

****

Energy flowed through me as soon as the sun set. I dug myself out of the ground, shaking dirt off my clothes and washing my hands, face and hair in the lake. I sat on the bank, letting the cool breeze dry my skin, staring at the sky. It was clear, stars growing brighter as the last glow of the sun faded.

As was my routine, I headed to the city. The streets I travelled were now familiar from walking them on a nightly basis.

Three rhythms beat on the lower floor when I reached the house. I wandered around, peering through the curtains. In the living room, two humans sat in chairs next to each other, their backs to me. Had to be my aunt and uncle. My brother sat on the couch, a heavy book next to him and a thinner one on his lap. He looked up when my aunt and uncle laughed at the TV.

"Danny," my aunt said and I softly growled at her. "Did you take the trash out after dinner?"

"Um, I forgot. I can do it now." He set his books aside.

"Best to wait until tomorrow; don't want any parasites sneaking up," my uncle said.

"It's just to the end of the driveway, I'm sure nothing's gonna snatch me." My brother turned his gaze towards our uncle, his eyes widening when he saw me through the curtains. "I... I'll go do it real quick."

"Take your thrower," my aunt said.

"Got it." My brother darted out of the room. "What are you doing?" he demanded when I met him at the front door.

I took the bag from him. "I always come here when I wake."

"But standing outside the window?" He sighed as he led the way to the end of the driveway. He pulled a lid off a large tin can, releasing a foul smell.

"I was trying to figure out how to get your attention." I set the bag in the can. "This stinks like a homeless human."

He laughed and replaced the lid. "Well, you definitely got my attention. See you upstairs."

I darted around the house, scrambled up the side and waited. He appeared a few minutes later, sliding the window open and leaning out.

"Can I see your mini flame-thrower?" I asked.

He nodded and plucked the device off his dresser, handing it to me. The device was simple, a black cylinder with a nozzle at one end and a trigger. I turned it over, seeing a white sticker full of writing and symbols.

Warning: Flammable contents. Store at room temperature. Do not freeze! Do not put in fire! To ignite, hold upright and pull trigger. Hold away from face and body. If burned, called 911. Keep out of reach of children.

"Do you want to light it?" he asked, giving me an encouraging nod.

I held the thrower out, following the instructions and pulled the trigger. A foot long flame shot out and heat burned my skin. I yanked my hand away and the thrower rattled down the roof and off the edge. I followed it to the ground, scooping it up and climbing back up.

"Are you okay?" he asked as I handed the thrower back. "I saw a second of flame and you disappeared and reappeared. I think I need a slow-mo switch for you."

"I'm fine," I replied. "What were you writing downstairs?"

"Homework – school work assigned to do at home."

"How does school and homework help you survive?"

"Some jobs require you to have certain knowledge. And a good job means lots of money, which makes surviving easier," he replied.

I nodded, understanding him for once. "And if you don't have money?"

"You've seen them on the streets, homeless people, begging and asking for spare change."

"They do seem to be struggling. Do you have lots of money?"

He chuckled at me. "Aunt Dee gives me an allowance, but that's the beauty of being fifteen. Money's not that big of a problem, that's the parents' worry."

I frowned. "I murdered our parents."

Grief flashed through his eyes. "Yeah, they used to worry about money for both of us." He gave me a forced smile. "Aunt Dee and Uncle Dick worry for me now and money probably doesn't matter to you anymore."

"Next time I hunt, I'll check the human. You can have that money," I offered.

His words were chosen carefully, trying to explain. "No, I won't take any money you give me, not if it's off some dead person you killed. That would taint the money. Do you understand?"

"Like our home?"

He nodded.

"I won't take any money off my prey then," I vowed.

That got a weak smile from him. He settled against the window frame, staring past me. "You know, as hard as it is seeing you like this and trying to deal with you, I'd rather have you with me as a vampire than dead. I don't think I could deal with everyone being dead. I'd truly be alone without you."

"I don't want you to feel alone."

"Good to hear." Amusement filled his voice, like the fact I felt I had to state the obvious to him was humorous.

A smile crept up on me and I prolonged it for him.

"That's creepy," he sighed and I laughed. His eyes widened and he sat up. "Okay, now that I can't handle."

"What?"

"You smiling *and* laughing. Holy crap, that was too much creepiness. Go back to being void and emotionless. I can handle that creepy look better than what you just did. I swear, my heart just tried to run away."

I laughed and smiled more.

****

Only two rhythms beat, both in the lower level of the house. I peeked in the windows, looking through cracks in the curtains. My aunt and uncle sat in their chairs, eyes glued to the TV, but there was no sign of my brother.

I froze with my fist hovering centimeters from the glass, remembering a promise. Not of how I promised I wouldn't kill any more family members, but of another. I promised I wouldn't linger outside the lower floor windows. It was so important to my brother that he used my name, ensuring I would listen.

Whatever you do, whatever happens, don't let them see you. Promise, Tommy!

I lowered my hand, feeling hurt. He didn't trust me, felt he had to use the power of my name to ensure I listened. I wanted him to trust me, to believe that when he asked something of me, I'd do it out of love for him and not because the power of my name bound me to the request.

I sank back into the shadows, moving silently to the back of the house. I darted up the side, perching myself outside his bedroom window to wait. To the west, light from the sun lingered on the horizon. I watched it fade, realizing how stupid that had been to wander around the house. Humans might have seen me in the dim light; their eyesight was good enough to detect movement in twilight. They'd misunderstand when they saw me too. Assume the reason I was there was to *finish the job*.

Didn't it occur to any of them that if I wanted my brother dead, he'd be dead? I would have done it the night I murdered our parents.

Something crinkled as I leaned back into the shadow. Tilting my head, I tugged the paper free.

Tommy,

I honestly have no idea if you can read this. I'm assuming you can since you remember how to walk and talk. If not, I'm sure I'll find you ranting and raving about my whereabouts when I get home. I went to a dance. Not sure how to explain it to you in writing. It's actually pretty pointless, survival-wise. Something us human kids like to do for fun. I'll be back around midnight (does time even matter to you anymore? Probably not, eh?) Hopefully, I'll have good news to tell you (about a girl we both used to like.) See ya in a few and remember what you promised me.

Peace, Danny

"I promise," I murmured, rereading the note. Idly, I wondered if my handwriting looked the same, but, disappointingly, there was nothing to write with at hand.

My patience grew thin as time ticked by, the glowing red numbers of a clock in his room taking forever to change. At some point, my aunt and uncle left. That made me happy, their presence in the house annoyed me. Why did I ever promise not to kill them?

A short time later, my aunt and uncle returned. I growled as the car pulled into the driveway. That was too short of a time for them to be gone. Why couldn't they stay away longer? Or better yet, forever?

"Danny," my aunt said as car doors slammed shut. "You were awfully quiet, is everything okay?"

"Yeah, just tired. I'm going to bed, night." I perked up at the sound of my brother's voice. Time slowed to a crawl as I waited. When the door to his room finally opened, I was practically clawing at the window. He headed to me, opening the window and leaning out. His voice was heavy with sadness. "Read my note?"

I nodded. "What's wrong? Wasn't the dance fun?"

He rubbed a hand over his face, sighing. "Yeah, I had fun. Mostly. It went a little downhill at one point and that ruined the night a bit. Completely ruined it, actually."

"Want to talk about it?"

"Will you care?"

"Danny, what happened?"

He lifted his head up, propping his chin in his palm. "I've been trying to work up my nerve to talk to Sally Marshal. I figured after what happened with our parents, I couldn't let my life slip by. I know she's has a boyfriend, but I had to talk to her and tell her she's the most beautiful girl in the world."

"And?"

"She laughed." His head fell back down. "Then her boyfriend, Justin, and his friends showed up. At first it seemed fine, he asked how I was doing, said he was sorry about our parents. He said he and a few friends were going out after the dance. They were going trapping in the city. That's, uh, when a group of people go searching for a vampire in hopes of catching it. You'd be surprised how often people catch one."

I frowned. "They were going to look for me?"

"I told him that was okay, I didn't want to go. He asked if I was afraid. I said no, Aunt Dee and Uncle Dick would be upset if I got hurt. But they kept asking, didn't I want to turn the monster that killed my parents to ash? It felt like everyone was watching me, expecting me to break out a pitch fork and torch and lead the way. I lost it. I screamed at Justin, told him to shut up, that you were still my brother." He gulped down a breath, torment in his eyes. "Everyone was so quiet, even the music stopped. They looked at me like I was some kind of freak. Then Sally looked down her nose and called me a sympathizer – that's someone who believes vampires are still human. She walked away and everyone followed. I hid in the guy's bathroom the rest of the night." He put his head in his hands. "How am I going to face everyone on Monday?"

I moved as close to the window as possible. My chest felt tight, a mixture of emotions welling. He had stood up for me, defended me and called me his brother. But because of what I was, he was hurt by it.

"Should I leave?"

He looked up, tears in his eyes. "What?"

"I'm hurting you," I replied. "My presence is causing you trouble, it pains you. I can feel it. Here." I pressed my hand to my chest.

"You feel there," he whispered and met my gaze. "We could always tell what the other was feeling; I always knew when you were upset. Even apart, I knew."

"You're my brother and I love you. I'll do whatever I have to so you'll be happy and if that means I have to leave, I will."

"No!" His voice was urgent, almost a yell. He stared at me with wild and tear-filled eyes. "Don't leave. I've lost everything else, I can't lose you too. Please, Tommy, don't leave."

"Don't you trust me?" The words flew out, sounding like an accusation.

He nodded, blinking rapidly. "Of course."

"Ask me again, but not with my name."

"Please don't leave."

****

Each night was spent at my brother's window, spending every second with him. The first night, he was quiet, sitting opposite of me and working on more homework. The following night he was anxious. He constantly rose and paced his room, packing his bag, unpacking it and picking out clothing before putting it back. The next day he'd be facing the humans at school. He feared what would happen. When I left as the sun threatened to rise, no words had been spoken between us.

I wished I had known what to say.

My steps were urgent. The sun had set moments ago, twilight still fading. I ran at full speed, a tight feeling in my stomach. I couldn't shake the feeling, couldn't push the thought to the back of my mind. It persisted, growing louder and louder, burning through me like fire.

I needed to feed tonight.

But my hunger could wait, had to because another feeling coursed through me. One that rivaled the need: concern. Concern for my brother and the feelings of anguish, which had nothing to do with my mood, racing through me.

I darted up the side of the house and was outside the window like a flash of lightening. The curtains and window were open; my brother's back to me as he played a game.

"What's wrong?"

He half turned, giving me a relaxed smile that contrasted with the churning emotions that drove me to him. He grabbed another controller and pushed it into my hand. "Let's play."

I didn't argue, taking the controller. Each round we played, I kept a careful eye on him. He grew more cheerful, the tension melting off him to match the smile on his face. Soon, he started laughing and making remarks about my lack of game skills.

"Aw, come on. You totally could have blocked that. Did you forget how to use your thumbs? What's that? What are you trying to do? Oh! That was cheap."

"I won one," I replied smugly.

"Maybe we should quit while you're ahead," he laughed, tossing the controller down and turning to me.

Our eyes met, only for a second, but long enough for me to see horror fill his. He slapped a hand across his eye, covering the splotch of blue, purple and black that had surrounded it. Wincing, he turned away. "Don't worry about it."

The ugly mark burned in my brain, infuriating me. I hissed, baring my fangs. He jumped, scrambling away from me, fear filling his scent. His heart beat out a furious rhythm, thudding so loudly I was certain our aunt and uncle downstairs could hear it.

My voice came out a low hiss. "What happened?"

"It's nothing, no big deal." His voice was barely a whisper.

I looked away, staring at the roof and reining my fury in. Once I was sure my face was void of emotions, I looked back up. "I'm sorry, I didn't mean to frighten you."

Voice weak, body shaking, he crawled back on the bed. "It's okay, you just shocked me." He kept his face half turned, hiding the bruise.

"Let me see," I pleaded. "Come closer."

He cringed and fear flashed across his face, but only for a second. He moved closer, leaning out the window. My fingers hovered over his skin, hesitant to touch the ugly mark. Fury still boiled in me, just under the surface. I focused on keeping my face and voice void of emotions.

"What happened?"

He blinked back the tears in his eyes. "When I got to school, everyone knew. Even the people who hadn't gone to the dance heard what I had said to Justin. They just stared and whispered. I thought if that's all they were gonna do, then I could deal with it. At lunch, the guidance counselor stopped me. He wanted to talk to me, make sure I was okay." He scoffed, a bitter look on his face. "I wanted to punch him, but I didn't. I said thanks, I was fine. By last period, I was sure I was in the clear. No confrontations, no one yelled names at me. Hell, no one even said hi to me. Then Sally and Justin walked up. Justin announced he and his friends hadn't found you, but they were going to try again."

"Justin did this?" I interrupted.

My brother chewed on his lip, clearly debating telling me for fear of what I'd do. Finally, he nodded. "I tried to explain why I didn't want you destroyed. I thought maybe if I explained it, people would get it. He started laughing. He told me I was a loser and a suck wannabe – that's the term used for people who want to become vampires. He punched me and I got suspended for causing trouble. Aunt Dee and Uncle Dick were so mad at me, wanting to know why I was defending you." He slumped back against the windowsill. "No one gets it. You're my twin! We were *always* close, *always* together. Mom and Dad practically had to tear us apart. You becoming a vampire hasn't changed how I feel. I still feel it. That weird twin bond that girls think is cute and other guys find odd. It's still there, still telling me you're okay. I swear I'd go nuts if it was gone." For a long moment he was silent, then he looked at me, eyes pleading. "Please tell me you understand. That you feel it too."

I slowly nodded. "While I was resting, I felt something was wrong. I knew you were upset over something. I understand for once."

He smiled gratefully at me. "Thank you."

"You're not going to let me kill him, are you?"

"No."

"Please?"

He shook his head, still smiling. "I should not be laughing at that."

****

I needed to stop putting hunting off. It had been over a week since I last fed. I was weak, tired and a bit sick. My focus was scattered, mind drifting to the rhythm beating near me, gums aching as my fangs strained to extend.

Next to me, my brother chatted nervously. His suspension was over and he would be going back to school in the morning. "I bet I have a ton of homework to catch up on. Do you think I missed much? Where am I gonna sit at lunch? No one's gonna wanna sit with me. I have to talk to the guidance counselor too. Guess everyone is worried about my mental health."

"You should move your bed from the window," I interrupted.

He looked at me as if just noticing I was outside his window. The bruise over his eye had faded, the black lightening to a softer purple. "Why?"

I stared into his eyes and pressed my will against his. His eyes turned blank, a hint of shock glimmered in them as he leaned forward, tilting his head. The vein in his neck throbbed, tempting and easy.

I broke the stare, looking anywhere but at him. "That's why."

He let out a breath of air, his voice weak. "Whoa, what was that?"

"A point," I replied. "At our home, my bed was by the window and yours was against a wall. That had to be how the vampire got me. It must have looked in my window and made eye contact. I wouldn't willingly go with a vampire."

"How do you know that?" he asked, a hint of hope in his voice.

"It makes sense. Humans don't like vampires and therefore wouldn't go willingly."

"Oh... Might as well do it now." He cleared the way, moving clothing, games and books. Pushing, he inched the bed against the wall. Once it was in its new spot, he sat back on it, looking at me thoughtfully. He jumped up, disappearing behind the desk before dragging it over to the window. "Happy now?" He rolled his eyes at my nod. "You hang outside my window all night. What are the odds of another vampire showing up when you're not here and catching me?"

"About the same odds as the one that turned me," I threw back at him.

"Meh," he replied.

"I have to go."

"Why?"

"I'm hungry and you look tasty."

"Funny. You said you go on smell." A flicker of panic flashed across his face.

"I do, but I'm hungry. I haven't fed in over a week."

"Oh, well, have fun," he awkwardly replied.

I tilted my head at him, waiting for him to explain how I was supposed to have fun hunting. He remained silent, avoiding my tilted gaze. Finally, I slid down the roof, dropping off the edge and let my need lead the way.

Tonight I felt bold, taking to the city to hunt instead of the highways. Like usual, most humans were in packs, staying in well-lit areas. Except for the homeless, but I remembered the first and only one I fed on. I wasn't that desperate.

In a run-down neighborhood, a lone human sat on the steps of a shabby house. A dim light shone above her, casting sharp shadows on her face. Streetlights kept the shadows small and I carefully picked my way towards her. I froze when her head snapped up, eyes falling on me. There was no to time reach her, the distance between us too great. I expected her to scream, alert other humans and run inside the shabby house. Instead, she continued to stare. Then, just as quickly as she looked up, she looked away.

I remained frozen in my spot, confused. She saw me. Why wasn't she running to safety?

"Aren't you going to come closer?"

I walked over to her. She looked up at me expectantly, right into my eyes. Her gaze didn't waver, letting me see her thoughts.

"Why are you waiting for a vampire?"

"No questions, just do it."

I could have listened to her. She wasn't fighting, she wanted to die obviously. It would have been so easy to sink my fangs into her neck and feed. But her compliance confused me. Why did she want to die? I couldn't see that when I looked in her eyes, only the desire to die.

"Why are you waiting for a vampire?" I repeated.

When she refused to speak, I grabbed her arm, intending on forcing her to speak. She cried out in pain, tears springing in her eyes. Dark bruises covered her arms when I pushed her sleeve up. I looked back at her, noticing more bruises covering her face, the make-up she caked on flaking around the edges of the wounds.

"What happened?"

She refused to meet my eyes now. "I walked into a door."

I grabbed her chin, forcing her face up. I locked eyes with her and willed answers. They filled her eyes, pouring into my head, telling me what I wanted to know. I looked at the shabby house, listening. A rhythm beat inside, steady and strong.

"He's inside?"

Her eyes widen and she tried to break my grip.

I pulled her back to me, trying to understand. "He hurts you, threatens to kill you, but you want to die. He should be the one that dies."

"No," she whimpered.

"If he's dead, he can't hurt you," I replied darkly. "Welcome me in."

"No."

"Why not?"

"Because it will upset his mom, she doesn't know. It's better if I die, then she'll be protected from the truth and I'll be free," she whispered.

"You'll be dead," I stated. "And I don't care about his mother," I added when she opened her mouth.

Her eyes widen in horror, thoughts speaking loudly. *The rumors are true. Vampires are monsters that kill whoever they want. He'll kill me, then her!*

I glared at her. "You don't know anything about me. You think I don't have feelings or that I don't care. If I didn't care, I would kill you. I'd kill you, then him and anyone else I came across tonight. But I'm not going to do that, I'm only going to kill him, he deserves it. That human needs to see the truth about her son. She needs to see that *he* is the monster." I focused my will, hissing my next words. "Welcome me in."

****

"Guidance counselors suck," my brother sighed.

"Why?" I asked, only half paying attention. I was almost winning this round. His character's health meter was nearly empty and mine was half full. This would be the first time I won the first round. With a tap of a few buttons, he sent my character flying out of the ring. I tossed the control down with a growl. "How do you do that? How do you knock them out of the ring?"

He laughed. "I thought you said video games were pointless."

"They are. I like winning. It's nice."

"Sore loser, that's a human trait."

"I am not human," I indignantly replied.

He laughed harder. "Now you sound like a human in denial."

"Why do guidance counselors suck?" I asked, not caring for his observations.

His face turned serious as he started another round. "He just asks me stupid questions. How do I feel about our parents' deaths? How do I feel about you being a vampire? What makes me think I need to defend you? Do I know you'd kill me if given the chance? Stuff like that. And I've tried to explain it, the twin bond. He says that's only a myth, there's no proof that twins have a psychic bond that lets them feel the other's emotions. I get to sit my whole free period talking about my feelings so Mr. Vargas can feel good about himself."

"Lie," I replied. "I know lying is pointless, but not for that. Lie to the human and tell him you want me dead. I won't mind if it keeps you happy."

"I'm happy."

"You're not. What happened with that human caused you pain and not just physical. Tell them what they want to hear and they will leave you alone. You can be happy," I insisted.

"That won't make me happy," he sighed. "Being honest about you makes me happy. I want people to understand what I see when I look at you. Sure, I see a vampire, but I also see my brother. You do things my brother did, say things he did. You are still him. Even if you don't remember or feel like it." He slumped back, eyes distant. "You make me wonder if we've been misjudging vampires. Maybe there is something human left in them. It's small and vague, but it's still human."

"There's nothing human left in me."

"Then why are you the only one of us who refers to our parents' deaths as murder? Every other time you've talked about hunting or feeding or blood, you say kill," he pointed out. "In your mind, you *murdered* our parents. How is that not human?"

"That's how I see it."

"That's why I accept you now. So indifferent at times, but I can still see my human brother. *I recognize you.* That's what I want everyone else to see."

For a long time, neither of us spoke. We played the video game. I won a few rounds, a grin filling my face each time. He snickered at my smile – along with shuddering. I felt content in the moment, happy to be with him, overjoyed at his feelings for me and at ease with our location. I was starting to feel like we had both found a new home.

"Danny." The door opened, my aunt froze halfway through, gaze locked on me.

"Tommy, run!"

My body jumped to action, instincts telling me to listen to my brother's order. I slid off the roof, my feet hitting the ground running. Once tall buildings surrounded me and not a human in sight, I skidded to a halt.

What happened back there? The sudden noise had shocked me, caused my thoughts to freeze in their tracks when I should have automatically melted into the shadows. Now my aunt had seen me with my brother. What would she say to him? After what happened to him at school, I was sure her words would be anything but kind. She might even hurt him.

I whirled around, heading back. My mind raced through everything he had told me about humans and vampires. Any human that sought out a vampire was frowned upon and usually wound up dead. But what happened to the humans that consorted with vampires and survived?

When I reached the house, red and blue lights flashed in the driveway. Humans stood in doorways of homes or watched from windows. I lingered in the shadows, not daring to move any closer.

"And you're sure, Ma'am?" the cop asked my aunt, writing on a small pad of paper.

"Definitely, it was trying to get in," my aunt replied. She hugged my brother tightly. "Trying to finish what it started and kill poor Danny."

"No, he wasn't." My brother pulled free. "He wouldn't hurt me."

"Now, son." The cop's voice was patronizing. "I know it may seem like that, especially if it caught your gaze. Those parasites can make you think anything. I need you to remain calm and tell me what happened."

"We were playing video games."

"Don't lie!" my uncle snapped.

"I'm not lying," my brother insisted. "If you'd listen to me, you'd know he doesn't mean any harm. He's my brother."

"That's enough!" my uncle roared. He grabbed my brother by the arm, almost propelling me out of the shadows. "We've been through this before, when you were suspended. Tommy is dead and you need to stop this nonsense. Mr. Vargas says–"

"Mr. Vargas is an idiot," my brother interrupted. "He doesn't have siblings or kids even. How exactly is he qualified to be a school guidance counselor?"

My uncle pressed his lips together before speaking. "Dee, take Daniel inside. We will discuss this later."

My aunt silently led my brother inside.

"Your nephew believes the vampire's harmless," the cop noted. "That happens. Some people find it hard to believe someone they love is dead. Especially when there's a monster out there that looks like them."

"What do I do?" my uncle sighed.

"I know of a therapist, helps victims of vampire loss." The cop wrote on the paper and tore it off. "Give him a call; I'm sure he can help."

"What about the vampire? It's going to come back. If it already hasn't." My uncle peered around.

"We can post a car outside if you want. VF will be over shortly too," the cop replied. "They'll probably relocate you and set a trap. Vampires can be slippery leeches, it takes time to bait and catch them. If it wants your nephew dead, you don't want to give it the chance."

The cop left and my uncle and the other humans disappeared back into their homes. I stayed in my spot, listening to my brother and uncle argue. Finally my uncle ordered him to his room.

I darted out of the shadows and across the street. Hugging the shadows of the next house, I moved around the back. Gauging the distance and scanning windows for faces, I headed across the lawns and up the side. "Danny."

The window opened a fraction of an inch, curtains still closed. "I'm here."

"I'm sorry."

"It's not your fault."

"Yes, it is, she shouldn't have seen me. I promised you they wouldn't!" I insisted. "What's going to happen now?"

He was silent for a moment. "They're making me leave. Aunt Dee has wanted to move out of the city for a long time and now she has the perfect excuse. But they won't tell me where."

I stared at the rows of houses. Lights glimmered in them, but tonight those lights lacked warmth. Every human in those houses hated me. The ones below me hated me. None of them knew me, knew what I felt. All they knew was I was a vampire, and because of that, thought I was a heartless monster. In their opinion, I was only good if I was ash.

The only human that didn't feel that way was my brother, filled with a pain that transferred through our bond and into me.

"You have to go with them," I whispered.

"Why?"

I leaned over, seeing him through the curtains. "Because I'll find you."

****

The smell of my brother lingered in the air, faintly drifting on the breeze. I inhaled deeply, the scent as familiar as the house before me. I cautiously moved closer, aware of the truth. My brother wasn't in that house. Or my aunt and uncle. The humans inside were ones I didn't know, would never know. They were decoys, sent to the house, carrying items saturated with my brother's scent in hopes of luring me. Vampire Forces.

I scrambled up the side of the house, leaning next to the window. The spot comforted me, reminding me of the nights spent talking with my brother, learning about him and about myself as a human.

Footsteps thumped into his room. "Hey, brought dinner."

An irritated sigh. "Not more fast food. I'm so sick of that crap. When is this stint gonna be over?"

"Stop your complaining," the first voice sighed. "We're seven days into this and already you're whining like a child."

"I'm sick of sitting in this room, pretending to be some deluded kid. Did you see the interview tape? I've never seen that much denial. That kid's lucky to be alive," the second voice said.

"I know. Why the parasite didn't kill him is beyond me. What was it thinking?"

"It's a vampire. It was probably playing a sick game of cat and mouse, torture the boy, then kill him." The second voice grew more and more irritated.

"True, those monsters are ruthless. Want to grab a beer when your shift ends?"

"Sure. Hey, thanks for the food."

"No problem."

I slid down the roof, slipping into the shadows. Each night I made a trip to the house, checking to see if Vampire Forces was still there. I hid in the shadows, hoping they'd mention where my brother had been taken. They never did. Afterwards, I'd go to my home, the house where I murdered my parents. I wasn't sure why, I just did.

After, I'd resume my search for my brother. I roamed the highways around the city, venturing into nearby towns. I kept my nose open. He knew I'd be looking for him, knew I'd be able to smell him. He had to know leaving his scent would lead me to him.

Tonight, though, I had to pause my search to hunt.

It took most of the night, but I found a human. He was breaking into a home, face covered in black. When he was dead, I dragged him to the curb and set him next to a trash can. Taking out the trash. I laughed at my own joke.

My cheer faded as gray and pink tinged the sky. There was no time left to search the next town before the sun rose. A bit disheartened, I headed to the cabin.

Rhythms beat inside the wooden walls. I wandered around the building, eyes narrowing. Had the Vampire Forces sent humans here? I knew my brother wouldn't tell them about the cabin, so how did Vampire Forces find out? Maybe my aunt and uncle told them. Would my brother still be mad if I killed them?

Yes, I decided and headed up the steps. My brother's scent was absent and that told me it wasn't Vampire Forces waiting for me.

There were ten of them, huddled into a group. One stood apart from the group, well-muscled arms folded across his broad chest and a smile on his face. "Look at that, he wasn't kidding."

"Justin, are you sure this is a good idea?" a human girl whimpered.

"Don't worry, babe, there's more of us than it," he said confidently. He looked at me, smirking. "I told Danny I'd find you. Offered to let him come, but he didn't want to. He thinks you're still his brother. His freaky twin. Did you know that? Out of the two, you were always freaky, creeped the girls out. It's no surprise you're a leech now."

The humans behind him chuckled nervously.

I flashed my gaze to each one, watching them look away in fear. I looked back at him. "Justin."

"Am I supposed to be afraid of my name?"

"You are afraid," I replied. "I can smell it. It smells good."

"Is the big bad vampire is trying to frighten me?" Justin laughed. The others laughed as if on cue. He looked back at me, still smiling. "Danny kept insisting he wasn't afraid of you. He said and I quote, *He's my brother, he'd never hurt me.*"

I snarled. "My brother does not sound like that."

"Oh, you called him your brother too, isn't that cute." His laughter was cut off as I grabbed him around the throat and slammed him against the wall. He choked, clawing at my hand as his eyes bulged. The fear he had worked so hard to hide rushed to the surface.

I grazed my lips against the pulse pounding in his neck. "You want to know why you're not dead yet?" I whispered in his ear. "Because the human you put down, mocked and hurt doesn't want me to."

Justin gasped, the air whooshing out of his lungs as I slammed him against the wall again. The girl screamed when I appeared in front of her. I pinched her chin, brushing my lips against hers. "Let's see what the humans at school will think of you now," I whispered and disappeared.

I watched from the roof as the humans flew from the cabin, feet thudding as they ran to their cars. The one I kissed sobbed as she was half-carried, half-dragged to the cars. Justin appeared last, grumbling as he climbed into a car.

"Gonna come back when the sun's up with shovels and chains, dig it up and watch it burn to ash."

"You wish," I quietly hissed as the cars drove away.

Another home tainted.

****

Bright lights illuminated the streets in a sun-like glow. Where the lights didn't reach, darkness gathered like pools. A group of humans ventured down the streets, staying in the light. Their voices echoed, bouncing loudly off the brick walls. Their strides were slow and casual – in no hurry.

"Hey, I got an idea," one blurted out, his greasy hair hanging over his thin, pimple-covered face, obscuring his eyes. "Why don't we break into the principal's office? I bet he has all the confiscated drugs and porno mags stashed in there."

"No," the one in the middle sighed. "I don't want to get in trouble with my aunt and uncle."

A tall and thin human gave the one in the middle a shove, propelling himself backwards in the process. "Come on, Dan, you're always using that excuse. Be adventurous for once."

"It's the truth, Aunt Dee will crap kittens if I get in trouble again."

"Again?" a short, stocky human asked.

He seemed uneasy, shifting at the attention that hadn't bothered him before, eyes quickly looking around for a distraction. "We should do something, though."

The thin human stretched his limbs and yawned. "No, you're right. I need to get home before Mom throws a hissy fit. She needs to chill."

"I should probably head home too," the pimple-covered human sighed, wiping the hair out of his eyes.

"Yeah," the short, stocky human agreed in a sad voice. He looked over, pausing. "Whatcha staring at, Dan?"

He didn't answer and all eyes followed his, their whispers filling the air.

"Dude, is that a?"

"No, it can't be."

"It's gotta be a costume."

"It's not."

Their eyes turned back to him. He smiled, a knowing look in his eyes.

It had taken two months of searching, fanning out and scouring the nearby towns. Each night I searched, putting off hunting as long as possible. I even procrastinated finding a safe place to rest, opting to bury myself wherever when the sun rose. I knew that one night I'd find him or he'd find me.

I smiled back.

"It's smiling," the short, stocky human whispered.

"Dude, it's gonna kill us," the thin human replied.

"I doubt that," my brother snorted and their eyes turned back to him.

"Is it just me or does it look–" the pimple-covered human started.

"It's gone!" The thin human pointed to the spot I had been standing.

"I can't believe it, a real vampire! What's it doing here? People know to stay inside after dark," the short, stocky human gasped.

The pimple-covered human cast a nervous glance at the others. "Except us. I don't know about you guys, but I forgot my torch at home."

"You guys are paranoid, vampires don't attack crowds." My brother stretched and yawned as he walked away from my hiding spot. I felt his relief as he left me, mirroring my own. Like a whisper in the back of my mind, I swore I heard his voice, *It's about time.*

I silently agreed.

Part Two: Friendship

My brother held out the brown bottle, his arm wavering. "Take a drink."

I shook my head, lips pressed together.

"Come on, take a drink."

"Why?"

"Because I want to know if you can," he sighed.

I leaned away from the bottle. The odor rising from it reminded me of a homeless human. "I don't care if I can."

"It's not like it can kill you," he insisted and started laughing. "Can't have liver failure," he continued, laughing more. "Or die from alcohol poisoning." He was roaring with laughter now.

I scowled at him. "You've been drinking this stuff, haven't you? You reek like it."

He stopped laughing, giving me a serious look. "Yes, before you showed up I was in the next dorm having a few beers with my classmates. Is that so wrong?"

"I don't know, is it?"

"Only because I'm under twenty-one," he idly replied and took a drink. He held the bottle back out. "Don't make me force you with your name."

I eyed the bottle, then him. We no longer looked identical. His hair had grown and his body was no longer lanky. *Filled out* was the term he used, flexing a few muscles as he grinned at the mirror. His voice was richer and deeper. He did something I'd never do.

He aged.

Three years had passed. Three years since I had been turned and murdered our parents. Three years since our aunt and uncle tried to separate us.

As far as they knew, they succeeded.

Now he attended college, living in the dorms and only calling our aunt and uncle once a week to let him know he was okay or going to visit. There was still a song and dance he had to play, but it was less restricted.

I was less restricted too. The dorms were open to me. I could enter any I pleased; no one needed to welcome me. My brother thought it was because the dorms were public buildings, and with so many humans coming and going, whatever kept vampires out was broken.

The human students knew I was there. In the first week, while my brother was asleep and I explored the campus, finding routes to and from my resting place, I stumbled across a human. She snapped a picture, then ran off while I blinked at the spot in my vision. The next day he said a girl approached him, asking why he was dressing like a vampire and scaring people. I don't know if I made things worse for him or not, but I found the human again and told her I wasn't the human she thought I was.

A fist pounded on the door and I was out the window in a heartbeat. "Yo, Danny," a voice called. "There's a party in Street Hall, tons of beer and girls. You coming?"

"Just a sec," my brother replied. He leaned out the window with an amused look. "I gotta go, but I'll be back before the sun rises." He set the bottle on the window ledge. "Have a drink on me. Peace."

Then he was gone, happily chatting with the human.

I sighed and crawled back through the window. He had been doing that more and more as the weeks passed. Leaving me to be with other humans. What was so great about the humans at college? If they found out he was my brother, they'd shun him. Like the humans back home had.

I grabbed the beer bottle, bringing it to my mouth. The taste was horrid, bitter and fizzy. I coughed as I swallowed. How had he drunk this?

Time ticked by as I sat on the inside of the window, watching and waiting. Below, the human students were out in force. They roamed the sidewalks, yelling at each other, even close up. Too many for my taste, I waited for a lull, and then slid out the window. I dropped into the shadows and headed to the only spot on campus void of humans at night.

The big, empty field stretched out before me, surrounded by rows of seats. My brother explained they played football games here. He said it'd fill with humans, all cheering for a touchdown. He tried explaining the rules of the game, but as usual, I didn't get the point. How would throwing a ball help one survive?

"It does, trust me," he had replied.

"Ah, if it isn't a dark brother."

I whirled around, startled at the three humans lounging on the lower rows of seats. The one that spoke watched me with mournful eyes lined in black. An equally pale and black-clad human puffed on a cigarette, his face unconcerned. The last human had draped herself across a few seats, arms lifted towards the stars.

"I would have thought vampires would be more aware of their surroundings," the first one noted.

"Maybe he was lost in solitude, drifting peacefully," the one lounging on the seats replied.

"What?" I asked.

"What a shame, he has no idea," the male said.

"I never understand how a human thinks. You make no sense to me whatsoever. This place." I motioned to the arena. "I can't even begin to understand why it's important."

"That's where you're wrong," the lounging female replied dreamily. "We don't understand the fascination either. It's back and forth, back and forth, get knocked down, get back up and repeat."

"Ignore her," the first one said, giving the other female a sideways look. "She's smoked too much tonight." She slid closer, holding her hand out. "I'm Fallen. He's Risen and she's Settled. I've heard vampires don't like using real names, so it's what I came up with on the fly. I've always loved the idea of fallen angels."

I looked at her hand. "What are you doing?"

Fallen took her hand back, a smile filling her lips. "Is the temptation of blood too much, perhaps?"

"No, you could slit your wrists and I wouldn't react," I replied. I always hungered – always craved blood – but in terms of being around it, I reigned in those wants. As long as I didn't need blood, I didn't take it.

"Interesting," Fallen said. "So what brings a dark creature like you here? We've heard the rumors of a vampire on campus. Our unofficial mascot. The paper is dying to get a photo."

The three humans laughed.

"I have my reasons."

"There haven't been any deaths," Fallen said.

Risen glanced at me. "Unless they're not reporting them."

I scowled at him, noticing he looked like he was half asleep, eyes shot with red. "I do not hunt here."

"Why? Do you have a resting spot nearby?" Fallen inquired. "My apologies," she said when I glared at her. "There must be something here that interests you. Vampires stay away from humans. We're too quick to call the cops and have Vampire Forces descend on us with their martial law."

"Mourning what you will never being able to enjoy? The college experience?" Settle suggested.

"No."

"No, I don't suppose that is a good enough reason either." Fallen watched me, a calm look on her face. Her calmness unnerved me, all three humans lacking fear of me. I had never spoken to humans who didn't fear me because I was a vampire.

"What are *you* doing here?" I demanded.

"Can see the stars and moon." Fallen stared at the sky. "It's so peaceful, makes you want to be up there."

I felt like the air had been sucked away. The sky always looked serene and quiet. Sometimes I wanted to fly up there, escape the busy human world for a few moments of peace.

"I understand."

"Of course, we're siblings in darkness," Fallen replied. "We prefer night over day, seeking the peace darkness creates and feeling at home."

"I stay in the dark because the sun would kill me."

"But if it didn't?" Fallen asked.

"I don't think about pointless things like that."

"You're a direct creature," Fallen replied. "I like that." She rose, the others following suit. She dipped down, bowing her head. "Until we meet again, brother of the night."

****

Tommy,

Sorry I didn't come back to my room like I said. I passed out in some girl's bed. Man, I wish I could remember last night. I wish I wasn't hungover too. I'll explain that next time I see you. There's another party and I wanna find that girl. She was cute, I remember that! Don't have too much fun without me and I'll try to make it back before sunrise. No promises.

Peace, Danny

I crumpled the note and threw it on the ground, then picked it back up. It had been taped precariously to the window, fluttering in the wind. I had scrambled to grab it before it blew away. Now I wished I had let it.

"Girlfriend dump you?" Fallen asked as she approached.

"I don't have a girlfriend. Where are the other humans?" I asked.

"Boozed up, passed out and detached from reality again," she replied, a bottle dangling in her hand. She held it out. "You look like you need a drink."

"I'd rather not."

Fallen smirked at me. "It's not like it can hurt you. Just give you a splitting headache the next day."

"Why do it then?"

Fallen took a drink and winced. "Ah, there's a whole list. Some do it to have a good time, others because everyone else is and some to forget."

I looked at my brother's crumpled note. Was he drinking the liquid that made humans forget? Was he forgetting me? "Why would someone say he'd do something, then leave a note?"

"He? I didn't know vampires swung that way." Fallen arched an eyebrow at me.

"I don't understand what you mean."

"Ah, guess I was wrong," Fallen replied. "So who is the person in question?"

"It's my brother, my twin brother. He's abandoning me," I replied, catching myself off guard. I hadn't meant to say that last part, but something about her eyes told me it was okay to tell her.

"And he's human?"

"Why is that so hard to believe?"

Fallen rolled her eyes. "Because you're a vampire, duh! Ever since vampires were discovered, the relationship between them and us hasn't been stellar. And a hundred years from now – maybe even a thousand – the relationship will be the same. All because us humans have a superiority complex and are afraid."

"Why aren't you afraid of me?"

Fallen stared at me a long moment. "I've never met a vampire or been to a torching. I heard about vampires, read about them, but that's it. Every little thing I've learned has been bad. But I see you and you don't seem evil. A bit creepy, but not evil."

"Maybe I'm luring you, willing you to think I'm safe so I can drink your blood."

Fallen traced her finger across the palm of her hand. "If vampires are monstrous bloodlust driven creatures, then why is humanity still here? Shouldn't they have wiped us out? I have a cut on me right now, sliced my hand open working on an art project today. If you were only interested in blood, wouldn't I be dead already?"

"I did smell blood."

"More fuel for my argument. May I see the note?" Fallen held out her hand and I passed her the crumpled paper. When she finished reading, she handed it back with a kind smile. "He's not abandoning you. This is college and a lot of us are away from our parents for the first time. It's a chance to experience life, but still have the safety of our family to fall back on."

"You don't think he's forgetting me?"

"Sounds like he's hoping to have sex." She held the bottle out. "Still don't want a drink?"

I took the bottle and gave it a sniff. The strong, spicy scent burned my nose and the taste was horrid, burning my tongue as fiery fingers clawed down my throat. I gasped, choking as I handed the bottle back.

Fallen laughed. "Another myth bites the dust."

"Huh?" I croaked.

"Some vampire myths claimed vampires couldn't consume anything but blood."

"This is the second time I've drank something besides blood," I replied, throat still tingling from the liquid. "I'm not making a habit of it."

Fallen laughed, stretching her arms high. "Well, this was fun, but I better get back to my room. If I'm lucky, Riley and Jamie aren't going at it on my bed."

"Who?"

"Risen and Settle. Forget the slip." She stopped next to me, lightly socking my arm. "Go find your twin; he might need to be nursed through a hangover."

I headed towards my brother's dorm, slinking through the shadows. He was sprawled on his bed when I crawled through the window. His eyes fluttered when I shook him, his voice weak.

"I think I over did it," he whispered. "The room's spinning. It was fun though, oh man, was it fun. I totally got some."

"Some what?"

He laughed and winced. "Kissed a girl. Well, a little more than that, but there's no way I'm going into detail with you. Where have you been? I got back and was shocked you weren't here."

I paused, wondering if I should tell him about Fallen. "I was by the football field."

He groped at me, hand waving through the air. His voice was soft and tired, fading into sleep. "Sorry if you feel like I've been ditching you, I'm not. I'm just trying to experience human life. You're still my brother and I won't ever abandon you."

"I know," I assured him.

****

Sunday signified the end of the parties, the night silent when I arrived on campus. The students were in their dorms, preparing for class the next day. The window to my brother's room was open, light spilling out. He didn't look up from his notes as I slipped through the window.

I leaned over his shoulder, looking at the numbers and symbols. I knew what this was. "Math."

"Yeah, Algebra I is required for graduation. I've been at this all day, popping pain pills and making up for partying all weekend. Maybe next weekend I'll take it easy, not party every night." He leaned back and rubbed his face. Dark circles ringed his eyes, his skin pale and mouth slack. His eyes blinked rapidly with fatigue. He tossed his pen down, popped a couple pills in his mouth and took a drink of water.

"You look tired."

"I am, but I gotta study a little."

"You're not doing a good job."

"You're distracting me."

"Maybe I should go."

"Maybe you should."

Hadn't I put enough amusement in my voice for him to hear? I turned to the window, thinking I'd wander around campus or see if Fallen was at the football field.

"You're so clueless." His voice stopped me. "I thought by now you'd know sarcasm. Sit."

Relieved, I sank onto the bed and he focused back on his homework. I slid closer to him, leaning on the desk. "What are parties like?"

"Loud," he snorted. "You have to yell over the music and noise at the person next to you. Things get broken and people fall down because they're too drunk to stand. You never, never, never want to be the first one to pass out; not unless you want to wake up with body parts tattooed all over your face with a marker."

"And that's fun?"

"Being drunk helps."

"What did you mean the other night about not being twenty-one? Twenty-one what?"

He yawned. "That's the number of years a person has to be to legally drink."

"You're breaking the law?"

"Yup."

"I kill humans who break the law."

He turned to me, a puzzled look on his face. "What?"

"You said some humans don't deserve to live, like ones that break the law," I replied.

He rolled his eyes. "I said that once three years ago when you wanted to know why people hit each other. I didn't mean it literally. I meant some people are bastards and you wished they had never been born because the world would be better without them."

"Maybe those humans should be killed at birth," I suggested.

"You can't tell if a person's gonna turn out bad when they're born. There are a million different factors that influence how a person acts. It'd be like trying to determine who a vampire will pick to turn. Scientists figure out of a certain number of people killed by vampires, one gets turned, but we have no clue as to why a vampire will turn one person, but not the next," he explained.

"Well, what humans can I kill?" I asked. "I thought you wouldn't mind that."

"Oh jeez." He shook his head, then fixed me with a stern look. "Does this have anything to do with the fact you that killed Mom and Dad?"

"No."

"Then this has solely to do with me?"

"I don't want to upset you."

"Tommy." Using my name meant he was serious. "I accept you, you know that. You will always be my twin, my brother, and I've gotten used to you as a vampire. I barely notice now, even when you do that creepy head tilt. But there's one thing I will never be used to. It doesn't matter if I know the person or whether they're a perfect stranger. I can't ever accept you killing people. I know and understand why you need to, but I wish you didn't have to."

"But I want you to be happy," I insisted.

"You're not always going to be able to keep me happy. Look, don't worry about it. You do what you have to do to survive. I won't condemn or hate you for it. I know you like it too," he said gently. He closed his books and stood. "I'm gonna hit the sack for the night. See you tomorrow?"

I nodded and slid out the window.

A mixture of feelings churned in me as I hit the ground. My brother's words floated in my head, confusing me. I had been sure he wouldn't mind me killing bad humans. They hurt other humans, beating, cutting and even killing them. For no reason! Humans didn't like that as much as they hated vampires. Wouldn't killing the bad ones be a good thing?

"They think I'm bad and want to kill me," I muttered as I settled down to rest for the day.

I no longer had to dig into the dirt to rest – not that it mattered. My safe place for the day was a small, enclosed cellar. The decaying house above was hidden by trees, grass covering what remained of the floor and vines crawling up the crumbling chimney. I would have missed the door leading to the underground room if I hadn't stepped on it and noted the different sound my footsteps made.

Despite the decay of the door, no light reached the room. A single ladder was the only entrance and exit, several rungs missing. Not that I needed the ladder, I could easily climb in and out. It was only a few minutes to the college and even less to the city where I hunted. I felt safe there, hidden from the burning sun.

****

I stared at the fourth story window. No light shined, the curtains drawn tight. I listened, but from the ground there were too many heartbeats to tell if my brother was in his room. Maybe he was asleep, in which case I didn't want to wake him. Or he could be gone, out to another party or visiting friends. He had all day to visit his friends though.

Sometimes I mused about killing his friends.

With a sigh, I headed back the way I came, passing dorms full of sleeping humans, lots full of cars and dark buildings. As I walked, a scent kept drifting by me. It filled the air with its fragrance, tickling my nose. I knew this scent; it was Fallen's.

Letting the scent guide me, I headed toward the football field. It grew stronger, fresher, making me think of blood. Desire stirred and I pushed it back. I hadn't given into desire since the night I chased that human. I wasn't ever giving into it again.

I found Fallen on the bleachers stairs. She stared at her arm and the mark across it. It stretched dark against her skin, beads of red dripping to the ground. Her face solemn, she took a knife, drawing it across her arm and creating a new mark.

My eyes followed the blood as it ran down her arm and dripped to the ground. The desire stirred more, hunger and thirst started gnawing at me. It'd be easy. She'd never know what hit her...

No. The word blasted through the desire, hunger and thirst. I did not want to hurt this human, she was kind to me. A rare way for humans to act when it came to vampires.

Had I made a friend?

I mulled the concept over. Fallen interested me. She helped clarify my brother's behavior this past weekend, but a friend? I always considered them pointless.

Even though I dismissed the idea as quickly as it came, when she lifted the blade to her arm again, I stopped her. "What are you doing?"

The knife fell from Fallen's fingers, a smile filling her face. "I knew the blood would draw you."

"I followed your scent." Which was true enough, I had followed her scent, made more potent by her blood.

"Where were you the other night?" she asked. "I waited for you."

"Why?"

"Why not?"

I tilted my head. I had never been asked that. I asked why and my brother always tried to explain. Why not... What a weird question.

"There was no point to wait for me; I had no intention of coming here."

"I didn't know that. I don't claim to know how a vampire's mind works. You might have decided to appear at any moment. Where were you?" she asked.

"Talking to my brother."

"So you smoothed out your problem with him?"

I scowled at her choice of words. "I did not have a problem with him. I didn't understand why he was doing what he was. You helped me understand."

Fallen nodded, looking thoughtful. When she returned her gaze to me, a sly look glimmered. She held out her arm. "Do you want a sip? You look thirsty."

"I am fine."

I wasn't fine. I had never been around fresh blood when I wasn't hunting. My gums ached, fangs straining to extend as I forced them to stay put. I felt like I was teetering on the edge of a cliff, desire waiting for me below.

"No."

"Oh, just thought you wouldn't want it to go to waste." Fallen innocently shrugged.

I put a scowl on my face, prolonging it to ensure she saw. "The only reason I drink blood is because I need it to survive."

"Interesting," she murmured, dragging her finger through the trails of blood.

I watched her, trying to figure her out. She wasn't anything like the humans in the city or the ones on campus or even my brother. He shuddered at my actions, mourned the humans I killed and I almost understood him at times.

Fallen was a mystery. Everything she said made no sense and her actions confused me. She wanted to interact with me even though there was no reason.

"I have to go," I said and turned to leave.

"Will I see you tomorrow?" A hint of desperation filled her voice. "You could come visit me at my dorm."

"I'm not doing that."

"Why not?" Her voice rose in pitch.

"Why?" I shot back.

Fallen pouted in reply.

I left her, heading to my brother's room to tell him about Fallen in hopes he could explain this strange human to me. Hopefully he wouldn't be mad I woke him.

Or mad I talked to another human.

Two rhythms on the other side of the glass froze me. Why was there another human in the room? My brother should be the only one.

My mind reeling, I dropped down. I wanted answers to my questions, but for the first time, I had no one to talk to. Long before the sun threatened to rise, I was back in my cellar, curled up in the corner and wishing I wasn't so alone.

****

Two rhythms beat on the other side of the window again. I scowled at the glass and my reflection scowl back. This was the second night in a row another human was in my brother's room.

Who was with him?

I dropped down and headed to the football field. I wandered up and down the bleachers, searched underneath, weaved across the field and looked in bathrooms and storage rooms, but Fallen wasn't waiting for me.

I never realized how much I liked having someone to talk to. I always said I didn't care if I had no one to speak with, it wasn't important to my survival. Now it was all I craved. I slumped onto a stone bench, not caring about the light glowing above. Maybe a human would see me, stop and talk to me.

No. I jumped to my feet and headed down the path. I didn't need to talk to my brother every night, I told myself as I passed by his dorm and saw his window still shut. I was fine by myself I decided as I doubled checked the football field for Fallen. I didn't need either of them.

Fallen's scent froze me as I stalked across a parking lot. Everything I had been trying to convince myself was forgotten as I whirled around and followed. I mused over what to talk about, but nothing came to mind. Something would present itself, I decided. She'd say something and I'd ask her to clarify.

Her scent came from an open window on the second floor of one of the dorms. I climbed up, peering into the cluttered room and seeing a human curled up on one of the beds. I turned my gaze to Fallen. "I told you I wasn't doing this."

"I have no idea what you mean, but if you don't be quiet, my roommate will wake," she replied innocently.

I concentrated, pushing hard against her will to make my suggestion last. Without a word, she stood and exited the small room. I jumped down from her window and waited in the shadows by the door, grabbing and pulling her into the darkness. She blinked in confusion when I released her.

"What just happened?"

"I forced my will on you."

"My head hurts now." She pressed her fingers to her forehead.

I considered apologizing, but dismissed the idea. I told her I didn't want to go to her dorm room. Maybe if she didn't have a roommate or the roommate was gone, I'd consider it. Even then, I wasn't sure. Instinct asked, what did I really know about Fallen?

"I don't care, take some pills," I replied.

Fallen's glare turned into a sweet smile, her voice matching. "Now you know where to find me so I don't have to sit out on the field freezing all night."

I scowled at her. "It's not wise to let someone know where you rest."

"Only for vampires." She tilted her head, watching me. "Is something wrong? It almost looks like you're upset."

"Past two nights there have been two heartbeats in my brother's room. I don't know who could be in there with him."

Fallen wandered around, a thoughtful look on her face and gaze cast up. "Maybe he's has a girlfriend. Or boyfriend."

"I know he has friends."

Fallen shook her head. "This would be different. More intimate." She strolled closer, tapping a finger against my chest. "With more touching, some hugging, lots of kissing and no clothes."

I stepped back, irritated by her closeness. "And that's more intimate?"

"Yes." Fallen coyly smiled. "Maybe he thinks he's in love and whoever the lucky girl or boy is consumes his thoughts. I imagine you're but a second thought to him now. Maybe not even. Maybe he's forgotten you."

I whirled around, Fallen's words mocking me as I dashed to my brother's dorm. No one stole my brother from me. No one made him forget me. Whoever this human was, I was going to kill them! I didn't care if he didn't want me to kill them. All I had to do was look in his eyes and make him forget. He trusted me...

He trusted me.

The thought stopped me, fist millimeters from the glass. My brother trusted me and I had been ready to use that trust to hurt him. Almost killed a human I knew nothing about. Maybe the human was a friend spending the night. He had told me stories of us doing that when I was human. I couldn't see through the curtains to confirm. And even if it was as Fallen described, I had to accept it, had to accept that I was forgotten.

I sighed, ashamed of myself.

"Dan?" a female voice whispered on the other side of the window. "I heard something outside the window."

The curtain moved and a sliver of my brother's face appeared. A smile lit his face and the curtain swung back. "It's nothing, go back to sleep. I gotta go outside a second."

"Why?"

"Go to sleep," he replied and I heard a door open and close.

I dropped down and paced under the lights, the second time in one night I didn't care if a human saw me.

"Hey," my brother padded over to me, barefoot, *with no shirt.*

"Who is that human?" I demanded.

The grin on his face faded and for a second I feared the worst. Then he sighed and shook his head. "I guess my note blew away." He looked back at me. "That's my girlfriend."

"But you have friends."

"Yeah, but she's special. She's my girlfriend and that's different from just a friend. It's a bit more intimate."

"With kissing and hugging and no clothes?"

He busted out laughing. "Hopefully there will be times like that, but we've only been dating a couple of days. Last night I invited her to stay, then tonight she asked if she could again. We're really hitting it off – getting along."

"So you haven't forgotten me?"

He sighed, shaking his head again. "Who have you been eavesdropping on? I suggest you find a new source for human information because whoever it is has got relationships wrong." He placed a hand on my shoulder. "No girl is ever gonna come between us, but there's gonna be times when I won't be around because I want to be with her. You panic too easily, worrying I'll turn into a normal human and chase after you with a torch and pitchfork."

"I wouldn't like that."

"Well, it isn't gonna happen. You have to remember while you're resting, I'm wide awake living my human life that you're one of many parts. My life doesn't revolve around you and your life shouldn't revolve around me."

I nodded.

"I'm sorry I worried you, I wrote a note, but it must have fallen. Next time I'll use duct tape." He looked up at the window, then back at me. "Are we good? Misunderstanding cleared up?"

"Yeah."

"Great, I'm going back to bed."

I grabbed his arm, stopping him. "That's the first time you've touched me since I murdered Mom and Dad."

He looked down at my hand gripping his arm and placed his hand over mine. "Yeah, it is. Guess I just avoided it unconsciously."

"Maybe," I agreed. I looked back up at the window, remembering the feeling of loneliness. "Can we talk tomorrow? I miss you."

"I miss you too. I'll try to be free tomorrow night and if not, I'll super glue the damn note to the window if I have to." He placed a hand on my shoulder again, shuddering. "You feel like death."

I shoved him as softly as I could. He still stumbled from the force. "Go to sleep."

"You're not my aunt," he teased back.

"I'm better than that," I said proudly. "I'm your brother."

"Peace," he called as he disappeared inside.

I turned to head back the way I came. I should have known better than to jump to conclusions. My brother would never forget me. Why had I believed Fallen? I shouldn't have, I decided.

And I won't ever again.

Fallen's face brightened when she saw me, but the expression quickly turned to shock as I grabbed her throat. I lifted her off the ground, my voice hissing. "You told me my brother forgot me. My brother would never forget, abandon or leave me. You lied. I don't like lying, it's pointless and I'll kill anyone who lies to me."

She struggled against my grip, her hand clawing at mine. "I didn't lie. Please, let me explain."

"What if I don't want to listen?" I hissed. "What if I just want to kill you?"

"You'd be killing an innocent human and you're not like that." Her voice rasped as I tightened my grip.

"I have no problems killing innocent humans."

"But I was trying to help. I didn't mean for you to think I was lying. Please put me down and I'll explain."

I debated her words. It'd be easy enough to catch her if she ran. Desire flared at the idea of chasing her down and drinking her blood. I pushed the desire back and let her feet touch the ground. Before I let go, I gave her fair warning.

"If you run, I will catch you and kill you."

She didn't move as I released her. Her voice shook as she rushed to explain. "I had an older sister; not a twin, but we were close. Then she met this guy and everything changed. She no longer had time for me and I felt abandoned, like I had lost her forever. We haven't talked in years."

"And you thought my brother was going to do that to me?"

She shrugged, refusing to meet my gaze. "I wanted to spare you the hurt. I wasn't lying, I swear."

How did I know if her words were the truth? She could be lying in an attempt to save her neck. But if she was telling the truth and I killed her, I'd be destroying the only other human I talked to. I debated for a long moment, watching Fallen stand as still as possible.

"Fine," I finally said. "I believe you and won't kill you."

Fallen fell to the ground, a wavering smile on her face and her voice trembling. "I'm very glad to hear that."

I didn't reply, my mind drifting to my hunger. I'd be lying if I said the thought of drinking her blood hadn't excited me. The anticipation rolled through me; every part of me ready to hunt and the need was strong enough that I could argue I had to. "I want blood now."

Fallen looked up, eyes going wide. "Oh."

"I said I wasn't going to kill you."

"Oh." She quickly looked away, cheeks turning pink. "I thought maybe you'd want a sip."

"Why would I want only a sip?"

"I dunno," she replied and fell silent.

I shook my head. Fallen never ceased to confuse me. "I'm going now."

She jumped to her feet, grabbed my arm and looked into my eyes, no signs of her earlier fear left in their depths. "Can we get together tomorrow night?"

"I haven't thought that far ahead."

"I'll wait for you here," Fallen called as I disappeared into the night.

I headed down the highway at a quick pace, heading to the nearest city, blending with the shadows as much as possible. This city was different from New York City, their Vampire Forces was more tenacious and the humans didn't hesitate to raise the alarm when I was seen. It made the hunt more thrilling as I hid in the shadows, stalked the human and delivered the blow that knocked them out.

The streets were like the highway, quiet and deserted. A breeze blew, sending debris dancing around my feet. I felt alone, the only creature in the darkness as I searched for any signs of bad humans.

It came out of nowhere, the blow throwing me to the ground. My chin smacked the pavement, teeth slamming together with a loud snap. Pain throbbed through me as I scrambled to my feet to face my attacker.

The vampire glared at me, flashing long fangs. His eyes narrowed, a glint of light making the black depths look evil. Twitching his fingers, he moved from side to side. A slow hiss escaped his lips, his message obvious. These were his hunting grounds.

A small part of my mind told me to back away carefully; this wasn't a fight I should get into. But another part spoke louder. It urged me to not back down; this vampire wasn't older than me. *Fight!*

I dropped into a defensive crouch. My lips pulled back to show my fangs, hands clenched into fists as I met the vampire's challenge. For a long moment we stared each other down, waiting for the other to make a move. My mind raced, trying to predict where he'd strike and how to counter him.

With a snarl, the vampire lunged. I threw my hands out, twisting around and knocking him down. I jumped at his exposed back, teeth clamped onto his shoulder, trying to rip flesh away. He snarled in pain, pushing back and crushing me against the wall. My grip on him loosened and he grabbed my neck, throwing me into a telephone pole. Each blow he struck sent pain racing through me. My instincts cried at me and survival kicked into over-drive.

I sprinted into motion, trying to escape, but the vampire grabbed me and threw me into another building. My vision spun around, dizziness slamming into me like a gale force wind. I slumped against the wall, watching as he came at me, fangs bared. The two needle sharp teeth raked across my face, creating a fiery path of pain. More pain laced down my neck, the vampire biting again. I felt flesh tear away, too weak to stop it.

Vaguely, through layers of pain, I heard a noise. A quick chirp. The vampire wailing on me disappeared in an instant. Red and blue lights flashed across my pain-filled vision. What an unlikely savior.

But not if I remained here.

I forced myself to move, stumbling down the street and away from the flashing lights. Voices yelled from behind, ordering me to freeze. I kept running, ignoring the pain my movements caused. I didn't stop until I was safe in my cellar. The cool floor eased the pain throbbing through me as I stretched out on it. Quickly, I drifted away, feeling closer to death than my turning three years ago.

****

It was almost surprising I woke. While resting, my mind had been blank and my body teetering on actual death. The pain had lessened to something more tolerable, a steady throb that I found relatively easy to ignore. The injuries on my cheek stung as I traced my finger along one. I had never been injured before. How much blood it would take to heal? Since I was no longer at risk of dying and my need only murmured softly, I decided I could spare a few moments to see my brother first.

The window to his room was open, causing yellow light to spill out. The sight was a relief. I hadn't wanted to find a closed and curtained window with a note for me.

Checking for humans, I stepped out of the shadows and limped across the sidewalk into the shadow of the dorm. Another quick look around confirmed still no humans in sight. My climb took a little longer, my energy and strength weakened by my injuries. Another thing blood would fix. Finally, I slid through the window, wincing in pain.

"What the hell?" My brother jumped to his feet and his face turned a few shades whiter. "What happened?"

"I got into a fight with another vampire. I was on his hunting grounds and he didn't like that."

"But you're ripped to shreds and." He paused and moved closer. "There's no blood," he whispered. "You don't have any blood in you."

"Why do you think I drink it? I need it to survive."

His hand hovered over my injuries. "I just figured you'd have something in you. Plasma or I dunno. Does it hurt?"

"Yes, I think I almost permanently died during the day."

His Adam's apple bobbed. "I thought I felt something today. A weird, crawling feeling and it freaked me out. I didn't think of you, I figured you were resting safely."

"I was safe," I assured him. "I was simply closer to death than I liked."

"Aren't you always close to death?" His lips quirked up.

"I can be closer."

He shuddered and slumped into his chair, tapping his fingers. "Are you gonna be okay?"

"I need to hunt and heal."

He looked at me out of the corner of his eye. "So you got your ass handed to you, almost died during the day and first thing you do, instead of fixing yourself, is come find me? Aren't I a temptation? I can see your fangs."

I shrugged, ignoring the pain. "I wanted to talk to you first. I'll survive and you will too."

"What if you were hurt bad enough? Would I still be safe?"

I shook my head. "It wouldn't be a choice, it'd be survival."

He gulped down a breath and weakly laughed. "Don't ever put yourself in that position and if you do, do not come find me."

"I'll stay far away," I promised with a laugh.

"Don't laugh, it's freaky and double freaky because you look like you got into a fight with a razor and lost. The way the skin moves, bleh." He shuddered again. "Don't touch it!" he added when I ran a finger along the lacerations.

I dropped my hand. "I should go."

"Wait a sec, I have a crazy and stupid idea and I'm curious enough to try." He darted into his tiny bathroom and back. "Hold still." He instructed and pressed a blade against his thumb.

Our eyes met when a tiny bead of blood appeared. We both knew what he just did was dangerous and insane, but he was safe. My need and hunger remained calm within me, the tiny bead of blood not enough to tempt me – not if the blood was my brother's. I stopped my breath, keeping the scent out of my nose as an extra precaution.

He pressed his thumb against my cheek, spreading the blood along a wound. Goosebumps covered his arms, his skin turning white, and sweat broke out on his forehead.

"No offense, but I feel like I'm going to hurl," he muttered between tight lips.

"Why are you doing this? What are you trying to figure out?" A whiff of blood filled my nose and tingled on my tongue.

"Because I've lost my mind," he said with a forced laugh. "I wanted to see if this would heal you."

"I think I have to drink it."

He pulled his hand away to inspect. "Guess so. And now that I've filled the room with the smell of my blood while my injured vampire brother sits two feet away, I'm going to get a bandage."

I grabbed his hand, my eyes riveted on the tiny slice across his thumb. There was something else I was curious about. And even though I knew this was a crazier idea than what he just did, I drew his hand closer and opened my mouth.

He gasped as I scraped my fangs along the side of his thumb. Blood burst onto my tongue from the shallow, twin cuts. I ran my tongue across his skin and injuries along my face tingled.

"Tommy," he whispered. "Should I be afraid?"

I released his hand as an answer. He cradled it against his chest, his heart pounding and the smell of his fear thickened the air. I dashed to the bathroom, finding a box of bandages. He resisted when I pulled his hand free to wrap a bandage around his thumb.

"I didn't mean to scare you."

"I wasn't scared, just shocked," he replied, pulling his hand free.

I looked at him, frowning. "Don't lie. I don't like it, especially if it's you. I can handle any truth you tell me."

"Even if you don't like it?" he asked and I nodded. "I guess I was afraid. Terrified is more like it. You had this intense look on your face and when you actually bit... I nearly pissed my pants."

"I didn't really bite. Made shallow scrapes; I didn't want you bleeding too much."

He rolled his eyes and I saw relief in the action. "Whatever. Your injuries look a little better."

"I need more to fully heal."

"And you're going elsewhere to get it?" he asked uncertainly. I scowled at him and he threw his hands up. "Just making sure. One day you might change your mind and have me for dinner. I'm too young to be dinner."

"You know I'd never do that to you," I replied.

We rose together, heading towards the window. He stopped me before I climbed through. "I'm glad you stopped, it was a real learning experience."

I rolled my eyes, repeating what he said when he thought something was crazy. "You're insane, the humans should lock you up."

"Get out of here." He shoved me. "And don't get into any more fights," he called after me.

****

I saw the questions coming, had figured out something about Fallen. She liked to ask questions. A lot.

"How often do you kill? Is it every night? Because the belief is that vampires kill every night because they are always hungry."

I glanced at her out of the corner of my eye. I also figured out why sometimes my brother sounded exasperated when I asked questions. It really was annoying. "I only hunt when I need to."

She stopped her skipping. "Need, you've used that word before. What does it mean exactly?"

"It means what it implies. When I need to feed, I hunt. When you get hungry you eat, correct? You *need* to eat. I *need* to hunt." I replied and glanced around. "Where are you taking me?"

We were on the far side of the campus, in an area I never traveled through because of the amount of lights. They were everywhere, at each door, along the sidewalks and spaced out among the parking lot. There were few shadows for me to hide in and I felt exposed.

Fallen glanced around as if she just noticed our surroundings. "I dunno, I wasn't paying attention."

"That's how a vampire could get you."

Fallen shrugged. "If one does, I can only pray it is painless or I wake back up."

"Why would you want to wake back up? You'd be a vampire then; that's stupid."

"*You* woke back up."

"I never said I wanted to."

"Maybe it was a secret wish," Fallen replied. "You can't deny it. You said you forgot being human so maybe deep down you wanted to be a vampire."

"I had denial," I retorted. My eyes snapped away from her, ears picking up the sound of fast approaching feet. "Someone's coming." I disappeared up the side of a building before she could respond.

Two humans hurried along the path of light. Their pace quickened when they spotted Fallen. They were her two friends who I had met on the football field. I often wondered why they never came with Fallen to see me. I wanted to talk to them; I liked the idea of having more humans to interact with.

"There you are," Risen panted when he reached Fallen. "We've been looking... all... over..." His voice faded, stopping both himself and Settle as I dropped down from my perch.

I paused in my own tracks, confused. Didn't they recognize me from the night we met? I took a step forward, prolonging my smile. "Hi."

They didn't reply as they inched closer to Fallen. When she was within arm's reach, Risen grabbed her and pulled her away. The distance between us was about the length of the parking lot when they stopped and began talking.

"Are you insane?" Risen whispered. "Do you want to die?"

Fallen scoffed, her voice much louder. "Please, if he wanted to kill me, he would have done it the night we met."

"There were three of us!" Risen's voice jumped in pitch. "Vampires never attack crowds."

"That was hardly a crowd," Fallen snorted.

"Enough of a crowd," Risen replied. "It could have killed you, then me or Riley. All of us could have died!" He leaned closer, lowering his voice more. "There's been some talk around campus. There haven't been any deaths, but the college heads are thinking about calling VF. They don't want a vampire on campus, bad publicity."

Fallen scoffed again.

Risen's scowl deepened. "This is serious, you know what people will say."

"I don't care what people say and I thought you didn't either," Fallen challenged.

"I don't," Risen said defiantly.

"No one in their right mind wants to be seen as a sympathizer," Settle said softly.

"I don't want to be a sympathizer!" Fallen hissed.

"We know what you want, *Fallen*. You've made that perfectly clear," Risen snapped. His eyes narrowed when she didn't respond. "Fine, if you've made up your mind. Guess we'll start treating you like one. Come on, Riley."

"Find them first," Fallen muttered as the two humans hurried away.

I walked to her, watching her friends disappear. My chest felt crushed, the whispered conversation revealing. "They don't like vampires; they don't like me."

Fallen scoffed. "That night at the field, they were too high to realize you were a real vampire. They said it wasn't possible, that you would have killed us instead of talked. They don't know anything, they don't know me." She sighed, wiping the anger away and quickly changing the subject. "Halloween is coming up and there's this place I go every year; they have a party to celebrate the spirits. Want to come?"

"Why?"

"Why not?" she replied with a grin.

"That won't work on something that pointless."

"Fine, because it's fun."

"Do I look like I care about fun?"

"You'd do it if your *precious brother* asked," Fallen muttered.

"My brother wouldn't risk my safety by insisting I go somewhere with humans. In case you haven't noticed," I motioned the way her friends had retreated. "Humans hate vampires. You should hate vampires."

"Why?" Fallen demanded. "Because you drink blood?"

"Because if I was inclined, I'd kill you. It wouldn't bother me and I wouldn't feel guilty or mourn you. The only reason I haven't is because I like talking to you. I like having a..." My voice died.

I finally understood a human behavior. Friendship. I understood why humans made those connections with each other. I didn't talk to my brother just because he was my brother. That was the reason I didn't kill him three years ago. I talked to him because I enjoyed his company. He was my friend and so was Fallen.

A smile filled my face and I was sure my brother would be proud of my human discovery. "I won't kill you because you're my friend."

****

"Tommy." My name drifted like a whisper in the wind. I froze and listened closer, hearing leaves softly rustle and cars driving in the distance. Around me, human heartbeats called like a siren. My name didn't repeat, the voice falling silent.

Fallen watched my frozen form, eyes boring into me. "Is someone coming?

"Something's wrong," I replied. Feelings churned in my chest, growing with each passing moment. Annoyance and anger bubbled, tugging at me. I let the emotions pull me, leading me across campus as Fallen hurried behind.

"Tommy!"

There was no mistaking the voice this time. It grew louder with each step I took, my brother calling my name again and again. His voice ended at the dorms, a group of humans filling the doorway of one and more clustered inside. A few were pleading with him, trying to convince him to go back inside.

"Come on, Dan," a short, stocky male I recognized said. "You drank too much and don't know what you're saying."

My brother jerked away. He wavered, almost falling, as he jabbed a finger at the short, stocky human's chest. "I know exactly what I'm talking about. I'm talking about my twin brother, who's a vampire."

"You don't have a brother," the short, stocky human insisted.

"Yes, I do!" my brother snapped, his words slurring together. "Whyou... why do you think I live with my aunt and uncle? Because my brother got turned and came back and killed our parents. He killed our parents and he can't even give me the decency of showing up on the night he did it. Tommy! Where are you, you leech bastard?"

"You shouldn't say stuff like that, Dan," a girl said. "It's not right."

"You're not right," my brother snapped. "Why don't you go have a few more shots and kiss the next guy you see? It's what you've been doing."

The girl made an offended noise and anger flashed across her face. "Since you're drunk, I won't take you seriously."

"Whatever," my brother snorted. "Why won't he come? I said his name. Can't he feel my pain? Doesn't he care what tonight is?"

He started to sag, letting the short, stocky human grab him and maneuver him towards the door. "Let's get you inside and to bed."

"My room's open. He can crash there for a few," another human offered.

"Thanks," the girl said. "We'll get him back to his room later."

My brother was led through the door, the rest of the humans following. They muttered and whispered as they piled through, discussing his behavior.

"He always rambles about a brother when he's drunk."

"Tony said he never met a brother."

"Maybe the brother was killed by the vampire and he's in denial. They say it happens."

"Who knows, he's wasted and people say crazy shit when they're drunk. Probably won't remember what a fool he made of himself tomorrow."

Fallen pulled on my arm. "Come on, he's drunk. Let his friends take care of him."

I looked back at the dorm, at the scene through the glass door. Humans crowded the lounge, huddled in groups, cups in hand. The short, stocky human and girl rejoined the crowd. One by one, their voices halted, the loud music forgotten as the humans noticed what was among them.

I had never been around so many humans, not in an enclosed area. I should have stayed closer to the door, giving myself a clear view of my only escape route. Pushing my instincts and nervousness back, I made my voice loud enough to be heard over the music.

"I'm looking for my brother. He wants to see me."

No one answered and I wasn't surprised. Humans were thrown off when I let them see me. Even more when I talked to them, asking for help. But it didn't matter if these humans were struck speechless, I caught my brother's scent. I dashed up the stairs, footsteps following as a voice yelled in panic.

"Don't let it find Dan!"

It took me seconds to find the room that held my brother. I dashed to the bed, sliding onto my knees. "Danny."

His eyelids fluttered open. "Tommy, what... When did I get back to my room? My head is pounding, how much did I drink?"

"You called me, you're not in your room and I have no idea how much you drank."

"I'm not in my room?" He bolted up. "Ow!"

"What's hurt?"

He gripped his head. "My head, sat up too fast. Damn. Why did you come? Are you nuts?"

"I heard you call my name. You wanted me to come," I replied weakly.

"I'm drunk. I say and do a lot of stuff I don't mean when I'm drunk." He looked sideways at me. "How many people saw you?"

I glanced at the door full of fearful humans. I looked back in time to see his eyes follow. "All of them."

"All right," he muttered and threw his legs over the side of the bed. He pinched the bridge of his nose, squeezing his eyes shut. "Did anyone call VF?"

"No, we didn't want to get busted," the short, stocky human replied.

"Good, go downstairs and tell everyone it's cool. He won't hurt anyone. He's like a pet tiger."

"Tigers eat people," the short, stocky human said.

"Only if you piss him off, so don't give him a reason."

Slowly, the humans disappeared. The short, stocky human was the last to leave, eyes darting between me and my brother. He dismissed the short, stocky human with a wave.

He rubbed his face, groaning. "I'm still drunk and it's fading, which is good. Usually I pass out and forget what happened. I'll remember everything I said for once. Damn. You've never shown up before when I've gone on a rant."

"You've called me before?"

"Yeah, we get talking about vampires and I mention my vampire brother and insist I can prove it. No one believes me, then I pass out and forget what I said until someone tells me."

"Did you really think I didn't know what tonight was?"

He shrugged. "You don't pay attention to dates and you've never said anything about it before."

"I didn't think you wanted to remember. You always say anything related to Mom and Dad's death is tainted, so I figured the night was tainted."

He gave me a weak, tired smile. "You can mention that night. Aunt Dee and I always make a trip back home to visit the graves and lay some flowers. I always wished you could be there too."

"I like that idea."

"Mean it?"

"Would I lie?"

He snorted, then winced. Wobbling, he pushed to his feet. I grabbed his elbow to help keep him steady. "Oh this sucks, everything is spinning. Don't let go or I'll fall flat on my face."

"They're going to separate us again. Take you away and try to destroy me. What if I don't find you again?"

He turned to me with a serious look. And fell forward. His face smacked into my shoulder, his hands flailing. For a moment he stood there, face buried against my shoulder, hands gripping me. Then he started shaking with laughter.

"What's funny? I think you bit me," I informed him.

He laughed harder. "I wish I could have seen myself. Oh, I just drooled on you." He dissolved into fits of laughter, barely staying on his feet. Finally, he tried to calm himself. "I'm sorry, I'm still a bit drunk and that was funny. Now, come on, you're walking me through a room full of drunk college students."

The humans fell silent when we appeared at the top of the steps. Their eyes followed us, watching and waiting to see what I'd do. I wondered who was more nervous: them or me.

"Dan, what are you doing? That thing will kill you." the girl from outside whispered, a hint of annoyance in her high voice.

I growled at her, irritated at being called a thing.

"Stop it," my brother ordered me. He looked at the girl who had shrunk behind the short, stocky human. "If he wanted to kill me, he'd have done it already." He planted himself firmly, refusing to let me take him to his dorm. Instead he raised his voice, eyes daring any of the humans to speak. "This is my brother. He's very real, very dead and mostly harmless."

I smiled, trying to look harmless.

"Don't do that. You'll freak everyone out," he ordered.

I dropped my smile.

"Now you look like you want to eat everyone."

"I do."

"I should smack you." He looked back at the humans. "I'd appreciate everyone not calling VF. Tommy's–"

"Hey!" I interrupted.

"Rick, Kate, Linda, Susie, Jerry, Casey, Arik, Kel, Tyler, Vinny, Matt, Scott, Michelle and Charissa. Now you know their names." He jabbed a finger at me. "You're not going to eat any of them." He turned his finger at the humans. "And no one is going to call VF. I'm not crazy or a sympathizer or any of that crap. If anyone can't deal with my association with my brother, then don't talk to me."

I felt he wanted to march out of the building on his own, but he had started to shake. Sweat covered his forehead and a green tint was creeping into his skin. I kept one hand on his elbow, supporting him with as little contact as possible as we walked out the door.

The humans watched us from the building, hiding behind the glass doors. The short, stocky human looked conflicted, like he wanted to break away and help my brother, but didn't want to break away from the group of humans at the same time.

"I don't think anyone's calling Vampire Forces."

"No one wants to get busted." My brother weakly laughed, grinning. "That felt great, showing people you're real. I don't have to make up excuses for leaving early. I can say, *My vampire brother's coming to visit tonight.*"

"They could still call."

His smile faded and he shuffled to a bench, huffing as he fell onto it. He leaned forward and rested his elbows on his knees with his head bowed. "I know. They could call as soon as we're out of sight. It just felt liberating doing that. I struggle with you and how I know people see you. And their perceptions aren't wrong; you kill people. I wish it weren't true, that I could change that truth. I wish I could turn back time, keep you from being turned, then life would be normal. I know it may not matter to you, but I wish people could see past the vampire and see you like I do."

Anger bubbled up inside me. I shouldn't have done that. I should have listened to Fallen and stayed away. Why did I keep ruining my brother's life? My fists clenched. "I need to leave and stop ruining your human life."

"We've been through this. I don't want you to leave."

"If I was gone, you could get on with your human life, be with your girlfriend and forget about me," I insisted.

"I don't want to forget you!" He sprang to his feet. "Don't you get it? There is no one else. Aunt Dee and Uncle Dick took me in because they were the only relatives I had left. They never even wanted kids, it's why they don't have any. You're the only family I have. I need you."

"You need me?" I echoed.

He slumped back onto the bench. "When everything's messed up and I feel like I'm going crazy, there's you. Always on time, always there, even more now you're a vampire."

I sat onto the bench next to him. "But you said your life doesn't revolve around me."

"It doesn't," he assured me. "But you're the thing I cling to when I feel like everything's being swept out from under me. I need you to survive."

That was all he needed to say for me to understand. I helped him back to his feet and we hurried as fast as he could to his dorm where we took a back stairway up to his room.

He groaned as I laid him on his bed. "Think my stomach has decided to hurl. I kinda like it better when I pass out and I'm not sick until morning." Another groan had him up, tentatively sitting on the edge of his bed. He sat a moment, then laid back down, only to sit back up. "Maybe I better stay awake a little longer. Every time I lay down, that's when I feel like hurling." He looked up at me. "Will you stay until the sun rises?"

****

The humans didn't call Vampire Forces. I had been certain they would as soon as I was out of sight. Instead, what they did was talk about it. The story of the party I crashed spread over campus, quickly turning into a legend with many versions blown out of proportion. My brother thought it was amusing, laughing as he told me the latest tales. Give it time and something will distract them, he assured me. Fallen was sullen about it. Said it was dumb to risk myself like that and when I stopped finding her, she'd assume I had been destroyed and would mourn my death.

Being the center of human conversation made me nervous. All it would take was one human calling Vampire Forces and I'd have to run. I started laying low, melting into shadows and trying to be invisible to human eyes. Sometimes the effort didn't feel worth it, hiding in the shadows as I waited for the humans to clear out, and then darting up the walls.

Only to find a sentence long note that said, *Went to a Halloween party. Peace, Danny.*

I folded the note, placing it in my pocket with the others. I wasn't sure why I kept the notes. Once read, I wasn't forgetting the message. Maybe it was part of the friendship concept I finally understood. My brother wasn't available to talk to me, so I reread his notes instead.

At least I had learned when he left notes, that meant he wouldn't be back to his dorm that night. It was disappointing coming back to check over and over, each time seeing a dark window.

That left Fallen, who was always willing to talk, but I wasn't finding her tonight. She had been insistent on her Halloween party. Begging until I pushed my will on her and forced her to leave. But the next night she was at it again, arguing I needed to go. After all, I went to a party my brother had been at, so why couldn't I go to her party too?

"Nice costumer, loser!" The voice came from behind me. "Hey, I'm talking to you! What are you, a suck wannabe?"

I turned, a bit shocked. The human was talking to *me*?

There were six of them, all dressed oddly. Some in bright colors, a few wearing odd hats, there was even a male in a dress. Their smiles and jeering faded when I moved towards them.

"Dude," the one in the dress whispered. "I think that's a real vampire."

"Do you think it's the one that was at that party a couple weekends ago?" another human whispered.

The rest of the humans muttered, each stating what they had heard.

I tilted my head at the one in the dress, stopping a safe distance away. "Why are you wearing a dress? Those are for females."

They backed up a few paces, looking anywhere but my eyes. That was what I was used to. As much as I enjoyed talking to Fallen, I didn't understand why she didn't shy from me.

"It's Halloween," the human in the dress said. "You dress up, go out and have a good time."

"You need an excuse? You have good times on a weekly basis. Every Friday and Saturday."

"There you are!" Fallen rushed over and gave the group an apologetic look. "Forgive my little brother, he thinks it's a riot to dress up like a leech and scare people." She gave me a stern look, not giving me a chance to speak. "That's not funny, Billy, people might mistake you for an actual vampire and then you'll be in big trouble with Mom! I'm really sorry again. Don't tell anyone what a little twerp my brother is." She pulled me away, her voice lowering so only I could hear. "What is wrong with you? How could you let them see you?"

"I didn't mean to, I thought this part of campus would be empty. It usually is," I replied. "How did you find me?"

She gave me a blank look. "Luck."

I didn't believe in luck. Luck didn't help me survive. Luck didn't help me find my brother three years ago. Persistence did. But what else described Fallen's ability to find me? She always found me as I was leaving my brother's dorm. Sometimes she found me before I talked to him.

"Come on." She tugged on my arm. "We gotta hurry or we'll miss the party."

"No." I pulled out of her grip and fixed her with a long, icy stare. "Just because you think I'm gentle and not like other vampires doesn't mean you can drag me around like your pet. And I know what a pet is, apparently I had one as a human. Another pointless human activity, but that's beside the point.

The point is I'm not your pet and I have no objections to turning you into my meal. In fact, I think I will. Right now."

"You won't."

"You don't think so?" I pulled my lips back, showing her my fangs.

"No," she defiantly replied.

I growled, knowing she was right, but not wanting to admit it. "This is why sympathizers always end up dead. You're too stupid to know what's good for your own survival."

"I'm not a sympathizer!" she shouted, giving me a hard shove. "I want to be a damn vampire!"

My annoyance disappeared. "What?"

"I want to be a vampire. Being human sucks. We're slow and we age every day and one day I'll die."

"That's how it should be."

She shoved me again, pounding her fists against my chest. "Says the vampire! What? Are you the only one who gets to be a vampire and live forever? Is that how it should be?"

"You wouldn't last as a vampire, you'd die by the end of the first night," I told her with certainty.

Silent fury shook her body, fists clenched at her sides. "If you don't turn me, I'm calling VF."

"Go ahead," I replied and walked away.

****

Like the humans at the party, Fallen didn't call Vampire Forces, but for different reasons. The desperation in her voice told me she'd say anything if she thought it'd get me to turn her. I had to give her credit. She was tenacious.

She passed my hiding spot, walking along the sidewalk. Every few feet she stopped, holding her hand out and letting red drops fall to the cement. Then she moved on to a new spot and repeated. I watched until she disappeared, then darted in the opposite direction. I knew what the red drops were. That was begging me to kill her, not turn her.

I wasn't doing either to my friend.

I followed the red drops, a bloody trail, to her dorm. I hoped to find her two friends – the ones who hated me – and tell them what she was doing. Maybe they could explain to her what I obviously couldn't.

Through the door, I spotted Risen and Settle in the lounge, laying together on the couch and their eyes on the TV. A few other humans were present as well, but they sat at a table with their backs to me. Now I hoped luck was real and mine would last.

I ducked through the door, staying low to the ground as I darted up to the couch. I crouched behind it, keeping an eye on the humans at the table. Risen and Settle jumped when I appeared in front of them. I grabbed Settle's arm, pressing my finger to my lips, nodded towards the door and whispered my request before darting back out.

"Please, I need to talk to you about Fallen."

"What? Did you kill her?" Risen demanded as he approached me.

"No," I said. "But if you don't talk some sense into her, I will out of annoyance. She wants to be a vampire."

Risen scoffed. "We know."

"You do?" If her friends knew, why weren't they discouraging her?

"She talks about it all the time," Settle sighed. "At first she acted like she wasn't serious, but the more we hung out with her, the more we realized she was serious. We've tried talking to her, but she won't listen."

"That's what you meant that night you said you knew what she wanted," I realized.

Risen fixed me with a cold, hate-filled glare. "Why haven't you turned her? I'm sure you leeches must want more of you around."

"More would mean more competition and I don't like fighting for my meals."

Risen scoffed again, his favorite thing to do. "So she finally asked you to turn her?"

I nodded. "Now she's walking around campus, leaving blood everywhere. I've been hiding from her for the past four days. She's my friend; I don't want to do that."

The glare in Risen's eyes softened. He sighed and for the first time met my gaze. "Look, we've tried talking to her, but she won't listen. The only good thing was she didn't know how to find any vampires."

"But now she knows me," I muttered, then winced. "Damn."

"What?" The sharpness returned to Risen's voice.

"She knows about me. Knows about my hunger and how often I hunt... my name..." A knot of dread formed in my stomach. I snapped my head up, making the two humans jump. "What's her name? I have to counter any power she has over my name!"

Both humans looked doubtful, but finally Settle muttered, "Amber, Amber Tally." She gave me a pleading look and a tiny hint of trust shimmered through the fear. "If you are her friend, please don't kill her. She needs help."

What was I going to do? I couldn't have Fallen following me around, begging me to turn her, threatening when I refused. Killing her would be easy, a quick solution, but I didn't want to kill my friend.

I was turning into a human.

"I know someone who might be able to help," I replied and left the two humans standing in the light. I crawled up the side of my brother's dorm, sliding through the open window of his room. "I have a problem."

"Does your problem consist of figuring out what Y and X equal?"

"No."

"Then it's not that bad of a problem. I am way too close to failing this class and I'm not taking it again," he replied without looking up from his homework.

"A human knows about me."

"Everyone knows about you. Our little fiasco is college legend now."

"No," I said. "A human *knows* about me. I've been talking to one."

His head snapped up, his pen slipping through his fingers. "What?"

I always felt bad not telling him about Fallen, but never understood why I was hesitant. Now I knew. I feared his reaction. "Don't be mad, but I've been talking to this human since the start of college. I kind of stumbled upon her. She helped me understand a few things about humans, about you."

A long, silent pause as my brother looked at me.

"Okay, lemme get this straight, not only have you been talking to another human, but this human knows about me too?" he sighed, sounding exasperated. "You know, everyone at the party was really nice and didn't blurt out it was me who called you to the party. I couldn't believe that a single person didn't drop my name at some point, but by some miracle they didn't. By some miracle no one called VF. And you blurt everything out to the first human you see. What else?"

"She knows my name," I mumbled.

He placed his hands on his head. "Anything else?"

"She wants me to turn her."

"Jeez, a suck wannabe, those people are the worst." He cast a glance at me. "What did you tell her?"

"I told her she wouldn't last as a vampire and now she's following me."

A laughed escaped him. "Sorry," he said sheepishly. "What do you know about her?"

"I know her name," I replied. "Amber Tally."

"What does she look like?"

"Long, black hair, pale skin, tall and thin. She wears a lot of black."

"I've seen a few girls on campus that always dress in black, lit or art majors I think." He rocked back in his chair, tapping his pen on the desk. "Is there any risk she'll call VF because you rejected her?"

"She threatened, but it was a lie."

He relaxed a little. "If you're sure she's not going to call VF to spite you, I think we can relax. We have her name and I'll see what I can dig up on her while you're resting."

****

The next night Fallen was absent from campus. Her scent hung in the air, but it was fading. I slipped through the shadows, on edge from her lack of presence. What if I had been wrong? What if she was at Vampire Forces, telling them about me, saying I hung around the college on a nightly basis? That I'm the vampire the humans on campus gossip about? What if Vampire Forces made the connection between me and what happened in New York City three years ago? I dreaded a repeat of that.

"I don't like girl problems," I sighed as I slumped to my brother's bed.

He snorted. "Get used to it. Girls are a nightmare to deal with." He leaned forward, homework discarded. "Okay, I snooped around and found what dorm Amber Tally is in. I sweet-talked Mrs. Fable, the housing director, saying I needed to return something to Amber and she forgot to tell me her dorm room. Then I asked any black-clad people I saw if they knew her. There were two that looked at me funny when I asked." He raised an eyebrow.

"Those were probably the two friends she was with when I met her. I found them last night and asked them to talk to her, but they said they tried and she wouldn't listen to them either. The girl asked me not to kill her," I replied.

"That definitely explains the stares." He held up a finger, making sure I didn't interrupt. "Then I noticed something while standing in line trying to decide did I want tacos or pizza for lunch. This girl was staring at me. She was tall, thin with black hair and sad eyes."

"That's her!" I jumped up. "What did she do?"

"Calm down, killer," he laughed. "She didn't do anything, just watched me the whole time. It was creepy, she didn't move much, like she was pretending to be a vampire. Or practicing."

"Then what?"

"I ate my food and left. She didn't follow."

"Did you see her again?"

"No, I had class, and then I got sucked up doing homework and forgot to look for her. I think I need a math tutor," he said apologetically. "I did learn a few things about your girlfriend. She's an art major, not from around here and an only child."

"Wait," I interrupted. "She told me she had an older sister."

"Did you tell her I was older?"

"No, I told her I was worried about you always being with your girlfriend. She said she knew what it was like because her older sister abandoned her for another human." I felt anger shake me. "I believed her. She told me she wouldn't lie to me."

"Tommy." My brother placed a calming hand on my shoulder. There was a mixture of concern and fear on his face. "You know why she lied?"

I shook my head, too angry to speak.

"Because she wanted to get close in hopes that when she finally told you what she wanted, you'd do it because you were connected in a way."

"I thought she was my friend," I hissed.

"I know and in a way she was."

"But she lied."

"She lied so you'd be her friend."

"I don't like liars. I should have killed her the first time I thought she was lying."

"You don't mean that. You're mad and hurt."

"Yes, I do! I'm going to find her, make her think I'll turn her, then kill her. It's what she deserves."

He added his other hand on my shoulder, wiping the fear from his face. Even the usual goosebumps were absent from his arms. "I know for you when something goes wrong, you instantly want to kill it, but think about it. Do you really want to kill her?"

"No," I admitted after a moment. "I want to know why. I want to understand."

"Okay." He released me.

"I don't know where she is right now, her scent has faded. This is a mess," I sighed.

"That's what you get for talking to anyone else but me," he teased, bent over his homework again.

"You said my life shouldn't revolve around you," I protested.

"It shouldn't," he replied. "But you have to be careful around people. Do a little research, push your will against theirs and get them to tell you why they aren't afraid to speak to you first. If it's a sympathizer, fine, but anyone else, get away."

"Can I kill them?"

"You should know what I'd say by now," he sighed. "Do whatever you want, just stay safe, for me."

"Okay." I fell silent, letting him work on his homework. For a few minutes, then I wondered something. "Why do some humans sympathize and others want to be vampires?"

"Sympathizers believe vampires are still people, there's human in you. I think they're right, but I'm not about to buddy up with any more vampires. You're enough of a handful. Plus, any other vampire, I'd probably wind up dead," he replied without looking up from his homework.

"You trust me?"

"I trust you," he agreed. "I think what happened with you was you saw me and our connection sparked what human was left in you. Now it's growing, helping you still be the brother I know."

"You still think I can be human?"

"You get more and more human every day."

"Maybe," I admitted in a small voice.

He looked up at me, smirking. "One day, when I'm old and you still look the same, you're going to do something incredibly human and I'm gonna say, *I told you so.*"

"I do understand friendship now. I like having friends to talk to." I made another admission. "What about the others? Suck wannabes. Why do they want to be vampires?"

He sighed, tapping his pen on the desk. "Guess they think being human is boring. They get caught up in the glamor of old myths, thinking that's how it will be. Or sometimes, they want to be immortal at any cost."

"She did say humans were slow and one day she would die."

He snorted. "I bet she's got a nice life. Both parents, no worries and all she does is whine about how one day she will get old and die."

"I told her dying was normal."

"Do you really believe that?"

"Of course." I motioned to myself. "Do I look normal?"

"You look like a walking corpse."

"Exactly, I should be six feet under."

He laughed and shook his head. "Do you even know what that means?"

****

The rest of the night I spent with my brother. After he finished his homework, he went to bed, tossing and turning before settling into sleep. The sleep was fitful, like he was unconsciously aware of the danger I presented.

When the sky started to lighten and the air slowly warmed, I didn't move from my spot. The unknown was outside my brother's room. Fallen was out there. I expected her to try to force my hand and make me turn her. Which wouldn't happen; if my fangs punctured her flesh, it'd result in her death.

"What are you still doing here?" my brother muttered sleepily.

"I can't go out there, not when I don't know what's waiting for me out there."

He sat up, shuffled to the window and looked out. "Sun's gonna be up soon. Whatcha gonna do?"

"...Can I stay here?"

His eyes widened in shock. "You serious? What are you gonna do? Rest on the bed? I'm sorry, I don't think I could deal with that. Not without thoroughly washing my sheets."

His worry was a little trivial in my opinion.

"I wouldn't sleep on the bed," I replied. "I just need someplace dark."

He relaxed instantly. "Um, the bathroom doesn't have windows. Maybe you could crash in the shower and I could cover you with some blankets? It won't be pitch black, but you should be safe from the sun."

I peeked out the curtains, seeing pink tint the sky. "It will be fine."

"All right." He pulled a thick and dark blanket off his bed.

I followed him to the bathroom, wrinkling my nose. "It kind of smells bad."

"Yeah, well, cleaning the bathroom is a bit low on my to-do list." He cracked the shower door, peering in. "Floor's dry, that's good. You want some towels to lay on anyways?"

"Doesn't matter."

"Of course not. Get in and I'll cover you up. I don't know how I'm going to manage taking a piss with you in here."

"I'm not sure I want to be in here when you have to," I replied warily.

He smiled wickedly. "Sweet dreams, lil' bro... or rest," he said and tossed the blanket over my head.

I settled against the tiled wall, staring at the threads in the blanket and feeling unease settle into my stomach. A new resting spot that was *above* ground? As safe as I felt with my brother, it'd be a lie if I said I didn't feel a little exposed. It took some time, but I managed drifted away, falling into half awareness.

True to his word, my brother was back in the bathroom, trying to move quietly as he prepared for his classes. After running a lot of water and generally making the room smell worse, he snuck back out.

When the door to his room clicked shut and his footsteps faded down the hallways, I fully woke. Anxiety joined the unease sitting in my stomach. What would happen if a human came in and found me? What would happen to my brother? A vampire found in his room. The other humans would be outraged.

As time ticked by, the day grew hotter and hotter. The blanket was no help. It trapped heat, drawing it in and holding it against my skin. My instincts started screaming at me, pleading for me to go underground where it was always cool and the sun's rays couldn't reach me. That was impossible though. I was stuck in the smelly bathroom and trapped under the hot blanket.

At one point, my brother returned, but he left quickly and without checking on me. I wished he had, I was desperate to know how much longer the day had.

What if the sun never went down?

"Tommy?" The scorching blanket fell away, my brother leaning over me. "Hey, what are you still doing in here? The sun's been down for almost an hour. I figured you'd want to be out of this room."

How could the sun have set an hour ago? I would have known, would have felt energy return to me. All I felt was heat.

I opened my mouth to speak, but nothing came out.

Worry filled his face. He knelt before me and he placed a hot hand on me. His lips moved, but a thumping sound drowned his words out. A pulse accompanied the thumping, both beating against me. My eyes were drawn to his arm, stretched across my vision. I could see his pulse throbbing, beckoning me. He cried out, trying to tear his arm from my grip when I grabbed his wrist and sank my fangs deep.

"Tommy, stop! Please, Tommy, listen to me. *Tommy, I'm your brother!* You know you'll regret it! ...I don't want to die."

The last words were a terrified whisper, but a loud roar in my ears.

His hand slipped through my fingers and he scrambled back until he hit the wall. There was no color in his skin and terror filled his eyes. His chest heaved with each breath. When I moved towards him, he jerked away.

"I'm sorry!" The words burst from me and I knew I meant them. "Please, I'm sorry, I didn't mean to. Please, don't be scared. Please, I'm sorry." It wasn't something I had done often, maybe once or twice, but I had seen enough humans do it. I hugged my brother, trying to reassure him. "Danny, don't be afraid of me, I don't want you to."

He pulled away, leaning against the wall. He kept his arm close to his chest, the blood from the punctures on his wrist running down his arm and dripping onto his clothing. He took a deep, shuddering breath, leaning his head back and closing his eyes. "Never gonna be afraid of my little brother. I'm okay, I'm okay."

I wasn't sure who he was trying to reassure more: himself or me.

I reached up, gripping his hand, unsure if *I* was trying to reassure him or myself either. "You are okay. It was a little prick, barely any blood loss. You'll be fine in a few minutes."

He smiled weakly. "I'm not the only one that took by surprise, eh?"

"I told you survival was stronger than anything," I replied. "I felt your pulse and heard your heart and couldn't stop myself."

"I guess you spending the day above ground wasn't that great of an idea."

"Guess not," I muttered. "I told you I'd never put you in a situation where survival would trump you."

"Yeah, you did. What the hell?" A trace of a smile was on his face, his voice growing stronger. He motioned for me to sit next to him. I settled against the wall, our shoulders pressed together. His fear was melting, maybe dripping off him like the blood on his wrist. He held his hand out, the tips of his fingers puffed up and red. "You burned me. Your skin was so hot when I touched you, my skin blistered."

"Does it hurt much?"

"My fingers hurt more than my wrist." He curled his fingers up, twisting his wrist this way and that. "It feels numb now, like when your foot falls asleep. It's like there's something on your teeth that numbs skin."

Carefully, I took his hand. He flinched, barely, but let me examine his fingers, and then his wrist. His face remained calmed, even when my fingers lingered over the drying blood.

"You said survival was stronger than our bond, but you stopped. As soon as I said I didn't want to die, you stopped," he said softly.

"I know, but I..." I thought back, trying to understand how I had been able to stop. I had never done that. If I needed blood, I took it until there was no more. Stopping never entered into the equation.

"You don't know how I made you stop," he finished my thought.

I looked into his eyes, being truthful. "I shouldn't have stopped."

"I bet I know why you did." In the dark, his eyes sparkled, a sliver of light from outside the door catching them. "It's much sooner than I thought, but I told you so."

****

Gray and pink lined the horizon, the tree line slowly becoming visible. The air warmed, chasing away the chill of the night. Birds started chirping, rejoicing the start of the day.

I saw no reason for happiness. After spending the whole day above ground, my aversion to daylight had multiplied tenfold. I refused to stay above ground for a second of it. Fallen waiting for me or not, I had to get underground now.

"I imagine you don't want to spend the day again?" My brother yawned, silencing the alarm that beeped next to his bed.

"No."

He laughed and yawned again. "I figured as much. Well, gimme a minute and I'll drive you to wherever."

"What?" I asked as he shuffled to the bathroom. I followed, peeking in.

"I'm gonna drive you to your resting place." His speech was muffled, a toothbrush in his mouth. "What?" he asked when he noticed me staring. "You spent all of yesterday in here; it shouldn't be a mystery to you."

"What's the point of doing that?" I motioned to the toothbrush.

He rinsed the toothbrush off and spread more toothpaste over it. "To clean your teeth."

"Why do you need to clean your teeth?"

"Because if you don't, your breath can smell really bad. Sometimes I keep my distance because your breath could knock over an elephant," he replied and held the toothbrush out. "Brush."

I stuck the toothbrush in my mouth, instantly pulling it out. "It tastes nasty."

He pushed the toothbrush back in my mouth and wiggled it. "Just do it."

I obeyed, making a point to show my dislike for the taste. Why he put something that tasted this horrible in his mouth was a mystery. How it would make my breath smell better was a bigger one. "Do you do this all the time?"

"Every morning. Girls will be more willing to kiss you if you don't have nasty breath. Okay, spit and rinse," he instructed, filling a glass of water. He exchanged the water for his toothbrush, dropping it in the trash. He never used something after I did.

I rinsed and spat, wiping the water away in amazement. It worked! The bad tasting paste and foam was washed away, leaving a clean feeling in my mouth. It was oddly refreshing in a non-satisfying way. "I don't care about girls."

"One night you might care about a girl. Then you'll be glad I taught you how to brush your teeth," he said with a grin.

"Why would I care about a girl? Humans are only food to me."

"Maybe you'll meet a vampire lady." He clasped his hands, fluttering his eyelids. "You'll fall madly in love with her and run off into the sunset."

"You're making a joke right? I can't run off into the sunset, I'd die," I replied slowly.

He dropped his hands, shaking his head. "Yes, I'm joking. But you never know, you may meet a special someone one day."

"I doubt it. If you're taking me, then we need to go. The sun's about to come up."

He paused by the door, pulling a dark shirt down and tossing it at me. "Put this on and the hood up. Oh, and try to act human."

I smirked at him. "I thought you said I did act human."

"You occasionally do human things. You don't move like one though. Watching you move, it's pretty obvious you're not human. Although, anyone out might be thrown off by how close to sunrise it is." He poked his head into the hallway looking both ways. "Coast is clear."

I followed him as he rushed down the hallway and stairs. At the door to the lobby, he peeked out again, checking for humans. We made it to his car without seeing a single one. The small sedan came to life with little coaxing and soon the college was shrinking behind us.

"You cool with this?" he asked. "I know where you rest is something you don't want anyone to know, not even me."

I watched cars pass, most heading to the college. "I trust you. Besides, I won't show you the exact spot."

"As curious as I am, that's a good idea. That way I don't risk letting it slip while I'm drunk. You have no idea how often I'm threatened to have my mouth duct taped at parties," he laughed.

I laughed with him. "You do talk a lot. Left."

"Maybe you don't talk enough," he teased, following my direction.

"I only talk when I need to."

He snorted. "How much farther?"

The road stretched straight ahead of us. Thick trees surrounded us on both sides. Other than a few reflective markers, there were no other signs on the road.

"See up ahead, about four markers, there's a driveway. That's it."

The driveway we turned down was overgrown. Grass grew thick between twin ruts of dirt that were marred with potholes. The car bounced as it hit the holes, crawling to a stop out of sight from the road.

My brother turned to me, eyes full of questions. "Do you want me to go farther?"

I shook my head. "This is fine."

"And you just dig into the ground?"

"No, there's a cellar that's perfect."

"Ah! I've been wondering. It used to be you'd show up and your clothes would be caked with dirt." He picked at the tattered fabric of my shirt. "You need some new ones. I'll pick up some up for you this weekend."

"Thanks."

"Well, I figured if I didn't, you'd strip your victims or something equally disturbing."

I didn't reply.

He shook his head at my silence. "After three years, I shouldn't be shocked. They find bodies drained and naked all the time."

I scrambled for something to say, something not typical of my vampire thoughts that would wipe the shocked look off his face. If I was lucky, maybe I could make him laugh.

I jabbed a finger at him. "You should be ashamed for thinking such a horrible thing. I'd never do something like that. Those humans were my meals, why would I degrade them like that? I can't believe you'd think that!"

His face wavered. A grin filled his face, laughter cutting up his words as he shoved me out of the car. "Get out of here. Go rest."

****

It felt good to be back underground. I didn't feel like I was being slowly baked alive or vulnerable to discovery. I curled in the corner of the cellar, resting peacefully and debating whether I should hunt or not.

I was border line on the idea. The day above ground had whipped me bad. I was weak from the draining heat, but the small taste of my brother's blood had staved off the hunger that had roared to life. If I wanted, I could skip.

But if I wanted, I could hunt.

"Decisions, decisions," I muttered to myself.

As the day progressed, I thought of hunting less and less. Unease curled through my stomach and I knew the feeling wasn't mine. I had no reason to be agitated while I was safe in my cellar. Something had upset my brother and it resonated through our bond.

Hunting could wait another night.

At sunset, I took the shortest route back to the college. Recklessly, I darted under lights and across open parking lots. I scrambled up the side of the dorm, forced to stop by the closed window. I lightly tapped on the glass, but the window stayed shut, the other side dark. I pressed my ear to it, only hearing the rhythms in rooms around me.

I looked for the note my brother always left, then dropped down to scan the ground where it must have fallen. Frustration welled as my search yielded nothing. Why hadn't he left me a note? He always did, always let me know if he wasn't going to be around.

Maybe something happened to him.

I scrambled back up, tugging at the window, trying to open it, but it refused. Feeling frantic, I broke it and crawled through. I searched the small, dark room, scouring every inch in my quest for clues to my brother's whereabouts. I paced back and forth when nothing appeared out of place. Where was he? Had someone taken him? Grabbed him while he was on his way here? Why would a human want to take him? Had Vampire Forces found him?

I whirled around as the door slowly opened, expecting Vampire Forces, but seeing my brother instead.

"Tommy!" he yelped, quickly shutting the door. His eyes stopped on the shattered glass at my feet, eyes widening. He rushed to the window. "Did you break into my room? Ah hell, how am I going to explain that?"

"I didn't see a note and you always leave one," I replied.

"So you broke my window?" He fell on his bed, gripping his hair. "Do you know what *overreaction* means? Because you do it. All the time!"

I stood there, not knowing what to say. Finally I said the only thing I could. "I'm sorry, I was worried."

"It's fine." he muttered, picking up large pieces of glass and tossing them in the trash. "It's just been a long, eventful day."

Should I be helping him clean the mess? I decided yes and started picking up pieces. "What happened?"

"Your girlfriend," he replied and I growled. "She followed me all day. Even went to all my classes. That's why I'm so late; I was trying to lose her. I finally did when I ran into the admin building and found a spot to hide. But that's not the worst part." He held out his hand, showing me his bandaged wrist. He pulled it off. Dark bruises surrounded the two punctures that had scabbed over. "The worst part was she saw this."

"What did she do?"

"Apparently, you're not very fair," he replied icily. "I told her it was nothing; I banged my wrist up on something stupid. She didn't believe me. She said I didn't deserve that *honor* and *why did you pick me* and all this other crap that wasn't true. The only good thing was she knew to keep her voice down so everyone wouldn't hear. Her two friends tried to calm her down, but that made things worse. She told us, *Just you wait until he turns me.*"

A cold feeling settled in my chest as I remember other words she said.

Find them first.

I understood what that meant now. If Fallen was turned, she'd find her friends first. The memories would be there, fading, but that would be enough to get her to her friends and kill them. Would the memories also get her to my brother?

The cold feeling died, replaced by heat. I was done hiding from her and trying to salvage the fragile friendship. I knew what I needed to do.

I stayed all night with my brother. A few times he tried to sleep; tossing and turning only to turn the light back on and talk to me more. Worry was etched on his face, his eyes darting to the door. He worried Fallen would finally call Vampire Forces. His reasoning was if Fallen couldn't have what she wanted, then she might believe no one should.

As the sky started to lighten, he climbed out of bed. "Come on, I'll drive you back again. I don't want her sneaking up on you and catching you as the sun comes up."

"She was good at sneaking up on me."

He shook his head. "I thought vampires had super senses."

"I have good senses," I protested. "She was lucky."

He scoffed. "It wasn't luck, it was stalking. She probably camped out, watching my room and waiting for you."

Like the other night, we snuck to his car and escaped the campus and Fallen.

"I think I'm skipping classes today," he sighed, eyes checking the mirrors.

"You didn't sleep much."

He yawned. "This whole thing with her is unsettling. I've never heard of a wannabe being so..."

"Insane?" I offered.

He laughed. "She's something. You know, I think everything that's happened lately proves people aren't as scared of vampires as the news makes us out to be. I mean, no one called VF when you crashed the party. I think people could learn to co-exist with vampires."

"Can you learn to live with something that might kill you?"

He shrugged. "Animals in the wild do it. Maybe the most people could do is learn to accept the existence of vampires.

We'd never be able to truly live together, but we'd learn to deal with each other without the fear."

"I think vampires and humans should stay separate."

"It is kind of hard to imagine vampires and people going to school together." He pulled into the over-run driveway and turned to me, apprehension on his face. "I wish you had a phone; then if something bad happened, you could call."

"What would go wrong?"

"You might get caught and destroyed."

"You'd feel it."

"I'd rather not."

I touched his shoulder, feeling him shudder. "I'll be there tomorrow night. Safe and alive."

He snorted. "Alive, right. I'll leave the window wide open – after I get it fixed." He gave me a weak smile, reluctant to leave. "Have a good rest. Peace."

"Peace," I echoed as he pulled away.

I wandered to the cellar, jumping down. My energy drained as the sun broke the horizon above and I started to drift away. Fallen didn't know where I rested, she'd have to wait until sunset to try to find me and convince me to turn her. Until then I was safe.

"Tommy."

****

It wasn't a choice. It was survival.

The weight on my shoulders was uncomfortable. Not because it was too heavy or because I had been carrying it for miles, but because of what – who – I was carrying. Satisfied with the distance between the college and us, I set her down. Blank eyes stared at me, but I swore I saw betrayal and a plea asking why.

"I told you what would happen. I said I'd kill you!" I told her.

Fallen had found my resting place. As the sun slowly moved across the sky, she appeared. In the darkness, she smiled and curled against me. I was too weak to push her away. She knew I was powerless too; I had told her that myself. She talked the whole time, voice gentle. She said finding me was a sign, she was supposed to be a vampire and once the sun set I had to turn her.

Then she leaned forward and pressed warm lips against mine. She told me she had been longing to do that since we met. She continued kissing me, my ears, my neck and my cheeks. She even gently bit me.

I longed for the sun to set and have energy course through me so I could move. I wanted her away from me, to stop touching me with blood filled hands. It was torture, feeling her warm body, unable to do anything. Hunger and need raged in me, desire building. I tried to tell her to stop, explain how much her touch hurt me, but I didn't have the strength.

The moment the sun set, I was on her. She bared her neck, a smile on her lips. I inhaled her scent and let myself fall into desire. Relief was instant when I bit and I sucked hard to draw each drop out of her.

"When do you do the turning part?" she had asked at one point.

But I had no intention of turning her. She found my resting place and invaded it while I was vulnerable. I was caught up in desire, but need was fueling it. Survival trumped everything.

"Hey, when do you do the turning part?" she repeated. Then she pushed at me, but I gripped her tighter, digging my fangs deeper. Fear surged through her blood and fueled the desire more. "Tommy, stop!" she shrieked, then screamed for help.

I grabbed her by the forehead, slamming her head against the wall. The crack echoed in the tiny room and she fell limp. When the blood was gone, I let her fall to the floor. I knew it had to be done, but it still didn't feel right.

I knelt next to her, touching her cheek. Her skin was cool, her arms and legs stiff. She felt like me, but unlike me, she wasn't waking back up.

"I am sorry," I told her. "But I can't stop surviving."

I left her where she wouldn't be found, surrounded by nature. If the humans found her, they'd link her back to the college. I couldn't risk both my brother and myself being discovered again.

His window was open and fixed, like he promised. Warm light spilled out, inviting and friendly. I stood in the shadows, staring up. I didn't want to face him and tell him what I had done. I was too ashamed.

Head hanging, I returned to my resting spot. Her scent hung heavy in the air, reminding me of what I had done. I curled in the corner, my head tucked in my arms to cut the smell off.

I spent the night that way, surrounded by memories of the night before. The day was a curse. At night I had the choice to leave, but during the day I was stuck. My only consolation was her scent faded, lifting into the air and drifting away.

When night fell, I continued sitting in my corner, not wanting to move, but at the same time wanting to run away. I had tainted this cellar and put bad memories in it. Now I understood why my brother said our home was tainted. I understood how he felt about me murdering our parents.

"Tommy!"

His voice cut into my thoughts. The walls behind me vibrated from his footsteps. He called again, closer this time. I listened to him walk above me, felt his anxiety and worry for me. I said I'd be there last night and I never showed. He had to be fearing the worst, like I had time and time again.

I waited a few minutes, letting him move farther away from the cellar door, then climbed out and trudged after him. "I'm here."

He whirled around and ran to me, hugging me tightly. "What happened? I waited up half the night for you. Fell asleep next to the window. My neck is killing me."

"Can you not use that word?" I kept my face turned into his shoulder, reluctant to look at him.

He bent his knees, lowering to see my face. Slight apprehension glimmered in his eyes and a knowing look that said his mind already guessed what was wrong. "It's okay. You know I won't judge you."

"I had to," I muttered. "She found where I rested during the day."

His face paled. "She found you during the day? How?"

"I don't know."

"She spent the whole day with you?" His eyes roamed over me, searching for something. "Did she hurt you?"

I shook my head. "No, she mostly talked about how finding me meant I had to turn her."

"Mostly?" His face darkened, something flashing in his eyes. "Did she touch you?"

I wasn't sure why that upset him. "Yes."

His lips pressed into a tight line. "She found where you rested, spent the day with you, did... things, then what? What happened when the sun went down?"

I looked away. "I killed her."

"Okay," he said in an emotionless voice.

"You're not sad?"

"I have no sympathy for her. Everyone knows people who look for vampires get killed. She asked and you said no. You did what you needed to do to survive," he replied.

"She was my friend and I didn't want to kill her," I said softly.

Some of the hardness left his face. "I know, I felt your pain all day and knew something was wrong. It's why I came looking for you."

"I'm glad you came looking. I tainted this place. Where am I going to rest now?"

"Do you really want to find a new spot?"

I shook my head.

"Then don't let the bad things chase you away from what you want. You want to know what I realized I want to do one day?" He smiled at me. "I want to go back home, to our house, and replace the bad memories with good ones."

I mulled over his words. Could I wash bad memories away with good ones? Leaving the cellar behind wasn't what I wanted. It was a good resting place.

"Come on." I pulled him back the way we'd come and dropped into the cellar.

He peered over the side, eyes wide. "You've got to be kidding."

"Just jump."

"It's like a twenty foot drop! I might break a leg!"

"There's a ladder."

He looked at the broken ladder. "I don't think so."

"Come on," I pleaded. "I want to replace the bad memories."

"I think you're doing fine as it is. I'm good up here, you're great down there."

I rolled my eyes and climbed out. I flung him over my shoulder, dropping back down. He gasped and swore as I sat him down. Fishing into his pocket, he pulled a lighter. The small flame flickered as he wandered around the cellar.

"So, this is it? It's… empty."

"I don't own anything."

He turned to me with an amused smile. "Maybe I'll buy you a poster for your next birthday."

****

My brother was waiting for me the next night. He sat on the hood of his car, his face vacant and arms folded tightly. Without a word or looking up, he tossed a newspaper at me.

I flipped the paper over and revealed the one human I didn't want to see. Her skin was white in contrast to her black hair and her face was full of life with a happy smile filling it. For a brief second, the image changed. Dead eyes accused me from the face of a corpse. I tore my eyes away as a surge of regret rolled through me. Calming myself, I opened my eyes and read.

College Student Missing

Police are searching for Amber Diane Tally, age nineteen, who went missing late Wednesday night. She was last seen by fellow classmates leaving her dormitory and gave no word to where she was going or when she'd return. Friends say she frequently missed classes and often disappeared for long periods of time, but never more than a day.

Unconfirmed reports say a vampire was spotted on campus and an investigation is underway to see if the two are related. Witnesses said, on many occasions, a vampire was seen talking with students. Others suggest vampires have been drawn in by sympathizers, easy targets for a ruthless vampire.

Police say many disappearances are thought to be vampire victims. Victims go missing for days before their bodies are found, drained of blood. The police urge anyone with information on Miss Tally or the vampire sightings to please call Vampire Forces.

There is a candlelight vigil being held on campus for Miss Tally's safe return.

"I can feel your dread," my brother said. "Campus was crawling with VF and cops today. I saw them talking with her friends and they must have told VF everything because they knocked on my door shortly after. They asked if I had heard anything about a vampire on campus or someone calling to it. I could tell by their tones they thought it was me. They knew who I was, kept bringing up what happened three years ago. It took all I had to answer their questions and not slam the door in their faces. Before I came here, I drove around for an hour, paranoid I was being followed."

"What do we do?" I asked, glancing nervously at the overgrown driveway.

He sighed deeply, rubbing his face. "I dunno, my mind's fried from the stress. I can't even add two and two right now." He pushed off the car, pacing back and forth. Anger flared in my chest, his anger. "This is high school all over again. Everyone knows I'm the one with connections to a vampire, thinks I'm a sympathizer and will wind up dead. VF is breathing down my neck, wanting to relocate me again and set a trap. Aunt Dee and Uncle Dick have already decided I need to go back into therapy. It was such a pain convincing that shrink I was rehabilitated. I don't want to go through that crap again."

"Sorry," I offered, knowing this was my fault.

He slammed to a halt, his face tightened with a mixture of emotions I wasn't quite able to catch. "Don't apologize or regret coming to see me that night. I'm the one that called you, I'm the one to blame." He reached out and placed a hand on my shoulder. "No matter how far they drag me this time, I'll find you." His lips quirked into a grin. "I know where you rest."

Part Three: Monsters

Home.

Familiar scents filled the air and the few memories I had floated in my head as I stood in the doorway of the house before me. I felt for the key, finding it hidden along the top of the door. It slid in, the door soundlessly opening.

The living room was dimly lit, the only source of light a small lamp next to an overstuffed chair. Long shadows from the rest of the furniture stretched across the room. I moved around the couch, past a coffee table with newspapers littered on it, a TV along a wall and over a stack of video games.

In the kitchen, a small human girl sat at a table. Her feet dangled inches from the floor, swinging back and forth. She softly hummed, clutching a bright red crayon in her delicate hand, a partially colored image before her.

I silently moved closer, stopping inches from the girl. She froze when I swept her long, brown hair aside and leaned in. Goosebumps rose on her neck and her small body trembled. I opened my mouth.

"I'm going to eat you."

She shrieked, whirling around and flinging her arms around my neck. "Uncle!"

I pulled her up, cradling her against my chest.

Laughing, she flung her arms out. "Acrobat!"

She screamed with delight as I flipped her up and around, dangling her by her feet. I swung her back into my arms, somersaulting over the table. Her half colored picture fluttered to the floor as I bounced her around the kitchen. I cradled her head, always aware of the sharp corners of surfaces as we moved in a blur. I bent my knees, preparing to spring up onto the counter.

"Tommy!"

I fell motionless in an instant, setting my niece down. She scurried to the human woman scowling at me in the doorway.

"I swear," my brother's wife, Rissa, sighed, gathering my niece. "I finally get Mackenzie settled down and ready for bed, promising she can stay up until her uncle gets here and when you do, you bounce around the kitchen like springs are attached to your feet. I can't imagine what the neighbors think when they hear her screaming and shouting every night."

"Sorry," I obediently replied.

"He was doing what I asked," my niece said. "I wanted to be an acrobat."

"Well, someone needs to learn to say no to you," Rissa sighed. She kissed my niece, setting her down. "Give your uncle a kiss, then go tell Daddy goodnight."

My niece ran to me, arms outstretched. I pulled her up, presenting a cheek for her warm, wet lips. "Night, Uncle," she giggled, then disappeared into the living room.

Rissa finally let the smile she was fighting to hide free. She shook her head at me and picked up the drawing. "Is it really that hard for you to say no to her?"

I shrugged and wandered around the kitchen. I ran my fingers along the smooth counter, a feeling of ease settling in me.

My brother had kept his word about our home. He graduated from college, married the human girl he had dated for three years and when it came time for him to buy a house for his new family, our old home was the first and only one he looked at. Now the house was filled with life again and the bad memories were washed away by new ones. I no longer saw the house I murdered my parents in. I saw my brother's house, my brother's family.

My family.

"I see no reason to deny her request."

"But before bed?"

I shrugged again. "Where's my brother?"

"Where do you think?"

I headed through the house, following the voices out the back door. A tall fence now surrounded the back yard. A patio had been built against the house with outdoor furniture scattered across. My brother lounged in a chair, my niece on his lap and a beer next to him.

He grinned at me. "I thought I heard an acrobat a few minutes ago. Did the ringleader shut the circus down?"

My niece giggled. "Yes, Mommy's no fun. Uncle and I were having fun."

My brother gently smiled. "I'm sure you were, but you shouldn't be so hard on Mom. She's making sure you have a good rest and peaceful dreams." He looked up as Rissa wandered out.

She sat on the arm of the chair and draped her arm around his shoulder. "My knight, always sticking up for me." She leaned down, kissing his lips. "Come on, Mackenzie, let's get you tucked in."

My niece let her mother gather her up. "Night."

"Peaceful dreams," I called. I took the beer my brother offered, twisting the cap off. "How was work?"

He laughed. "You sound so serious when you say that, it's hilarious."

"You have an odd view of what's hilarious."

"Well, I have an odd family. A beautiful wife and daughter and a vampire brother." He held out his bottle and I clinked mine against his. "To family."

I grinned. "To family."

We stayed outside a long while, talking. I watched my brother out of the corner of my eye, aware of what had happened again. He had aged again, grown and changed while I continually stayed the same.

When we were done talking, we gathered the empty bottles and headed inside. My brother joined Rissa on the couch and I slipped upstairs to my new way to kill time during the night. Instead of stalking around cities, watching the humans risking the night, constantly confused by their actions, I stayed in my niece's room and watched her.

I wasn't allowed up there while she was awake. She'd never sleep then. But once she was fast asleep, and my brother and Rissa were watching the nightly news, I'd silently slip up and watch the small human toss and turn.

She reminded me of my brother, the resemblance clear. She had his eyes and nose, same round face and rosy cheeks. Her hair was lighter than his dark brown hair, falling in soft, feathery waves. The only thing that wasn't like his was her smile. When she smiled, it looked exactly like Rissa's smile.

Light from the hallway spilled into the room, voices from the TV downstairs grew louder, the news reporting on a disappearance as Rissa edged around the door. She perched on the bed, a tender look in her eyes.

"She was fighting to stay awake tonight, didn't want to miss you."

"I needed to hunt first," I replied.

Rissa's face showed no signs of sadness or anger. She'd rather I hunt and be sated before coming to visit. She said she wouldn't think about the humans I killed.

I watched her, a question brewing to the surface. "Why do you trust me?"

Rissa was silent for a long moment. "I'm not sure," she finally said. "I could argue I don't entirely trust you, but that would be a lie. If I didn't trust you, I wouldn't let you anywhere near Mackenzie."

"I wouldn't like that."

The smile Rissa gave me was sad. "I know. Sometimes I wonder if we should have kept you away. That way when we enrolled her in preschool, we wouldn't have had to explain to her why she can't mention her Uncle Tommy who only visits at night. But keeping you away would have made Dan sad and I wouldn't want that. He always told me the perfect woman for him was the one that accepted his brother."

****

The flames swayed, reaching for me. Heat licked at my skin and danger whispered in my mind. *Get away!* instinct urged me. I wanted to listen.

"Uncle, I need help," my niece declared.

"What do I do?"

"Blow," she ordered.

The skin on my face felt like it was burning as I leaned forward. Across from me, my niece leaned in as well, oblivious to the fiery danger that sat atop the colorful cake. With a great whoosh of air, she blew. I felt the heat burst, racing towards me and a flash of light filled my vision. With a choked snarl, I leapt back.

My niece laughed, clapping. "Uncle's funny. Let's do it again!"

"Once was enough," my brother chided, kneeling in front of me. He retracted his hand when I bared my teeth. "You're okay."

"I don't like fire." I touched my face, feeling smooth skin. My eyes darted back to the cake and the four unlit candles. I wanted to grab the candles, make them disappear and never be at risk again.

"Tommy, look at me," my brother ordered. His face and voice were calm. "You're not burnt. The flames were inches from your face."

I shook my head. "She blew the fire at me, why did she do that?"

"Mackenzie doesn't know what fire does to vampires," he said. "She wanted to have a candle blowing war with you."

"It was a game?"

"Just a game," he assured me. "Will you get up off the floor? You're cowering like a dog."

"But the flash, that was me catching fire," I insisted.

"Rissa took a picture."

Rissa held up the camera for me to see. Cautiously, I climbed to my feet and reclaimed my seat. My niece watched me with confusion and I smiled to reassure her.

"Let's cut this thing up," my brother declared. "Mackenzie, you get a small piece. You have bed in a half hour."

My niece sighed and slumped back in her chair. It didn't take her long to perk back up once she was handed her piece. She looked at the empty spot in front of me. "Uncle, don't you want some cake?"

I looked at the colorful food. "I've never thought about eating cake."

"Of course not," my brother laughed.

"That's because Uncle only likes blood," my niece proudly said.

My brother and Rissa exchanged a glance. His eyes flickered to me, warning me to keep quiet. "That's right," he said. "Uncle only likes blood, but only once a week."

"How do you get blood? Do you say please?" my niece asked me.

Rissa coughed loudly. "Eat your cake, sweetie."

"But–"

"No arguing."

The three humans ate their cake in silence. I watched them chew the food. A few times I mimicked the movement out of curiosity. It hurt pressing my teeth together like that.

"Can Uncle put me to bed?" my niece asked once she had literally licked her plate clean.

"Only if he promises not to will you to sleep." Rissa threw a glare at me. "She needs to learn to sleep on her own."

My niece giggled as I promised. She reached for me, clinging tightly as I carried her upstairs. I tucked her into her bed, pulling her favorite stuffed animal close. She touched my face, pushing at my lips. "You never smile. How come?"

"I smiled downstairs."

"I didn't see it."

"Sometimes my actions are too fast for humans to see. I'll smile slower from now on. Just for you." I poked her nose, slowly smiling.

She giggled, then leaned closer to whisper, "Will you tell me how you get blood?"

I glanced at the door, listening to the sound of my brother and Rissa's heartbeats downstairs. I turned back to my niece, pushing my fangs out. "See my teeth?"

Her eyes widened to saucers, trembling hand reaching to touch.

I pulled back, closing my lips over my teeth. "Now feel right here." I pushed her hair aside, exposed her neck and touched her fingers to the rhythm underneath. "Feel your pulse. It's strong right there. My teeth are made to bite through skin to reach that spot."

"You bite people?"

I hesitated, then slowly nodded. "When I need to."

"Does it hurt?"

"A little, but I try not to make it bad," I admitted. "I don't like it when they fight me."

"Why would they fight you?"

"I..." I faltered not sure what to say. My brother and Rissa didn't want me to explain how I hunted to my niece. They were worried it'd scare her. I understood that worry, I didn't want to scare her either.

The most important moment in my vampire life happened the day my brother introduced me to his wife and newborn child.

Not that he had much choice. I felt his emotions, excitement welling up like a fountain. What made him so happy? I raced to find out, sneaking into a clean smelling hospital and bursting through the door as soon as the coast was clear. He and Rissa fell silent, but the tiny human in his arms kept crying. I had never seen a human so tiny and noisy. My fingers itched, wanting to touch the tiny human.

My brother exchanged a glance with Rissa, then he handed me the tiny human. "Hold her head like that. Mackenzie, this is your Uncle Tommy."

She had felt so delicate! I could feel the life flowing through her. I touched my fingers to her chest, feeling the strong rhythm. Like I'd do anything for my brother, I knew I'd do anything for this tiny human.

From that moment, my life revolved around my niece. She was the first human I saw when I came home, the last one before I left to rest and the reason I made sure my need never got too strong. I had to protect her from everything. Even myself.

"Tommy."

My brother leaned against the door, watching me. He jerked his head, motioning me to go out to the hall.

I presented my cheek to my niece for a kiss, then hugged her. "Sleep well and don't let the vampires bite."

She giggled as I headed into the hall. My brother took my place on the edge of the bed, softly whispering to her. A few minutes later he wandered back out.

"Sorry."

"It's okay," he assured me. "She's curious and wants to know why you're different. Right now she's too young to fully understand what you are and what it means."

I looked down, understanding what he meant. "But one day she'll be old enough to understand when I bite, it's until death?"

"It may change her opinion about you and me."

"She won't like me?"

"She might be mad we sugar coated the truth about you." He placed a hand on my shoulder and shuddered. "Since she was born, you've been the most human I've ever seen."

I tilted my head and stared.

"In your own special way," he amended. "Your protectiveness is a bit feral. More like a wild animal than a person. It's why Rissa trusts you. She says if it comes down to it, she knows you'd kill her before Mackenzie."

That was true. If worst came to worse, I had planned who I'd kill if I had no choice. Rissa was first, then my brother and my niece last. I hoped if I ever put my family in a dangerous situation, killing Rissa first would enable him to get my niece to safety.

"I..."

"It's okay. My daughter's survival trumps everything."

****

"Recent violence between vampires and humans has increased. Hunting and torching have doubled in the past month," the news reporter stated. "The increase in activity is thought to be the result of a recent vampire protest. In the last ten years, vampires have been seen organizing, boldly going into public to demand fair treatment."

The TV switched to a dark street in New York City. Dozens of vampires stood motionless, some even clutching signs. The signs read, *We were human once! America, where EVERYONE has the right to LIVE!* The shot widened and revealed Vampire Forces closing in with torches. The vampires remained motionless, even when a Vampire Forces officer touched the flame to one. The reporter's voice commented over the images.

"No one knows why the vampires – after over thirty years of silence – have decided to seek human rights. Sympathizers state it is the humane thing to do."

"Vampires deserve rights! They were human once! They can remember being human and should be treated as such." a group of sympathizers chanted in another shot.

A scowling human in a black police uniform with a silver 'VF' embroidered on the chest appeared. "The vampire population gave up their human rights with the first life they took," he stated. "If a mass protest forms again, Vampire Forces will be there to eradicate the parasites and ensure *every* human's safety."

The camera turned back to the reporter. "And the debate continues. A bill in Congress would give Vampire Forces complete freedom to destroy vampires. With the recent rise in vampire torching, human deaths and turnings..."

"Daddy?" a scared voice interrupted.

"...many wonder how long the debate will last before Congress decides to pass the bill. In other news, the body of a five year old girl..." the reporter finished the first story and started on the next without losing a breath.

My brother quickly shut the TV off and turned to my niece with a smile. "What's wrong, sweetheart?"

"I had a bad dream."

He gathered her up and settled on the couch. "You made Uncle move." He quirked a smile at me. "It's unnerving when you stand *all* night."

"I don't need to sit," I replied.

My niece giggled into her hand.

I looked back at her. "What was your bad dream about?"

Fear crossed her face. "Bad people. They wanted to get you."

"No one's going to get Uncle," my brother said gently.

My niece shook her head. "People wanted to hurt Uncle. They wanted him gone."

"Who?" Rissa asked.

"The ones on the TV."

"No one on TV wants to hurt your uncle," Rissa assured her.

"It's okay," my niece replied in a solemn voice. "I know Uncle kills people."

Silence filled the living room. All this time I had been stepping on eggshells, worried about scaring her. My brother and Rissa assured me she would be scared if she knew the whole truth about me. But she wasn't, there wasn't a hint of fear in her scent or any on her face.

She wasn't afraid of me.

"Who told you that?" my brother asked.

"At school," my niece replied. "We do drills. What to do if a vampire comes. We're supposed to stay in a group and not let them look in our eyes. Miss Valerie said if a vampire looks in your eyes, the vampire can take your mind! I told her that's not true, that if a vampire looks in your eyes, you get sleepy." She frowned deeply. "I got put in time out for telling lies."

"Keep your mouth shut," my brother warned me before I could ask to kill Miss Valerie. He exchanged a tense look with Rissa, then turned back to my niece. "Does what you know about your uncle bother you?"

My niece shook her head. "Uncle wouldn't hurt us. He loves us. He tells me all the time. He says he even loves Mommy."

Rissa coughed loudly and her cheeks turned pink. "Mackenzie, do you understand what Tommy is? Why people may not like him?"

"Of course," my niece intelligently replied. "He's a vampire and it means he gets blood from other people by killing them and people don't like that because they don't understand. It's why I can't tell my friends at school about him."

Silence filled the living room again.

"Okay." My brother broke the silence. "As long as you understand. I guess."

"You won't let anyone hurt Uncle, right?" my niece insisted.

"Well, Uncle is pretty capable of taking care of himself." He rolled his eyes.

"We'll do our best," Rissa replied, throwing a glare at him.

My niece's face glowed with happiness. She hugged my brother then Rissa. "Thank you! Thank you! I love you, Mommy and Daddy!"

"Come on, let's get you back to bed." Rissa half laughed, half sighed. She picked my niece up and turned to me so I could present my cheek for another bedtime kiss.

"I won't let anyone get you," my niece whispered.

I looked at my brother, trying to comprehend my niece as Rissa took her upstairs. "She can't protect me."

He sighed. "It has nothing to do with whether or not she can protect you and everything to do with her feelings. She understands you, a lot better than both Rissa and I thought. She understands vampires are caught and destroyed and she's scared someone will catch and destroy you. She doesn't want that. In her mind, telling you she'll make sure no one gets you makes her feel better."

"I want her to feel happy," I said.

"I know you do." He wandered to the kitchen, returned with two beers and handed one to me. "Stop trying to understand humans. The ones who care about you will accept you as you are." His grinned widened as his voice dropped to a whisper. "Did you really tell Mackenzie you loved Charissa?"

"Yes."

He stifled a laugh. "Her face was priceless. It took all I had not to bust out laughing at her face."

"Why?"

****

"*Pssst! Pssst!* Hey you!"

She looked young, only a child. Her hair was blond, hanging past her shoulders, and her eyes dark blue. But for vampires, looks were deceiving. Her child-like face held eyes that, to another vampire, showed age. Wisdom in their depths that said she earned her survival. Her hands were held out, a cautious look on her pale face.

I growled and flashed my teeth when she moved closer.

"I'm not challenging you," she insisted. "I need to talk to you."

"You don't need to get closer to talk," I replied.

"But I do need you," she said. "You're young, I can see that. You don't know what it was like when the humans didn't know. That can't be undone, but there is something you can do. You can help. Be a voice. Don't let the humans destroy us anymore."

"No."

"We deserve to live.

"Do we?" I challenged. "Or should we have died instead of turn? We can't even remember our human lives."

"There's a lot about their lives they don't remember either," she said in an icy voice. "They are violent and hurtful. More than us at times. Why do they get to keep surviving? We deserve the same chance."

I agreed with that. I believed I deserved a chance to survive, but I saw no point in what this vampire wanted me to do. It only gave Vampire Forces another chance to destroy me. By staying hidden, I was giving myself the chance to survive.

"I will not help you." I turned to leave.

"I've seen you," she called. "With the humans. The little one, she is adorable. I had a younger human sibling like her."

She didn't fight when I grabbed her, letting me slam her against a brick wall and squeeze her neck until I heard bones crunch. "You *had*."

"She sat with me," she replied in a whisper. "As I hid in my room, fighting it. The hunger was bad, the need great and the desire overwhelming. I kept telling myself to leave, find another, not knowing why. But I was afraid if I left, I'd forget everything. Not only how to walk and talk, but her. I didn't want to forget her. Even as I forgot."

"You murdered her?" I asked, my fingers relaxing.

She nodded sadly. "The humans assume because we murder our families that we don't care and sometimes it feels that way. But when you refer to your family, you say murder and deep down, you regret it. You'd change it if you could. I don't know how you did it, but I'm impressed. I've never met another vampire who didn't murder their entire family."

"He is my twin."

"That doesn't mean much to me."

"Means everything to me," I replied and tightened my grip again. "You stay away from me and my family. I want nothing to do with your protests. I will not risk myself or hurt them that way."

She rubbed her neck when I released her, face showing no signs of discomfort or anger. I backed down the street, reluctant to take my eyes off her, finally turning when I rounded the block. As I dashed away, I heard her voice whispering, "When you change your mind, find me. My name is Amy."

I didn't stop running until I was home and in my niece's room.

Amy's words bounced in my head. Was it true she murdered her family, but didn't want to? I always wondered about other vampires and their families. Did they regret murdering their families like I had? If so, then maybe Amy was right. Maybe I should change my mind and help her.

No, that wasn't a possibility. If I protested, I was putting my family at risk. Another human could find out about me, learn my brother spoke with me. They'd think he was a sympathizer. I vowed never to put him through that pain again.

"I won't let anyone get you," I whispered, carefully brushing a lock of hair off my niece's face.

Faintly, an aroma tickled my nose. Hunger and need rumbled in me, drawing me closer, reminding me of why I had been out. I had been hunting when Amy distracted me.

Now all I smelled was my niece. She had never smelled this good before. Or maybe she had and I had never been around her when I needed blood.

A shudder ran through her when I placed my lips on her neck. Rhythm pulsed hot against me and I fell into it, imagining the way it would push the blood into my mouth. My fangs slid out as my stomach clenched in hunger. I closed my eyes, lost in the desire the rhythm beat out as it picked up its pace.

One small bite, I thought, my hands holding her head in place. One tiny, little bite to get the blood flowing.

"Ow! Dammit!" My brother's voice rang out after a loud crash down the hallway.

I jerked away, vividly aware of where I was and what I was about to do. Horror, disgust and revulsion slammed into me. I almost bit my niece, almost killed her.

I was a monster!

I whirled around, scrambling to get away. Dark houses and empty streets flashed by as I escaped into the night. I didn't slow until I reached my resting spot, wanting the safety and comfort of the dark cellar and earth. I jumped down, curling up in the corner, pressing my head against my arms and squeezing my eyes shut.

"I didn't do it. My teeth didn't touch her skin. She's okay," I whispered.

The words didn't console me. I knew what I had almost done and why. I had fallen into desire. I hadn't wanted my niece's blood because I needed it. I wanted it because I *desired* it. Nothing else would do. No other blood would satisfy me the way hers would have. If I had.

But I didn't.

But I could have.

That haunted me all day and into the night.

As the first glimmer of energy surged through me, I jumped to action. I raced to the city in search of a human to sate my need and cage my desire. My family would never know what I had almost done. But the human I found paled in comparison to my niece and when it came to the moment, I let her go. I didn't want her blood.

I wandered the city, starving with need and fighting the desire and confusion. Why was my niece tempting me? She was a constant fixture in my life and everything I did was for her safety. Now all I could think of was her blood and how I wanted every drop.

****

My stomach dully ached, my throat felt parched and my legs weak. It had been two weeks since I last fed. Each time I tried, I stopped before my fangs hit flesh and ran. I needed to feed. Hunger and need dominated my thoughts; my survival at risk each second I failed to feed. But stronger than the need to survive was the fear. Fear of what would happen once I tasted the blood.

The blood wouldn't be what I desired. And then what? I find my niece and sate the desire on her blood? I couldn't do that.

So I starved and avoided my family, digging into the ground far away from my cellar. I knew my brother would go there looking for me, maybe even bring my niece. When the sun set, I wandered the streets of the city, trying to gain enough courage to bite and growing weaker each time I backed away.

I stumbled to a stop, leaning against a large window. On the other side, dozens of TV showed scared eyes. How much longer could I go on like this? Would I drop dead? Permanently? I wanted to survive, but how could I if I was too scared to feed?

I resumed my walk, frequently stopping. If only I could get a little energy back. Maybe if I closed my eyes for just a minute... I jarred myself from that thought. The only way for me to get energy back was with blood.

Resolved to beat the desire, I headed to the part of the city that always had humans awake. Short, shabby buildings lined the streets, rusted cars parked under the unbroken lights. Debris littered the sidewalks and streets. Humans stood in tight groups, casting suspicious glances. I watched them talk, waiting for one to break away. That's all I needed, one to step away so I could swoop in, grab the human and feed.

"Hey, Darrell," a human called and separated himself from a group.

I blew out of the shadows like a gale force wind. The force at which I slammed into the human bent him over my shoulder. Behind me, the humans yelled in shock and feet pounded after me. My weakened state kept me from running as fast as I could, but even then the humans chasing stood no chance of catching me.

Down a dark and deserted alley, I threw the human to the ground, stalking back and forth, and trying to get the courage to bite. The human scrambled to his feet with a curse, yanking a gun free of his pants. His eyes widened, the whites almost glowing in the darkness, when he saw me. The gun swung around to face me and a crack echoed off the walls. Pain burned my stomach, spreading through me like a wild fire.

The injury ignited my need, propelling me at the human. I sank my fangs into his neck, the blood bursting into my mouth. I greedily sucked, unable to drink fast enough. Once his body was drained, I licked up the drops that had escaped my frantic sucking.

I left the body in the alley and raced home, eager to see my family again. I threw the door open, taking no care to be quiet, even trying to make some noise. I wanted my family to know I was home. Taking the stairs two at a time, I hurried to my niece's room. How mad would Rissa be if I woke her?

I didn't care.

The smell of my niece stopped me at her door. It hung heavy in the air, overpowering the other scents. Desire roared to life and the urge to feed on my niece filled me.

I backed away, not watching my step and tumbling down the stairs. A door above burst open, my brother flying from his room. He called to me as I raced away, darting out the nearest door and into the backyard. I paced the fenced area, trying to understand. Why did I still desire for my niece's blood? I shouldn't feel anything but minor hunger after feeding. Not full-blown desire.

"Tommy." Relief filled my brother's voice. He stopped my pacing, his eyes roaming over me. "What happened? Where have you been?"

I shook my head, refusing to speak. I couldn't tell him what I felt, he'd be furious and send me away. He said my niece's survival trumped everything. That had to include our twin bond.

"Come on, lil' bro, talk to me. You know you can tell me anything." His voice was soothing, easing the turmoil in me and making me speak.

"I don't want to leave! I want to stay and be part of the family."

"You are part of the family," he assured me.

I shook my head. "No, if you knew, you'd be mad, you'd hate me and send me away. She trumps everything. That means us too."

"You're not making any sense. Who trumps everything?"

I looked at him. "M-m-ma-mackenzie, I almost bit her."

His hands fell from my shoulders, mouth dropping open in shock. I braced myself, waiting for him to banish me from my family's life.

"Tommy, it's okay."

I shook my head. "No, you hate me. I can't be around her anymore."

He shushed me, his tone gentle. "You didn't touch her, she's okay."

"I wanted to. I was distracted from hunting by another vampire and I didn't realize how hungry I was until I came home. If you hadn't woken up, I would have killed her. I can't ever hurt her, I love her." The words were a relief to confess.

"I know how much you care about Mackenzie and I know you'd never hurt her."

His heart thumped loudly in my ears and the desire throbbed in time. I grabbed his wrist and bit. Blood oozed, coating my mouth, but I didn't suck. I didn't want his blood. I didn't know what I wanted. I released his wrist and bit into my own. No blood greeted my tongue or rhythm jumping as fangs sliced through flesh. I bit again and again, gnashing my teeth until he pulled my arm from my mouth.

"Danny, I'm scared."

He hugged me tightly, his voice soft. "I know, lil' bro, and I'm here for you."

****

My brother and Rissa were visible through the kitchen window. He softly groaned, his hand rubbing his chest. Rissa pressed her hand over his, worry filling her face. "Does it hurt much?"

"Feels like it did the past two weeks, like a bad case of heartburn. I'm just glad to know what's wrong so I can help," he replied.

"My knight in shining armor." Rissa smiled and kissed him.

"Why are you a knight?" I asked as he rejoined me.

He took the chair next to me, his eyes blinking to stay awake. "That's Rissa's way of saying I'm being noble."

I debated asking another question, wanting to keep him talking, but I didn't know what to say. Soon his eyes drifted shut, sleep claiming him. The fear slowly slid back, made worse by the silence around me. I wrapped my arms around my knees, terrified of losing myself to my feelings.

"He's been worried." Rissa stopped by my brother, brushing the hair off his sleeping face. "The only thing that kept him sane was he knew you hadn't been destroyed."

Guilt picked at me, worse than the fear curling through my stomach and the confusion filling me. I didn't want to feel any of it. I darted from the lawn chair and into the house. I rummaged through the kitchen, grabbing a beer. Ignoring the odor and taste, I drank it down.

"What are you doing?" Rissa grabbed the second beer from me.

"I'm getting drunk so I'll forget," I replied and grabbed another.

She snatched that beer from me and I snarled at her. She met my snarl with a glare. "You know I'm not scared of you."

"Give it back."

"It won't solve your problem."

"I want to forget," I insisted. "I don't like feeling human and I don't want to feel like him. I want to feel like me!"

Rissa sighed and shook her head. "Tommy, you're not feeling like Tommy the human, you're feeling like Tommy the vampire." She took my hand and led me into the living room. She pulled out a book from the bookshelf by the TV, flipping to a page and holding it out to me. "Read this."

Mackenzie smiled for the first time today. It lit up her face. The moment was bittersweet though. The smile wasn't for me or Dan, it was for her uncle. He was holding her, staring at her with that wide-eyed look he always gets when he watches her. He smiled back, a quick, barely there smile that one could easily miss. She started crying and Tommy panicked. I think he believes he needs to protect her, chase her fears away with a growl and some fangs. I took her back and he stayed by my side until her crying stopped.

I looked from the book to Rissa. "I remember that. Why did you show me?"

"Because this shows who you are," she replied. "I read this and I see a concerned uncle, ready to protect the ones he loves. You need to trust your feelings, trust the love you have for your family. It will protect us if you let it." She left me with those words, heading back outside to my brother.

I stared at the book in my hand. Had I been complicating matters and making my life difficult?

A vampire's life was straightforward. We survive, nothing more and nothing less. For me, it was the same with my family. I wanted to see them, so I did. If I didn't want to hurt my niece, I wouldn't, right?

Slowly, I walked up the stairs. At the top, I sniffed, searching for my niece's scent. It hung in the air, pulling at the desire. I hesitated, the book clutched to my chest. Footsteps creaked behind me. My brother yawned as he and Rissa reached the top. He smiled and patted my back and both disappeared into their room.

They trusted me.

I sank to the floor, afraid to go any farther and the book falling open on my lap. I leafed through the pages of pictures of my niece and read Rissa's commentary.

Under one picture of my niece wearing only a diaper, Rissa wrote, *Mackenzie managed to get her diaper off today. She laughed and laughed, running from Dan. Then she peed on the floor.*

A few commentaries mentioned me.

We let Mackenzie stay up until Tommy arrived tonight. The joy on her face was indescribable. I think he was happy too. We let him put her to bed. It turned out to be a bad idea. He willed her to sleep. At this rate she's never going to learn to sleep on her own.

Tonight, Mackenzie played hide-and-seek with Tommy. Dan explained the rules to him twice. He didn't understand either time and kept asking why. Then Mackenzie joined in, asking why too. I do not need two mouths constantly asking why in my life.

I was absent in the pictures. The flash always made me think of the sun, so I hid.

Jumping up, I rushed down the stairs. I rummaged through the desk in the corner of the living room, looking for the camera. The device was clunky and black with a long, gray strap. Flipping the flash up, I turned it on myself and pushed the button.

Nothing happened.

I frowned at the camera, turning it over. It was on, so why didn't it work? I held the button down again and a click sounded. Light filled my vision and seconds later a picture slid out.

Double-checking I didn't catch fire, I turn the camera back on myself. I held the button down longer, readying myself for the flash. I still flinched, the flare of heat tingling against my skin. Image in hand, I climbed to my feet, searching for a pen. I scribbled a quick commentary, placing the picture in the book. Then I set the book on the kitchen table, leaving it open to the page so my niece wouldn't miss it. Feeling content, I locked the front door behind me and headed to my resting place for the first peaceful rest in two weeks.

****

Giggles met my ears and a happy grin my eyes as my niece bounced to me when I arrived home at sunset. "Uncle, acrobat!"

Confusion filled her face when I stopped her at arm's length. Her scent curled around me, drifting up my nose. Desire and need flared, filling my mind. I tried to banish the feelings, reminding myself of the human I killed the other night. The human hadn't been enough, not after failing to hunt for over two weeks. I should have gone hunting again, but upon waking, all I wanted to do was go home to the comfort of my family.

What if the night before had been a fluke? The injury from the gunshot propelled me to do what I hadn't been able to. I wanted my fears erased, hear my brother or Rissa assure me I wouldn't hurt my niece. I looked from her to them. There was no fear in their eyes or scents. They still trusted me.

Pushing my uncertainty back, I managed a smile for my niece. "Did you see my picture?"

My niece looked behind me at her parents. When she looked back at me, her voice was serious. "Your eyes were closed and it's blurry."

"I don't like the flash, it makes me think I'm catching fire."

Little arms hugged my waist and my niece looked up at me with trust shining in her eyes. "Don't worry, Uncle, I won't let anything burn you."

How could she trust me? She knew what I was, how I survived, and wasn't afraid. When I first discovered she understood, I had been happy. I never thought there'd be a time she needed to be afraid of me.

As I raced out of the house, escaping into the night, I heard her ask, "Why did Uncle run away?"

"Family problems?" Amy appeared, keeping pace and a reasonable distance.

I slowed to a walk. "Guess so."

"Want to talk about it?"

"Do you care?"

"I don't."

"Yes then." I stared at her, tilting my head.

She mimicked me.

"I see what's creepy about that," I said. "Do you think about your sister a lot?"

Amy untilted her head and tipped it back to stare up at the sky. "She's always on my mind. I learned where she was buried and I visit her when I can, telling her about myself and making sure I don't forget. Forgetting is the only real fear I have, but I think we have to forget. If we don't forget what it was like to be human, we wouldn't be able to survive."

"But you still believe we have the same feelings as humans?"

"Do you laugh? Smile? Frown? The past couple weeks you've been expressing fear," Amy replied. "We feel the same emotions as humans, we just express them differently." She turned to me and reached up on her tip toes to gently place a kiss on my lips.

"Why did you do that?"

Amy shrugged one shoulder. "Maybe to see what the big deal about a kiss is. Have you ever been kissed?"

I nodded once. "During the day. This human–"

Amy cut me short. "It hurts to be touched during the day. Sometimes I wonder if that's what the sun feels like."

"I've been above ground during the day. It was too hot and when the sun set, I still felt hot, energyless."

"What had you above ground? Your humans?"

"My brother."

"Mmm," Amy sighed. "I can only imagine what that sort of trust must be like. Can't even trust other vampires. Makes organizing the protests hard, but sometimes I get help, another older one who's not threatened by the presence of other vampires."

"Why do you let them be destroyed? They don't move when Vampire Forces come."

"They're not supposed to let themselves get torched. Some of the younger ones don't get what it is us older ones are trying to achieve. We tell them not to fight the humans, it will hurt the cause, and they take it too literally," she replied.

"What are you trying to achieve?"

"That the sympathizers aren't wrong. That's there's some part of us that is still human: the part to survive."

I nodded. "I want to survive."

"But you still refuse to help me."

"I already hurt my brother twice by letting humans know he still talks to me."

"I can't argue with that. If I could, I'd abandon this to change the past. Leave my sister alive and forget about the hatred." Amy glanced at me. "We may not be human anymore, but somehow, family is more important than ever." She gave me another kiss, this time placing it on my cheek.

"You are young, with a lot left to learn. But know this: always trust your instincts. They will never lead you astray."

Then she was gone, leaving me alone on the street corner. I headed back into the night, ready to go home, but not before I did something. After all, I promised Rissa I wouldn't visit if I needed blood and if I was ready to put my fears behind me and trust my instincts, then I had to keep that promise.

****

My family was asleep when I returned. I made my way upstairs and slipped into my niece's room. She was sprawled on her bed, one foot hanging off the side and her stuffed horse on the floor. I picked the toy up, placing it next to her, then recovered her foot. I stayed by her side all night, escaping to the basement when I felt the first trickle of energy drain away.

I curled into a corner, my eyes on the small window on the far side of the basement that glowed with light. Above me the sounds of my family filled the air. My brother and Rissa shuffled about, their voices quiet and sleepy. When my niece woke, the noise grew louder. She ran across the floor, her voice filled with excitement.

"Can I go see Uncle?"

"No, we're not taking you out to see your uncle," Rissa replied.

"But Uncle's in the basement, I heard him go down. Do you think the monsters will get him? I hope not," my niece answered in a rush of words. She paused to take a breath. "The monsters are probably scared of him," she finished confidently.

"Mackenzie, stay here."

Footsteps thumped across the floor, then the stairs.

My brother threw up his hands when he saw me. "Jeez, Tommy, what are you doing?"

Rissa patted his arm. "I'll get a blanket for the window."

"I'm sorry," I mumbled. "I didn't want to leave."

He sighed, worry filling his face. "It's fine; I'm just remembering what happened last time you were above ground during the day."

"We're not above ground," I pointed out.

A sliver of relief showed in his eyes despite the stern look. "Okay, but if you feel even a slight urge…"

"I'm fine! I won't hurt my family," I cut him off.

He scowled at me, but a smile quickly cracked his anger. "You should see yourself, huddled like a lost puppy. I'm sorry I snapped; I know you wouldn't do anything to hurt us. We'll get the window covered and you can rest."

I nodded, already drifting away as they covered the window and left me. When the sun set, my niece stood at the top of the stairs, a smile on her face and arms reaching for me. "Acrobat, Uncle."

Desire flared, the urge to bite rising. I froze and pushed the feeling back. I would not hurt my family. The desire reigned in, I swept my niece into my arms and tossed her up. She squealed with delight, her arms spread as I ran through the house, vaulting over furniture and sliding under the kitchen table. We collapsed on the floor and she giggled madly. A laugh escaped me and I joined in her happiness until my chest ached and she panted for breath.

"Okay, you two," my brother said with a grin. He picked my niece up. "It's too late for your uncle to be getting you riled up."

My niece giggled more. I presented my cheek for a bedtime kiss and he took her up the stairs.

Rissa stopped by my side, a smile on her face. "I'm glad you're feeling better."

I glanced at her. "I don't know what to say to that."

She laughed. "Naturally."

****

It was time I started doing more for my family. Be a real family member that said and did things for them. I would stop doing things as well. Things that I knew upset my brother, like killing the humans I hunted.

I wandered down the city streets, searching. It didn't take long to find a human. She walked down the brightly lit streets alone, her purse clutched to her side. Nervousness churned in me as I closed the distance between us. How was I going to leave her alive? I didn't know where to put stopping into the equation.

Maybe this human wants to die, I thought. She was alone and vampires were still considered a threat in many cities. Maybe I could start not killing next time I hunted.

No, I was going to go through with this. I wasn't going to kill anymore humans. I just needed to bite and take a few sips to satisfy myself.

The human shrieked when I grabbed her and I clamped my hand over her mouth to silence her. Dull teeth bit into my flesh, the human continuing her screaming as I yanked my hand away. I whirled her around, catching her gaze and willed her silence. I looked at the faint mark on my hand, then back to the human.

"Why did you bite me?"

"I don't want to die."

"I'm not going to kill you so you don't need to worry."

She struggled slightly when I pulled her close and bit. The time I had wasted speaking to her had weakened my hold over her will. Her pleas for help grew louder and she pushed harder in an attempt to free herself. I grabbed her arms, pinning them to her sides and tried to figure out when to stop.

There were no clues. Her heart beat as fast as ever and the flow of blood was effortless. I slowed my drinking and tried to feel for a sign. Again, there was nothing to clue me in and I decided to stop while I knew she was still alive. Reluctantly, I let her go, a large part of me aware of how much blood I hadn't consumed.

For a moment, she stood there, eyes staring blankly. Then, without warning, she attacked. The life was back in her eyes and she shrieked loudly as her hands flew at my face. I reacted instinctively, slapping her hands away, and sinking my fangs back into her neck. I tore myself away after a few gulps and shoved her away. She thudded against a wall and her body slumped to the ground where she lay still.

Slowly, I approached, cautious of another attack. She remained still when I reached out to nudge her. Did I *accidentally* kill her? That was as unusual as leaving her alive.

I turned her over and pressed my ear to her chest. It heaved under me and a gush of air rushed from her mouth. I jumped back, watching as she rolled over and pushed herself up on shaking arms. Her eyes locked with mine and her head tilted to the side.

"Damn," I muttered.

"Weren't expecting that, were you?"

Amy strolled out of the shadows and to the human. Her hair fell over her face as she leaned over. With an absent gesture, she swept it back and faced me. "You turned her; did you mean to?"

I shook my head.

Amy sighed. "She won't survive as a vampire. You can always tell by the eyes."

I glanced at the turning human. A vacant look filled her eyes as she stared at our surroundings. The look said nothing was clicking in her mind when everything should be snapping into place.

When I was turned, I remembered looking at my surroundings and recognizing everything. My mind registered the trees around me, the ground below me and the sky above. Thoughts naturally came to me, my mind chaotically flitting through the events that were starting to fade as the denial set in and hunger started to grow.

None of that was happening for this woman. There were no thoughts or recognition, not even denial. She was nothing more than an empty shell incapable of surviving.

"You know what we gotta do?"

I looked at Amy. "We?"

She shrugged. "Why not? Follow my lead."

We moved around the vampire, Amy to one side and me on the other. At her nod, I grabbed the vampire, holding tightly. She grabbed the head, twisting and tearing it away as one last scream escaped. She dropped the head next to the body.

"Stand back."

I stepped back and Amy pulled a lighter from her pocket. She flicked it open and tossed it onto the body. Flames sprung to life, quickly consuming the corpse. I turned away, not wanting to see the bright flames or my failure.

A gentle hand touched my shoulder, Amy turning me towards her with a knowing look. She hugged me tightly, her voice soft. "Do you know how you did it?"

I shook my head against her shoulder. "I don't know. I was trying to leave her alive."

Amy sighed. "That's too bad, I've always wondered. I've never turned someone or even wanted too. Never even talked to another vampire that had turned someone. I've talked to ones that mentioned turning someone, but I don't know if they did. They disappeared and I assumed they were destroyed."

I glanced back at the smoldering remains. "Have you ever seen one like that survive?"

Amy's eyes followed mine. "No."

"Now what?"

"Go home to your family and stop worrying about being something you're not," Amy replied, already strolling away.

****

"Okay, lemme get this straight. You decided, for our family's sake, that when you hunted, you weren't going to kill the person, and you have no idea how, but in doing so you turned the poor woman into a vampire incapable of surviving." My brother rubbed the bridge of his nose, his expression torn between amusement and sorrow. He sighed, wiping the conflicting emotions away. "Is there any reason you're telling me this?"

I paused. "I'm not sure. I just thought you should know."

He laughed. "Well, thanks. Glad you like to keep me in the loop about the inner working of your freaky, vampire mind. Anything else?"

"I'm thinking of resting in the basement every day."

"Did something happen at the cellar?"

"No."

He took a slow breath before answering. "Let me discuss it with Charissa first."

I tilted my head. "Why? She's let me rest here before."

He fought another smile, patting my shoulder. "Trust me, lil' bro, it's better if I discuss it with her first. Come on, I need to get to bed."

We headed inside, rinsed our bottles out, clicked the stove light off and headed through the house. He led me to the basement and checked the blanket over the window. After arranging some boxes, he turned to me with an amused smile. "You want a blanket or pillow?"

"I thought you had to ask your wife first."

"I'm sure Rissa won't mind you sleeping in the basement tonight," he replied. "Don't worry, I'll talk to her tomorrow first thing. Night."

"Night."

He disappeared up the stairs, immersing me in complete darkness. I settled in the corner, curled against the cool wall. The boxes he arranged were piled next to me, obscuring my vision of the stairs. I stared at the neat letters on the side, deep in thought.

Amy told me not to worry about being something I'm not; my family did as well. When I tried, I failed. I turned the human instead of leaving her alive. Obviously I needed to listen to my family and friend's advice.

A grin tugged at my lips as I wondered if Amy thought of me as a friend too.

The night slipped by quickly and soon my energy faded and life sounded above. I listened to my brother and Rissa discuss me staying in the basement, and then listened to the noise my niece made when she woke. The house became nearly silent when she and my brother left.

Then she returned.

She raced across the floor above, talking loudly as she recounted her day to Rissa. "Today we played *Duck-Duck-Goose* and Billy Duncan smacked me on the head. And during story time, Billy Duncan kept poking me in my back. Then when we were painting, Billy Duncan smeared paint on my face. Miss Valerie put him in time out."

"Oh my," Rissa replied. "Sounds like Billy Duncan has a crush on you."

"What? Ew! Boys are gross, Mommy!" my niece shrieked.

Rissa laughed. "Hush, your uncle is resting downstairs. You don't want to wake him, do you? Anything else happen?"

"Jamie wasn't there again. She hasn't been to class all week. Miss Valerie looked worried."

"Oh. Well, I'm sure she's just home sick."

"Can I go see Uncle?"

"No, let him rest."

Silence filled the space above me. I drifted half away again, my mind musing on the girl my niece mentioned. The tone Rissa used wasn't unfamiliar, full of worry and fear. It was the same tone she got when the news reported something sad, like missing children.

"Mackenzie," Rissa suddenly warned. "Get away from the basement door." A few minutes later, the basement door opened. "Mackenzie, what did I tell you?" Soft footsteps on the stairs. "Mackenzie! Get back up here NOW!"

My niece rushed back up the stairs, giggling as the door slammed shut. She didn't try to make it down to me the rest of the day. When the sun set, she was waiting for me at the top of the stairs. A smile filled her face as I picked her up and carried her to the living room.

"Did you rest good?" she asked.

I nodded. "Yes."

She squirmed out of my arms and scurried to the couch to sit between my brother and Rissa. He tucked her against his side, pressing a kiss to the top of her head, then focused on the TV. It was a beautiful scene and I couldn't imagine life any other way.

My niece squealed with excitement as she pointed at the TV. "Look, Mommy, my school is on TV. It's famous!"

On the TV, a woman in a gray suit stood in front of a brown brick building. Large windows took up most of the walls and the doors were dull and yellow. Behind the building was a fenced in area with colorful swings, slides and other toys.

The camera focused on the woman, her voice serious as she started her report. "Four year old Jamie Bachand was taken last Monday afternoon. Happy Times Pre-School teacher, Miss Valerie, last recalled seeing Jamie out front, waiting for her parents with the other children. Witnesses didn't recall seeing Jamie leave or any strangers. If anyone has any information or has seen Jamie Bachand, please call the police immediately."

Silence filled the air as the reporter spoke, fear hanging like a sickly odor. My brother and Rissa stared at the TV, absorbing each word with solemn faces.

My niece looked from one to the other in confusion. "Mommy, Daddy, what's wrong? How come the TV was talking about Jamie? Is she okay?"

My brother took a moment to force a smile on his face. "I'm sure she's okay. They'll find her safe and sound and everything will be fine."

"Come on, let's get you up to bed and I'll read you a story tonight." Rissa hurried my niece up the stairs without handing out goodnight kisses.

I looked at my brother. "You lied."

Lines appeared around his eyes, making him look years older. "We don't want to scare her."

I tilted my head at him, growing more puzzled. "What is there to be scared of?"

He turned to me and looked in my eyes. Whispers of his thoughts filled my head and it was like he was pressing his will against mine. *We know her. Know her parents, talk to them almost every day. She played with Mackenzie at the school, at our home. And now she's missing, taken.*

"She's not scared."

"Mackenzie doesn't know to be scared or understand the danger," he replied. "This man, this... monster is faceless. We don't know who we can trust."

****

The flyer fluttered in the wind, barely held to the telephone pole by two flimsy staples. The face on the paper smiled, a bright, wide smile that lifted her cheeks. Tiny lights reflected in her eyes, making them sparkle. Her hair was pulled into pigtails high on either side of her head. She sat with her hands folded in her lap, feet crossed at the ankles and a giant teddy bear behind her. Underneath the picture was a plea for information, asking anyone that knew where the girl was to call the number.

I looked closer at the flyer, noticing the smile looked fake. Everything about the picture looked like it was staged and nothing was real. There were a few pictures like that at my brother's house. Family photos, he called them. Pointless, I called them.

More flyers were posted on other telephone poles, each one with the same plea for information. The sheer number of flyers felt desperate, like if there were enough posted, the little girl would appear.

I turned from the flyers and headed out to find my brother. He wasn't home when I woke, out with some friends according to Rissa. I followed his scent with a bit of difficulty, the taint of car exhaust trying to overpower his scent, to a house with cars parked in front, his among them.

Amy appeared as I snuck around the house. She stayed on my heels, silent, as I peered through cracks of curtains and stopped outside the largest window. I skimmed the edges, trying to see around the fabric, but it stretched past the sides and bottom of the window and hid the humans on the other side.

Feeling reckless, I knocked on the glass, then we dashed into the shadows. The curtain moved, a human appearing. Others crowded behind him, including my brother, all looking for the source of the noise. After a few seconds, the human released the curtain.

"Humans say curiosity killed the cat," Amy whispered with a quick smile as we crept back.

"I'm not a cat," I replied.

"I know, that doesn't make any sense to me either," she laughed. Using caution I never saw her use with me, she leaned in and pressed her ear to the glass. "Sounds like video games. I've played a few."

I was impressed. "My brother likes to make me play with him. I never win much."

"Sound a little sour about that." Amy smirked at me.

I shrugged and turned my attention to the conversation behind the curtains. As the game progressed, the conversation filtered through topics. Work, politics, cars, other video games, wives and kids, and finally, vampires. Amy's smile faded, a solemn look on her face as we listened.

"Did you hear about the latest sucker protest?"

"What happened?" my brother asked casually.

"It was messed up," the voice replied. "The suckers were standing there, holding their signs, not moving, looking creepy, and this girl was standing with them. VF kept trying to coax her away, get her to safety, but she refused."

"Said one of the suckers was her mother. Hugged it and everything," a second voice said.

"VF finally dragged her away," a third voice added.

"The sucker went nuts and attacked every VF there. It was like it believed the girl, thought it was her mother. They finally caught it, torched it and six other suckers," the first voice explained. "The rest disappeared before they could be destroyed."

"That girl had to be insane," the second voice said. "Suckers don't care about family. That's why they kill theirs."

Amy was silent next to me, her eyes closed. I placed my fingertips on her arm and an appreciative smile filled her face. On the other side of the glass, the humans were quiet too, only the music of the game filled the air.

"You gotta wonder." My brother broke the silence. "Was that vampire really that girl's mother? It's not impossible. If the girl wasn't home, that would explain why she survived or..."

"Or what?" the third voice asked when he fell silent.

"Maybe they were close when the vampire was human. Maybe it was enough to stop the vampire from killing her."

Another long moment of silence.

"What do you guys think about the kidnappings?" The first voice broke the silence this time. "I heard the police called the FBI to consult on the case."

"Kate's paranoid, won't let Emmett out of her sight. I told her not to worry. What are the chances of it happening to us?" the third voice said.

"I'm sure that's what Jamie's parents said too," my brother replied.

"You and Rissa aren't freaking out," the second voice commented.

He took a moment before he answered and I knew when he spoke, he meant me. "There's always someone with Mackenzie at night. I wouldn't be able to sleep if I didn't know she was protected."

"Gotta give one thing to suckers," the first voice said. "At least vampires only kill adults."

"Yeah," my brother replied. "Makes you wonder who the real monsters are."

There was that word again, monster. That was the second time my brother used that word to describe another human. Why?

When the humans left, Amy and I slipped back into the shadows. We watched them climb into their cars and drive off. I didn't hear her leave when she finally did, but I felt the space next to me become empty.

I took off after my brother, catching up quickly and climbing in. "I'm confused."

He jerked in his seat, his knuckles turning white as he gripped the steering wheel. "Jeez! Tommy, how many times do I have to tell you not to jump in the car while I'm driving down the road? What are you doing here anyways? Have you been following me?"

"I was curious," I replied. "I wanted to see what humans did to forget their fears."

"Fears?"

"You're scared of that human taking children. It stinks the house up." I paused. "That human, why do you call him a monster and not me?"

He stared at the road, silent for a long moment. When he finally spoke, his voice was low. "Because what he does... he doesn't have to do it to survive."

****

My family was afraid and the human that caused the fear was someone I didn't understand. I read every newspaper article, watched all the news reports, asked my brother to look up information on his computer for me to read. He explained everything to me, but nothing helped. I didn't understand. If this human wasn't doing these things to survive, then why?

Light glowed brighter, filling my niece's room as the door opened. Rissa leaned heavily on the doorframe, staring heavy lidded at my niece. She shuffled in and took my offered hand as I gave up the chair to her. She groaned softly as she settled into it.

"I haven't gone out and drank like that in ages – not since college," she whispered.

"Going to regret it tomorrow," I replied.

She laughed softly. "Look at you, finally learned something about us humans. I bet you nursed Dan through a few hangovers."

I nodded. "Yes. Sometimes I followed and watched, but I never understood the point of drinking."

She sighed. "Complicated species, humans. We make rules only to break them and sometimes we hurt each other." She reached out and placed her hand over my niece's smaller one. "We say vampires are the monsters, but how can that be true when there's a real monster out there who is hurting children?"

I knelt down, tentatively touching her knees. "I don't know, but I do know I won't ever let anything happen to my family. I won't let any monsters get you."

Her hand moved from my niece's to mine. "I know you won't." Her chin tipped onto her chest and her eyes drifted shut.

I found a blanket and draped it over her before backing out. My brother's door was slightly open; Rissa must have checked on him before going to my niece's room. I headed down the stairs, double-checking the lock as I left.

The night was silent as I stood on the sidewalk. Above, the stars sparkled and looked peaceful. There were no monsters up there.

I gazed at the bright dots, letting my mind wander. I may never understand the human my brother called a monster, but I did understand one thing. This monster would never be allowed near my family. I would find him and destroy him. It would ensure my family's safety and erase the fear that filled the house.

But how to find the monster? When I searched for my brother, I had a starting point. I knew what he looked like, what he smelled like and knew where to start. This time, I had no clue who I was looking for or what scents to follow.

How was I going to find the monster when I had no starting point?

I paced back and forth. There had to be something that could point me in the direction of the monster.

The fake smiling poster caught my attention. What if the image was my niece's? I'd tear the city apart to find her, wouldn't rest until I found her, I'd search every place she had ever been...

I whirled around and dashed down the street. I knew where to start.

The school was dark and the parking lot empty. Lights illuminated the sidewalk, a few more stationed around the fenced in area. I hopped over the fence, smelling the air as I walked. Dozens of scents hung in the air, on the scattered toys and seeped into the ground. I ran my fingers through the grass, sending up plumes of scents. Next, I picked up a toy and inhaled. My niece's was easy to find, the only familiar scent.

I moved around the play area, catching the scents of each child and growing familiar with them. From the scents, I could tell there were more boys than girls and what toys they played with the most. But outside nature had beaten at the scents, diluting them. I needed fresher ones if I was going to have a chance of finding the missing girl's.

I headed to the building, but the doors were locked. No time to search for a key, I slammed my fist against a window and broke it. Glass crunched under my feet as I stepped through and began searching again.

Inside, the scents were stronger and I roamed around the large room, picking up toys and smelling them. In the corner, a colorful blanket was spread before a bookshelf. I crouched down and grazed my nose across the fabric. The scents embedded in the fabric told me where each child sat and in one spot a scent struggled to cling to the fabric. This scent had to be the girl's.

I followed the faint scent around the room, drawing many breaths to keep fresher ones from overwhelming it. It led me across the room, down a hall and out the front door where I almost lost it. At the curb, I found it again along with another scent. Both scents disappeared, overwhelmed by the smell of exhaust and paint.

An annoyed growl worked up my throat as I stalked up and down the street. All car exhaust smelled the same, masking scents and lingering in the air for a long time. I wouldn't be able to pick up her scent again.

I went back to the spot I lost her scent, nose twitching at the paint smell. It stood out among the other scents – even the exhaust – shining like a brightly lit path. I had no clue if this scent would lead me to the girl and monster, but I had to follow. My thoughts focused on one thing, one goal that consumed my thoughts. Find where the paint scent led, find the girl.

Find the monster.

****

Lights were spaced at regular intervals, attempting to chase away the darkness. The pavement smelled like fresh tar and the lines of paint glowed. Lawns were manicured, shrubs and bushes trimmed into neat blocks. Shiny cars were parked in the driveways and equally shiny trash cans sat at the end. It was a suburb, a neighborhood where the humans were obsessed with organization. Everything had its place and everything was safe.

Or so these humans thought.

I flitted from shadow to shadow, still following the paint smell. I abandoned it when I caught the two scents from my niece's school. The scents were potent, telling me I had been right about my guess at the school and was closing in on my prey.

The scents cumulated around a house slightly smaller than the rest, but everything else about it was identical. The well-kept lawn, tended flower beds and the trash can that stank of garbage. The driveway was empty with oil spots marring the otherwise perfect cement.

Dozens of scents hung in the air around the house and I sifted through them for the girl and monster's, following theirs behind the house and to a small shed. Anticipation filled me as I yanked the door open. I wanted to kill this human, desired it even. Need was barely a thought, my mind set on enjoying the monster's death. It was the least he deserved for putting my family in fear.

But the shed was empty, only tools hanging on the wall. I turned away and followed the scents back to the house. Both scents disappeared behind an immaculate door. Annoyance welled and I slammed my fist against the door and a jolt rippled up my arm.

I shook the jolt away and lifted my hand again. The energy crackled as I pressed against it again, but it felt weak, giving as I pushed against it. Why?

I glanced at the still dark sky and decided it didn't matter.

Grabbing the doorknob, I shoved the door open. The energy snapped louder as I continued to push until my hand passed through. I yanked my hand back and examined the damage. Wisps of smoke drifted from my hand and small, shallow cuts covered my skin.

I pushed my hand back through, and for a split second, wondered if the energy would sever my hand if I held there long enough. Bad idea! Pulling my hand back, I lifted my shirt to cover my face and prepared myself. It took some effort, but I jerked my way through the energy and stumbled into the house.

Silence greeted my ears when the crackle of energy faded away. I moved through the house, clinging to walls and shadows as I explored. In the living room were the usual furniture and decorations. In a bedroom, a fan hummed quietly next to a large bed. A few more doors revealed more bedrooms and a bathroom, but nothing out of the ordinary. If another human came to this home, they would assume it was normal.

Yet there were things in the house that weren't normal. Scents. They filled the house and drifted along like pathways. Lots of humans had been in this house, causing the energy to weaken and allow me to force my way in.

The girl's scent stood out among the others. It was heavy with fear, turning the otherwise sweet smell almost sour. It led me back through the house and to the living room where it disappeared behind the couch. I pushed the couch aside, my nose grazing the wall as I followed. The scent stopped in the middle, but there was nothing. It was only a wall.

I sat back, puzzled. How did the scent end there?

Think like a human, I reminded myself.

I racked my brain and searched through everything I knew about humans and had learned about the monster. What he was doing was wrong and the other humans wanted him stopped, but were incapable of it. If the other humans knew what the monster was doing was wrong, then so did he. And if he knew it was wrong, he would hide it.

How did he hide the girl so her scent ended at the wall?

"He hid the girl *in* the wall," I muttered.

I pressed my ear to the wall and faintly made out a rhythm beating on the other side. A couple taps against the wall sounded hollow. The faint rhythm picked up its pace and I heard a frantic scratching. She was there, on the other side.

How did I get her out?

The wall didn't give when I pushed, too thick to break. I ran my fingers along the wall, examining the wallpaper. My fingers caught the edge of one tattered section and it tore away to reveal a door.

Dust puffed into the air, drywall crumbling as I pulled the door open. The smell of fear hit me hard and the aroma turned my stomach. A voice cried out in terror and feet scrambled to escape. I swatted my hand through the air to rid the dust and scents. A sick feeling filled me when I peered into the wall, my mouth going dry at the human cowering before me.

My niece was in the wall.

****

Every ounce of strength and energy I had drained away. I stumbled back, panic gripping my chest. No, it couldn't be her. She was home. Safe. Not huddled in terror behind a wall!

A few blinks and the horrible vision changed. My niece disappeared, replaced by the girl. She huddled in the corner of the shallow nook that was crudely carved into the wall, staring at me with wide, fear-filled eyes. There wasn't a strip of clothing on her, her thin arms wrapped around her trembling body. A whimper escaped her lips and tears sprung from her eyes when I reached for her. I dropped my hand and retreated as her fear hit me again.

"It's okay, I won't hurt you," I told her, reaching again.

She whimpered and tears rolled down her cheeks.

"I won't hurt you," I repeated slowly. "I'm here to..." My voice trailed off.

I was here to kill the monster. He was my prey. I hadn't given her any thought. I knew she'd be here, her scent helped me find him, but I never thought about what to do with her once I killed him.

Listening, I glanced over my shoulder at the vacant living room. There were no other sounds in the house, no sounds from outside that indicated a human was near or approaching. It was only me and her. I reached again, not backing down when she cried out and patted her arm. "I won't hurt you."

I took my hand back and tugged my shirt off. Carefully, I pulled her from the wall and dressed her in my shirt. Her shivering subsided, tiny fists clutching handfuls of fabric. I offered my hand again, letting her come to me. Cautiously, she placed her hand in mine and let me pull her into my arms. I cradled her gently, the fear easing from her scent as I rocked her back and forth.

"That's right, everything's all right." It was something my brother and Rissa always told my niece after bad dreams. I figured if my brother and Rissa said it to my niece, it was okay to say to her.

Gears creaked as a car pulled into the driveway, lights glowing through the curtains. The lights died, the car engine falling silent. Footsteps clomped on cement, a whistled tune drifted over the air and a key turned in the lock.

Her body turned rigid, head buried against my shoulder and she whimpered in terror. Curling back into the wall, I pried her fingers from my neck and pushed her behind me. I pressed my finger to my lips, then turned away to wait.

My prey had entered the house.

Lights flooded the living room, the footsteps stopped and the whistle died. A breath inhaled sharply, panic joining the smell of fear. He took one step, then another, making his way towards the couch.

I gave him a second to see me, a second for realization to hit and fear set in.

He whirled away, attempting to reach the door, but I grabbed his leg and jerked him back. Only to release him and allow him to scramble to his feet. I blocked him before he reached the door, forcing him to change direction. He slammed against the wall, sweat shining on his face as he panted for breath. With a cry, he reached into the wall, dragging her out. He shoved her at me, then struggled to his feet and raced down the hall.

I caught and set her on the couch, then took off after him. In the kitchen, I grabbed him again, knocking his feet out from under him. His head cracked against the counter, and he fell to the floor, crying in pain.

His fear filled the air, mingling with the fear of the children he hid in the wall. Their scents saturated the house, telling me a story of how their lives ended. He brought them here, terrified them, hurt them, and then killed them before throwing their bodies away like trash.

I didn't understand why, but I didn't have to. I circled around him and hissed one word, "Monster."

"No, I'm sick and need help!" he pleaded, crawling on his knees.

I threw him across the room, red seeping into my vision as I followed and pounced. Flesh tore and bones popped as he screamed in pain. I ripped into him, tearing and jerking until there was nothing left but red in front of me.

The fury drained out of me with his death and I stumbled back. I felt his sticky blood cooling on my skin, embedded under my nails. It covered the floor, flowing like a river to where she stood in the doorway.

Feet slipping through the blood, I swept her up. Her eyes were wide as she stared and I turned her head away knowing she shouldn't see any of that. She clung to my neck as I carried her away, leaving the fear and what was left of the monster behind.

Once home, I set her on the doorstep and unlocked the door. I knelt down, looking in her eyes, my hands on her shoulders. "I welcome you in."

She followed me inside, wide eyes following my movements. A growl rumbled in her stomach, her hand moving to it.

I crouched in front of her, tilting my head. "Are you hungry?"

She nodded once, her stomach growling again.

I led her to the kitchen, shifting through the food. I never paid much attention to what my niece ate. I knew she liked candy and cake, but Rissa always said she needed more than sugar to eat.

Finding the bread and a kind of dead meat, I made her a sandwich. If not for my brother's midnight snacks in college, I wouldn't know how to make one. She devoured the sandwich as I cleaned the blood off myself. She hiccupped a few times, so I filled a glass with water. She drank that quickly as well. When she finished, she yawned widely and blinked sleepily at me.

"Are you tired?"

She nodded, rubbing an eye with her fist.

I carried her to the basement, curling up with her in my corner. Her skin felt warm and uncomfortable as the sun rose, but I endured the pain. My family was safe and the monster was dead. The girl was in my arms, fast asleep and free of fear.

****

Each time the girl moved, I woke. And she moved a lot. One moment her arms were around my neck, the next her head against my chest, then she'd roll over onto her back, legs sprawled across mine only to roll back onto her stomach and curl up. Finally, I had to move her. As much as I didn't want to, the pain of her skin against mine was too much for me to bear. She didn't wake as I slowly worked on moving her from my lap to the floor. Once her body was no longer touching mine, I worked on reining in my need that had swirled to life from being touched during the day.

When the sun set, she stirred and softly moaned. I moved to her side and brushed the hair out of her face. My movement startled her, causing a whimper of fear.

"It's okay, just me," I assured her.

She stared with wide and uncertain eyes. I stared back, just as uncertain. She obviously needed care and protection. I could do the protection part, but caring for a human child. I barely had a clue.

"I don't know what to do," I informed her. "I need to go upstairs, my family will be wondering if I don't. Stay here and I'll be back."

She stayed silent, huddling against the wall and fear filling her scent.

I crouched down. "You're safe with me; I won't let any monsters get you again."

She nodded and the fear started to fade. I darted up the stairs and peeked through the door. My brother and Rissa were on the couch, watching a news report about a murder in a suburb. My niece was playing with her toys on the floor, absently humming. I slid through, racing up to the spare room for a shirt. Once it was on, I descended the steps at a slower pace.

Delight filled my niece's eyes when she saw me and she threw herself into my arms. "Uncle, acrobat!"

"Later." I set her down and disappointment filled her eyes.

"You don't need to get riled up before bed." My brother picked her up and swung her around.

"And that's not helping." Rissa plucked my niece from him. She looked at me. "You're awfully late coming up. It didn't get too warm down there today, did it?"

"I'm fine," I casually replied.

My brother turned to me, raising an eyebrow. "What emotion was that? You sounded like someone was squeezing your–"

"Dan!" Rissa cut him off, growling through her teeth. "Not in front of Mackenzie."

"What?" my niece asked. "What was Daddy talking about? I want to know."

"No, you don't," Rissa replied.

I inched back towards the basement, trying to look normal. A noise below had caught my attention, a weak whimper. Something upset her and she needed me. I had to get down there and make sure she was okay.

"Tommy, you okay? You look tense," Rissa asked and I froze.

"How can you tell?" my brother chuckled.

I nodded, then did it again slowly. "I didn't rest well; think I'll go back downstairs."

I hurried down the stairs, feeling guilty. I had never lied to my family before, but I was hesitant to let them see her. They wouldn't understand and want to send her back to her family. She couldn't go back to her family though. They couldn't protect her like I could. I could keep her safe from the monsters. She needed to stay with me.

She was crying when I reached her.

"What's wrong?"

She whimpered in reply. I pulled her onto my lap, searching for the problem. The bottom of my shirt she wore was wet, a foul odor soaked in. A small puddle lay where she had sat, the same odor wafting up. I moved her away from the puddle, tugging the soiled shirt off and offering her my fresh one.

How odd would it be if I asked for some of my niece's clothes?

"Why are you still crying?" I asked as I cleaned the puddle up and her tears continued. "Did you make this?"

She nodded, a mournful look on her tear streaked face.

"Did you mean to?"

She shook her head.

"That's okay then," I replied and gathered her up. I rocked her back and forth until the action calmed her.

"Tommy?"

I pushed her into the corner, making sure she was hidden before standing. "Yes?"

My brother slowly moved closer, eyes roaming over me. "Are you okay? You're acting weird, like you're trying to hide something."

"I'm not hiding anything," I said. "I just want to rest."

"Okay," he replied and headed back up the stairs.

"They can't know about you or they won't let me keep you," I told her, once he was gone. "But you need to stay with me. If you go back to your family, the monsters will get you. I'll make sure you're safe."

"Safe?" Her voice was small, timid and delicate. But beautiful. The one word chimed like little bells. Her first word spoken to me.

I nodded. "Yes, I'll keep you safe. Forever. If you need anything, you only have to tell me. You can speak. I'd like to hear you speak. It sounds nice."

She nodded and disappointment filled me. She settled on my lap again, head against my chest. I stroked her hair and touched her cheek, feeling the warmth and life in her. I wondered if this was what having a pet was like. A smaller being you took care of and kept alive.

So far I was doing well.

The door to the basement banged open. Feet scurried down the steps and my niece squealing with mischievous happiness. She jumped the last few stairs, landing with a huff. "Uncle, surprise!"

I pushed the girl behind me, growling.

My niece skidded to a halt, eyes widening in shock. Her lower lip trembled and moisture filled her eyes. Like a bubble, she burst and tears streamed down her face. "*MOMMY! Uncle growled at me!*"

"Tommy!" Rissa stormed down the stairs. "You better have..." Her eyes widened and her mouth dropped open. "Jamie."

I snarled when Rissa moved closer.

"Dan, you need to come down here," Rissa called. She hugged my niece, consoling her crying as she stared at the girl behind me.

My brother's face was pale as he rushed down. He skidded to a halt. "Jamie!" He jumped back when I growled at him. His voice turned gentle, hands held out in a peaceful gesture. "Okay, everyone calm down. Tommy, let us near Jamie."

"No." I growled the word, making him step back. "I won't let any monsters hurt her."

"But you know Rissa and Mackenzie aren't monsters and neither am I. Right?"

I turned my gaze to my niece who was huddled against Rissa. My growl died, fangs sliding back in as I relaxed my crouch, ashamed. This was my family, I trusted them and they trusted me. And what did I do? I hid her from them, lied to them and refused to let them near.

"That's right, Tommy, there's no monsters here," my brother said and moved closer to her. "Hey Jamie, remember me? I'm Mackenzie's dad."

She cringed and whimpered.

"Let me." Rissa gave me lots of space as she moved forward, placing a friendly smile on her face. "Hi, Jamie. Are you hungry? Would you like something to eat? A grilled cheese, maybe?"

She nodded, letting Rissa pick her up.

"I wanna grilled cheese," my niece whimpered.

"You can have one too," my brother assured her.

I silently followed them, feeling my emotions torn. Part of me was tense, on edge that another human was touching her. When Rissa picked her up, I desperately wanted to place myself between her and the danger. The other part was ashamed of the fear I caused my family. Fear of me.

"I'm sorry," I muttered.

My brother looked back at me, lips pressed into a tight line. "We'll get this smoothed out and everything will be fine."

"I already fed her," I added as we filed into the kitchen. "I made a sandwich last night. Bread and dead meat with a glass of water."

****

"She's a little girl who has a family. You can't keep her cooped up in the basement." My brother's voice grew more exasperated with each word.

"She doesn't have to stay in the basement all the time. Just during the day with me, where it's safe," I protested.

"She's not your pet," he sighed, rubbing his hands over his face.

"I know," I replied indignantly.

"You don't know how to care for a child," he persisted.

"I can learn," I insisted. "I know she needs to eat and sleep. Those are the important things."

"There's a lot more to raising a child than that," Rissa sighed. "Children need to eat at least three times a day with snacks, they need naps throughout the day, and constant supervision. You need to be there for them, every second of every day, even when you need to rest."

"I can do that."

"You can only do that at the night. She needs to be sleeping at night," my brother said.

"But–"

"Tommy, no," he ordered. He gave me a long, sad look. "I know you want to protect her."

"I can keep her safe from the monsters," I replied.

"Even yourself?"

I looked from him to Rissa. "What do you mean? I'm not a monster."

"You're a vampire," he replied. "And she's human. Survival trumps everything. Survival will trump her. You get hurt badly enough and you won't be able to stop yourself."

"I can stop. I did with you. Once."

"Can you stop before you hurt her? Or kill her?"

I looked at the girl playing with my niece in the living room. She paused, a toy in her hand and eyes wide with trust. A smile filled and brightened her face. She looked so happy and safe.

I sadly shook my head.

My brother placed his hand on my shoulder. "You did a good thing, you found her, alive."

I suppressed a growl at the word, remembering the fear in the monster's house.

"Who else did you find?" he asked.

I looked at him. "Giles Montgomery."

A shocked silence filled the air. I never used names unless I felt had to. In all my vampire life, I had said my brother's name nine times, never used Rissa's name and my niece's name I had only said once. Her name was the hardest to say. The fact I said a human's name, showing no remorse about it, meant a lot.

"They just mentioned him on the news. He was found brutally murdered in his home," Rissa whispered. "That was him?" She sunk into a chair, blowing out a breath of air. "How long did you look for him?"

"Last night."

My brother snorted. "Maybe the police force should hire vampires."

"But police would kill the vampires," I replied.

He shook his head. "Forget I said anything. We need to take Jamie home."

I darted into the living room and grabbed her. "No."

"Tommy, she needs to go home. Would you want someone refusing to bring Mackenzie home?" he asked.

I looked at my niece, who looked annoyed. "No."

Rissa reached for her. "Then we need to–"

"I'll do it," I said, refusing to let her out of my grip. "Please."

My brother and Rissa exchanged tense glances.

"You take her straight home, 415 Westwood Avenue," he ordered. "Knock on the door and leave her before anyone sees you, okay?" He stopped me at the door. "Be careful, lil' bro."

As the door swung shut, I heard my niece mutter, "I don't like Jamie anymore."

The address my brother gave me was only ten blocks away. Even moving slowly, the journey didn't take long. Cop cars were parked outside the house I needed and cops stood in the doorway as they talked to the humans inside.

These were my last moments with her. After tonight, I wouldn't see her again. Even as her savior, her family wouldn't let me near her. I couldn't even let them know I was the one who saved her from the monster.

"It's not fair," I told her. "I did something good, stopped him from killing you. No one will see it that way. All they see is a vampire who kills humans and hate me for it."

She clung tighter, pressing her head against the nook in my neck.

The wordless action comforted me and I pressed my cheek against the top of her head. I set her down and gave her a soft push. She clung to me, shaking her head.

"Safe," she whimpered.

The single word vibrated within me. I hugged her back, my voice stopped in my throat. She needed protection, protection I could provide. How could I let her go when she needed me?

I tipped her face up and did the only thing I could. The sparkle faded from her eyes as I pushed my will against hers. Her hands dropped from my neck and she turned towards the humans. When they noticed her, they grabbed her and rushed her into the house. The cops spotted me next and raced to their cars.

"Be safe," I whispered and disappeared as the cop cars roared to life.

Home was dark, a lone light on as my brother waited for me. I trudged to the couch and sat. "Danny, I'm confused. I didn't want to let her go. I wanted to protect her, felt like I needed to."

"Well," he slowly replied. "She's been through a lot and it's obviously affected you. When you first saw her, what did you see?"

"My niece, scared."

He leaned forward and rested his elbows on his knees. His eyes held a familiar light, an understanding that said he knew how to explain everything. "You finally understood why Rissa and I were terrified of this man, what we feared."

"But my niece was always safe."

"Didn't matter, you realized the possibility it could have been Mackenzie."

"I didn't drink his blood either, I let it waste."

He leaned back, watching me. "Why didn't you drink his blood?"

"What he was doing was wrong and he was planning on killing her like the other children he took. But it wasn't for survival or fun or anger, there was no reason. His blood was tainted," I replied.

"That's why you didn't want to drink it."

Part Four: Sunlight

I headed down the stairs and fell onto the couch. Feet kicked out, I slouched back and folded my arms across my chest. I sighed deeply, unfolded my arms and propped my chin on my hand. "I'm bored."

A smile cracked my brother's face, an eyebrow raised.

"She told me to say it."

Dan sighed. "Sometimes I wonder about that girl."

"Why?"

He chuckled. "Is that eyeliner?"

"Yes."

"Definitely wonder about that girl."

"But why?"

"If I explained, you wouldn't understand."

"Dan, have you seen where I put..." Rissa stopped short in the kitchen doorway. She stared at me, mouth hanging open. With a sharp turn, she faced the stairs. "Young lady, get down here now!"

Feet thudded on the stairs and a teenage girl skipped the last two steps. "What's up, Mom?"

Rissa folded her arms. "Where do I start? You..." Her eyes slightly widened. "Did you pierce his ear?"

My niece flopped down next to me, casually mimicking the moves she taught me. "It's not like it hurt him. Probably heal if he takes it out." She looked at me. "Uncle, don't take it out."

"Okay."

"How come he doesn't ask you why all the time?" Dan muttered under his breath.

My niece hugged me. "Because he loves me, don't ya, Uncle?"

I hugged her back. "Yes, love you lots and lots and lots."

"Mackenzie, don't try to teach him to talk like a teenage girl. It sounds creepy," Dan sighed.

"Why is it creepy?" I asked.

"Still as clueless as ever," Dan chuckled and picked up his newspaper.

Time had passed again and everyone in my family had changed. Everyone except me. My niece changed the most, surprising me on a daily basis. It had terrified me at first. I feared she would change into someone who might hate vampires. Dan laughed and assured me she was the same person, only bigger.

He changed the least. His hair had lightened and faint lines appeared around his eyes and mouth. Sometimes when he moved, he groaned, like the action was harder now that he was thirty-eight. He joked about looking like our father, but I never saw the resemblance. All I saw was my brother.

"Don't you have homework?" Dan asked my niece, looking around his newspaper.

"Yes, you need to get your butt back up there and finish your homework," Rissa ordered. "Not dress your uncle up like he's going to a funeral."

"It's called Goth, Mom, and it suits him. You can barely tell he's a vampire." My niece sighed and rolled her eyes.

"Go." Rissa pointed to the stairs. "Tommy, stay down here."

My niece grabbed my hand and her voice turned pleading. "I'll do my homework, promise. Uncle's just going to paint my toenails while I do it."

"Oh boy," Dan muttered from behind his newspaper.

Rissa sighed but didn't object.

My niece beamed and pulled me up the stairs. She fell on her bed and wiggled her toes. "Do black, I'm feeling dark."

"Why are you feeling dark?"

"And Dad says you never ask me why." She gave me the same pleading look she gave Rissa. "Just do it, pleeeease, Uncle."

I took the little bottle and shook it like she showed me. An acidic aroma hit me when I twisted the cap off and I wrinkled my nose. "It didn't smell this bad earlier."

"You didn't have your nose stuck in it," she laughed.

I looked at her, shocked. "You agree with me?"

"Of course, is that so hard to believe?"

"Yes, humans never agree with me."

She turned around so we were nose to nose. "I'm not most humans, am I?" She moved back when I shook my head and placed a foot before me. "There you go. Paint, please."

"Shouldn't you be doing your homework while I do this?" I asked as I carefully applied the paint.

"Mom's over reacting. It's not like anyone will kill me if I don't get my homework done."

I bolted to my feet with a snarl. "Who wants to kill you? I'll kill them first!"

She jumped back with a squeak of shock. "No one, it's a figure of speech. Oh jeez, Uncle, you broke the bottle." She rushed from the room and returned with a towel. "Mom is gonna kill us." Her eyes widened. "Not literally," she quickly added and took what was left of the bottle from me and tossed it the trash before wiping the black paint off my hand.

"I'm sorry, I didn't mean to break it."

She smiled at me. "It's okay, I should know better than to say stuff like that in front of you. I know the thought of someone hurting me upsets you."

"I never want you to be hurt or scared of monsters. I'll always protect you," I replied. "I love you."

"I love you too, Uncle."

"What can I do to help?"

"Besides going to the store and buying me a gallon of nail polish remover? Don't tell Mom and Dad."

"Okay."

"And don't go to the store to get me nail polish remover either."

One time. One time she told me to get her chips from a store. It's what she wanted, so why wouldn't I do what she asked me to? The humans in the store panicked and the one behind the counter wouldn't even take the money I tried to give him. In the end, I left it on the counter. When I returned home Dan accused me of losing my mind while Rissa waited for Vampire Forces to knock on the door.

"I wasn't going to. You don't need nail polish remover to survive."

My niece shook her head. "Dad is so right, you are clueless, Uncle. In high school, the right nail polish can help you survive. You don't wear the right clothes or say the right thing and you're singled out to be picked on." She pinned me with a serious look. "And no, you cannot kill anyone who picks on me."

"You and my brother are always telling me that," I grumbled.

"That's because we know how your mind works," she replied. "Don't worry, no one picks on me. I don't give them a reason to, but not everyone is that lucky." Her voice turned sad and soft. "Poor Jamie, she always gets the worst of it."

****

Poor Jamie, she always gets the worst of it.

The words stayed with me all day. Immobilized because of the sun again with nothing to do but drift half away and think. Think about what my niece said and about poor...

Jamie.

Was it her, the little girl I rescued from the monster?

The question kept repeating in my head, refusing to give me any peace. I knew I shouldn't wonder. I put her behind me, I had to. Dan and Rissa had been right, I had no idea how to care for a human child and they made sure I learned that lesson the hard way.

For one night, they let me watch my niece. They didn't say a single word or offer any guidance on what I should or shouldn't do. By the end of a half hour, my niece was crying her eyes out.

Apparently, even if a human child can, they should not be allowed to eat a gallon of ice cream.

While Rissa tended to my niece, Dan tended to me. He asked if I understood now why she had to go back to her family. She would be safe, he assured me. Her parents would protect her. It was best if I put her behind me. I didn't have to forget her, but I shouldn't dwell on her. She was with her family where she belonged and I was something I had never been before.

Sad.

I found it hard to smile and sometimes stayed in the basement rather than deal with the world. Even my hunger was affected. I couldn't concentrate on hunting and other times I didn't feel like it even though I needed blood. It was only when I listened to Dan and put her behind me that everything returned to normal.

Now she was back as I wondered what my niece's words meant. What did she get the worst of? As soon as I had the energy to speak, I needed to find out.

Once the sun set, I was up the stairs and outside my niece's bedroom door in a flash. Voices and laughter on the other side froze me. A hand grabbed me, Dan pulling me into the spare room.

"Rules, lil' bro. You're supposed to listen to make sure we don't have guests."

"Sorry," I replied and eyed the wall. "I wanted to ask her something. Will they leave soon?"

"Yes, and normalcy will descend again."

"I thought you said there was no such thing as normal."

Dan sighed. "Just stay here until they leave."

In my niece's room, one of the humans shrieked as the others started laughing. I moved closer to press my ear against the wall. They better not be picking on my niece. If they were, I didn't care what rules Dan and Rissa set for me, I was going to stop them.

Dan pulled me back. "Don't, you'll get confused."

"Why are they here again? They just visited her."

"They were over last month and Mackenzie likes to see her friends outside of school a little more often than that."

"But this is my time with her."

"Your time?"

"Yes, when I wake, everyone else is awake too, so I spend this time with my family."

"I didn't know you had your nights planned out," he laughed and I scowled. "I'm teasing, lil' bro. Don't worry, there's plenty of time left for you to spend with us."

"But you're aging and one day you'll die."

His smiled faded. "That's a long way away, Tommy."

"It scares me. I've always had you and I wonder how will I survive without you?"

He placed his arm around my shoulder. "I'll always be with you. It may not be in person, but you'll feel it, promise."

I nodded, even though I wasn't sure if I understood.

The door to my niece's room banged open and noise spilled into the hallway. Dan and I fell silent, not wanting to alert anyone to my presence. One thing hadn't changed over the past ten years.

Humans still hated vampires.

Not long after I rescued the girl, Vampire Forces was granted unprecedented power to stop the *undead plague*. Torchings were held nightly, vampires lined up to be destroyed. Lights filled cities and roads, blotting out the darkness so there was no place to hide. In public buildings, torches were placed alongside fire extinguishers, posters in schools showed how to spot a vampire. They were thorough in their crusade, working all hours of the night and trying to wipe vampires out.

Fortunately, vampires adapted if it meant survival.

I adapted to survive. One night, I walked up the stairs with my hands in my pockets and a passive look on my face. I blinked as I looked around the living room and shifted my weight like I was unable to stand still. Dan had stared at me, asking where I learned that. I shrugged and said I needed to. Then I tossed the hood on my jacket up and walked into the night like a human.

Pretending to be human was the only way to survive and as long as the humans didn't see my face, I could fake my way through a crowd and hunt. I had even started leaving humans alive. It was less risky than a dead body left in the woods.

When my niece came back upstairs, Dan stopped her and gave her a stern look. "Aunt Dee and Uncle Dick are coming for dinner tomorrow. I want you to be on your best behavior." He turned to me. "And you to be scarce."

"Aunt Dee and Uncle Dick are so boring," my niece groaned.

"You should let me kill them," I added.

Dan rolled his eyes. "You both are whining like a couple of teenagers."

"I am a teenager, Dad," my niece replied. "And Uncle will always be a teenager because he was one when he was turned."

Dan shook his head and disappeared down the stairs.

I grabbed my niece's hand and pulled her into her bedroom. "What did you mean by she got the worst of it? Worst of what?"

"What? Who are you talking about, Uncle?"

"The girl I rescued."

"Oh, you mean Jamie. It's nothing, don't worry about it."

"But I've been thinking about it all day and I want to understand."

She glanced away and shrugged, seeming reluctant. "It's just she's really quiet and everyone knows what happened to her and some people are mean about it."

"Are you?"

"No, of course not."

"But you said you didn't like her."

For a moment she stared in confusion, then a light dawned in her eyes. "Uncle, I was five when I said that and jealous of the attention you were giving her."

"You don't hate her?"

"No, but we didn't play much after you took her home. She became different, barely talking to anyone. Sometimes I think she's afraid of people, scared of what might happen. I feel bad for her, alone..." Her voice trailed off.

Or maybe I had stopped listening. She was alone and afraid, but she wasn't supposed to be! She was supposed to be safe with her family, that's why I took her back to them. I thought they would protect her. A tight knot formed in my chest as I realized everything I thought I knew was changing again.

****

Dan stopped me at the door. I tilted my head and he shuddered. "Never going to get used to that."

I untilted my head and relaxed my posture. "Is this better?"

A laugh escaped him. "I'm not sure; it's odd seeing you act so human."

I shrugged. "Did you want to tell me something?"

"Hmm? Oh yeah, if you're going out, be careful."

I crossed my finger over my chest. "Cross my heart and hope to die."

"I wish Mackenzie hadn't taught you that," he sighed. "Seriously, be careful, lil' bro."

"Don't worry, I'll survive." I gave him my usual assurance, then pulled my hood up and headed out to find the others.

Amy was the one who started gathering us. When Vampire Forces started hunting us to extinction, she found the survivors, brought us together and kept us from tearing each other apart.

She was perched on a tree branch with her legs dangling. When she saw me, she jumped down, a grin filling her face as she greeted me with the name I had given her, my brother's. As much as I trusted her, I couldn't quash the fear of having another vampire know my real name.

"Hey, Danny-boy."

"Hey..." My words turned into a growl as another vampire appeared too close for my comfort.

He glared at me, lip twitching. "He smells like human and I don't like it."

Amy pushed the vampire back into the trees to hide with the others. "We all smell like human, get over it."

I gazed warily at the trees, still feeling the vampire's anger. His hostility wasn't uncommon. He confronted every vampire about smelling human, but I received the brunt of it for smelling of human the worse. I swallowed my hostility and turned my attention to the only vampire I wasn't threatened by.

"Any new ones?"

Amy sighed. "No, I haven't found any more, but on the bright side, everyone is still here. VF hasn't torched any more of us."

"Do you want to go somewhere with me?"

Amy raised an eyebrow and laughed. "Are you asking me on a date? You know, I'm much older than you."

I frowned. "Why would I ask you on a date?"

"That's cold, Danny-boy. Sure, I'll go somewhere with you." She grabbed my arm and looped it in hers. "You need to work on being more human."

"You're my friend, I shouldn't have to fake around you."

"Still, practice makes perfect."

We walked out of the woods and headed down the brightly lit streets. No humans were in sight so we only faked enough, that if stumbled upon, a human wouldn't think twice. Hunger rumbled as we walk; the last time I hunted I had let the human live. If I didn't hurry and hunt, the night would be over and I'd have to sit through the day with hunger gnawing at me. I was reluctant to end my time with Amy. We didn't see each other much, too busy hiding and trying to survive.

"Do you have to hunt tonight?" Amy glanced at me.

"Yeah."

"I guess we better go our separate ways then." She leaned up and placed a kiss on my cheek. "Until next time, Danny-boy."

We parted ways and I melted into the shadows. There was one perk to Vampire Forces believing they were close to exterminating vampires: more humans out at night. I quickly located one, giving her no time to scream. I took her out of the city and deep into the woods where I drained every drop.

"Sorry," I whispered.

After burying the body, I headed home. I slipped back down the brightly lit streets, listening to the rhythms beating around me. As I walked, an aroma drifted like a graceful dancer. The faint scent stopped me, turning me around to race back the way I had come.

Memories flooded my mind as I turned down the street and stopped in front of the familiar house. Every window but one was dark, the light spilling onto the darkened lawn. A steady rhythm beat and a bell-like voice drifted from the half opened window. I pulled myself up the side and peered inside. She sat on her bed, a pad of paper in front of her and pen in hand. An image slowly formed as she drew and I watched with fascination.

Energy hummed when I pressed against it, reminding me I wasn't welcomed. I kept pressing, knowing if I pushed hard enough I could break through.

Anything for her.

My skin shredded as I forced my way through, stopping in front of her motionless figure, my hand on her cheek and said one word.

"Safe."

****

She was safe with nothing to fear. I took her from her dangerous home and tucked her into my old resting place. The cellar was a little neglected; I hadn't used it in ten years, opting to rest in my family's basement instead. I cleared away the dust, dirt and leaves littering the cellar floor and brushed clean the posters Dan had given me.

She huddled in the corner, eyes wide as she watched me. She whimpered when I moved closer, her voice timid. "Please don't hurt me."

I dropped my hand. "Why would I hurt you? I want to protect you, you need me to."

"I-I-I don't understand. Please, let me go. I won't call VF, I promise," she whispered.

"Don't you remember?"

"Remember what?"

"I rescued you from the monster who took you."

She was silent for a moment. "My parents told me a fireman found me wandering alone, but when I thought about it, that's not what I remembered. I remembered eyes staring at me and watching me." Her voice dropped to a whisper. "Eyes like yours."

"He had you in the wall, but I found you and took you back to your family," I explained.

Tears shimmered in her eyes and she sucked in a ragged breath. "I never met the person responsible and I always wondered why he never cared to know how I was doing. It didn't seem normal."

"I care," I assured her. "But I had to take you back because I didn't know how to care for a human child, but I do now. I paid attention." I jumped up. "Stay here and I'll bring you everything you need to survive."

I climbed out of the cellar and rushed home. The house was dark as I slipped inside. That was good; I didn't want my family interfering. They would object and tell me to take her back to her family. But her family couldn't protect her, so it was up to me to protect and care for her so she'd never be afraid or alone again.

I gathered everything I knew she'd need to survive. Some food, blankets, clothing and a toothbrush. Then I raced back to the cellar. "I got everything you need."

She looked at the objects I showed her and pointed to the food. "I can't eat that, it's raw... sorry."

My shoulders drooped, but I was determined. "I'll get more, don't worry."

She looked at me with those wide, brown eyes I remembered so well, her voice pleading, "Please, let me go."

"But I want to protect you," I replied. "You need me to because you're alone and scared. My niece told me you were."

"Niece?"

I bit my lip, realizing I shouldn't have said that. "Please," I said instead. "Let me keep you and protect you."

A tear trickled down her cheek as she retreated back to the corner. With a soft sigh, she rested her head on her arms. Short locks of ebony fell into her face and she swiped them away from her pale skin.

"Your hair was longer ten years ago. Why did you change it?"

She shrugged and looked away. "I like my hair short."

I inched a little closer. "It makes you look pretty."

Red stained her ivory cheeks and she buried her head in her arms.

I moved closer. "What's wrong? Your cheeks are red."

For a second, she looked up and her eyes locked with mine. More red crept into her face as she quickly dropped her gaze. "It's a blush. I was… embarrassed by your comment." She rose and moved to another corner.

I followed, knowing once I proved I knew how to care for her she'd calm down and stop being afraid.

I grabbed the toothbrush. "Want me to show you how to brush your teeth?"

"I already know how."

I set the toothbrush down and picked up the blanket. "What about the blanket? You're shivering and that means you're cold and need a blanket."

Still avoiding my gaze, she shrugged. "Sure."

I wrapped the blanket around her shoulders and silently congratulated myself for getting one thing right.

Silence filled the cellar as she huddled in the corner. The fear in her scent didn't ease as time slipped by. In fact, it grew with each passing moment. Her eyes darted to me, then raced to look away when she saw me watching. I racked my brain and tried to figure out what I was doing wrong. What was I missing?

I wandered to what I gathered, picking up the food and examining it. She couldn't eat it because it was raw. How did I make it unraw? Juices oozed onto my hand and I dropped it with a snarl. I glanced her way, seeing her looking fearfully at me. I picked the package back up, careful to avoid the juices spilling out.

"I understand why you can't eat this. I'll get rid of it and get something else."

I left her behind again and this time choose my food more carefully when I arrived home. A sandwich and a glass of water. Then I hurried back to the cellar, jumping with care so as not to spill the water. I pushed the sandwich into her hand, set the glass of water next to her and retreated.

For a long moment, she stared warily at the food. Then she nibbled on a corner. "Thank you."

She continued to nibble on the sandwich, refusing to look at me. I did my best to stay still, trying to be patient and wait for her to realize she was safe. When she finished, I moved closer.

"Do you feel safe now? I fed you and got you a blanket. That shows I can care for you and keep you safe like you need to be."

Her eyes widened with fear. "Please, let me go home!"

****

It had been simple. Find the girl, take her somewhere safe and keep her safe. Only it was turning out to be anything but simple. Even though I fed her, kept her warm and showed her she was safe, she was still terrified and pleading for me to let her go home.

I needed help.

Preparing myself for what I knew Dan would say, I headed up the stairs. I pushed the door to his bedroom open and slipped in. Giving him a shake, I locked eyes with him and pushed against his will. He rose and followed me without a word. Once he was seated on the couch, I released him.

He blinked a few times and glanced around the living room in confusion. "How did I get downstairs?"

"I willed you," I replied. "I need to talk with you... I don't know what to do."

He yawned and wiped the sleep out of his eyes. "What else is new? What's confusing you this time?"

"The girl I rescued," I said, shying from her name. I would never do that to her, never use her name against her.

"What about Jamie?"

I glanced at the window, gauging how much time I had before the sun rose. "I took her. She was alone and scared and needed me, but she doesn't remember me and she's afraid of me. I don't know how to show her it's okay." I looked away, hating the truth I felt coming. "You're going to tell me to take her home, aren't you?"

Dan sighed. "Where did you take her?"

"To my old resting place."

"Okay, let me get dressed and we'll take her home." He only took a few moments to get dressed, stifling a yawn as he headed back down. "Is there enough time for you before the sun comes up?"

I nodded. "What if she doesn't want me there?"

"You want her to not be afraid of you, right?"

I nodded, grateful I got the courage to tell him and he understood.

"Then you need to come. You need to show her you were only worried about her and want what's best for her and didn't mean to keep her against her will. And you were keeping her against her will," he replied. "That cellar isn't easy for a person to get in and out of. She couldn't get out herself."

I snapped my mouth shut and admitted he was right. She couldn't climb out of the cellar on her own and that was why I took her there.

The drive to the cellar was silent. Dan pulled up to the rundown house, then turn to face me, his eyes saying he knew what I felt through our bond. Over the years, it had gotten stronger. Sometimes we felt each other's pain.

Her voiced drifted through the door of the cellar, calling for help. She fell silent and sunk back into the corner when I dropped down. I pushed my sorrow back and reminded myself I needed to do this.

"I have someone who can take you home."

"Really?"

Now I was the one avoiding her gaze. "He'll take you home to your family. I'll carry you up."

She hesitated briefly, but allowed me to carry her. Topside, I set her down and stepped away to give her space. She rushed to the car, practically diving in. I stopped the door from slamming shut with my fingertips. Dan nodded and gave me a reassuring smile when I looked at him. I looked back to her, desperation pushing the words out.

"You know where I rest. If you want, you can come see me."

I pushed the door shut and watched as the car disappeared. Maybe I had gotten too hopeful and human, but I was certain, before the car disappeared, that she turned and looked at me.

Feeling the sun close to rising, I headed to my cellar. Her scent filled the air and I tried to ignore it, but the image of her felt branded in my mind. Memories rushed to be remembered and the sound of her bell-like voice echoed in my ears. I knew what I had to do, but I didn't want to put her behind me again. When the sun finally set, I dragged myself up and trudged home.

"Tommy!" Dan yelped when I slumped to the couch. "You're shredded. Still! Last night I didn't say anything because you were upset and I figured you'd go hunt and heal tonight."

I tilted my head and pain buzzed through me. "I forgot."

"You forgot? Well, don't you think you should go heal yourself?"

I shrugged and remained in my seat.

Dan's lips pressed into a tight line and I felt his worry vibrate through me. "Tommy, are you going to go hunting tonight?"

"I'll go tomorrow… maybe."

Dan sighed. "Tommy, please, not again. You reacted this way ten years ago when you took Jamie home the first time. I understand that you're upset about her, but you need to go out and hunt."

I threw as much human as I knew how into my voice and put to use every technique my niece taught me. "Fine, is my niece upstairs? I want to say hi first."

"No, she and some friends are walking over to Mandy's house and I don't want her to see you shredded."

I bolted to my feet. "She's out walking at night?"

"Calm down, it's only a few blocks to Mandy's and it's well lit. Nothing is going to get her."

I snarled. "That's how I hunt. I get into a crowd of humans and lure one away."

Not waiting for Dan to reply, I raced out the door as my emotions boiled. I didn't know what moved me faster, fear of my niece on the streets at night, Dan for letting her go, or the fact the little girl I rescued now feared me. I let those feelings drive me until I heard the unmistakable sounds of humans braving the night.

****

My niece and her friends were walking along the illuminated sidewalks, laughing and chatting. They made no effort to be quiet, their voices bouncing between the houses, unafraid of the night. I slowed my pace as I approached, clinging to shadows as I searched for the dangers I knew were hidden in the dark.

One girl paused and turned, a whiff of fear drifted through the air. "You guys, I thought I saw something move in the shadows."

"It's probably nothing," my niece replied in a confident voice. For a split second, her eyes stopped on me, but she gave no indication if she saw me in the darkness. "My family wouldn't let me walk at night if they knew I wasn't safe."

The humans resumed walking, my niece leading the way. As they neared a house, a shadow broke free, taking the form of a staggering human. A click sounded as a voice growled a threat. "Gimme all your…"

I cut the human off, slamming him into the ground, then throwing him against a telephone pole. The tantalizing aroma of blood filled the air and I dragged a breath in. Need roared through me and my injuries throbbed. A hint of desire tingled as I grabbed the human. Why had I waited so long to hunt? I could barely remember the confusing emotions of the day or the rage at the human for threatening my niece.

A noise made my head snap up and a growl rumbled in my throat. My niece and her friends were huddled nearby. They screamed, my niece's the loudest, when I locked eyes with them. They scrambled back the way they came, still screaming. Around me, lights flared to life, doors flying open.

I dropped the human and disappeared into the shadows, stopping once I was in the safety of the woods. There, I fought with my emotions, pushing the hunger, need and desire back until I was in control. When the sky started to lighten, I headed home.

My niece was waiting for me. She planted her hands on her hips and scowled deeply. "Why?"

"Isn't that my question?" I asked with slight amusement.

She didn't laugh or smile. "Why did you force your will on me and make me scream? You made it look like I was afraid of you and I'm not. I'm not afraid or ashamed that I know you."

"Neither was my brother," I replied. "He wasn't ashamed of me and he let humans know. They shunned him for it and that's what the humans will do to you if they know you talk to a vampire. They'll hate you as much as they hate me. I won't let that happen to you."

"But you saved us." she countered. "That man had a gun and could have shot us, but you stopped him. We shouldn't fear someone who saves us, we should thank you."

"I was going to kill him in front of you."

"I don't care."

"You should. You should understand what I am and what it means."

"I know what you are!"

"No, you don't."

"Fine!" She threw her hands up. "What does being a vampire mean to you?"

"Being a vampire means humans should fear me. You should fear me." Bitterness welled up in me. "She does, she only sees a monster that kills humans. I'm more than that, I know, but sometimes I wish I wasn't. Then it'd be simple. I wouldn't care about any humans, wouldn't get confused when I only want to understand."

"Uncle." Her voice turned soft. She placed a hand on my shoulder, pulling me into a tight hug.

"You never shudder when you touch me," I said softly.

"That's because the only thing you are to me is my uncle."

"You'd never think I was a monster, even if I killed a human in front of you?"

"No, but, I admit, I would appreciate it if you didn't kill someone in front of me."

"I won't kill someone in front of you then."

"Thanks." She lightly laughed and stepped back, her eyes wandering over me. Her skin paled as she touched a finger to my cheek and pain throbbed. "Uncle, what happened? Your skin is shredded."

"I forced my way into her home and it ripped my skin pushing through the energy."

The rest of the color drained from her face. "Will you be okay? Do you need blood to heal?"

"I'll be fine, I've had worse injures."

"I don't think I want to see worse," she replied, then held out her wrist. "Will my blood help?"

A long forgotten memory slid to the surface at the sight of the pulse throbbing under her skin. Her scent filled my nose, still as sweet and powerful as ever. I tried to get the smell out of my nose, but the desire glowed to life, fueled by the memories and the need to heal.

I stumbled back and raced into the fading night. I killed the first human I saw, slamming into the car and busting the front window out. Not even waiting for the car to stop, I dragged the human from the car, pulling her into the cover of the trees. I gulped every drop down greedily, letting myself fall into the desire and need. When the blood was gone, I took a moment to rein my feelings in. The desire fought, trying to control my thoughts, but my need obediently retreated to the back of my mind.

Once I felt a fragile peace of mind, I hid the body deep in the woods and piled leaves over it. I made it home as the sun broke the horizon, slamming the door and slumping against it as my energy drained away. The door to the basement felt miles away and a thought whispered I should have buried myself in the ground.

"Uncle!" My niece rushed to my side. "Are you okay? You're covered in blood."

"Don't touch me," I whispered. "Stay away, please."

Hurt filled her eyes and she blinked the tears back. "I'll go get Dad."

I slid to the floor, unable to support myself. I hated the day.

"Hey, lil' bro." Dan knelt before me. "What has you up here during the day?"

"I got home late," I whispered.

"Everything okay?"

"Yeah, I just want to get underground. It's so hot, how do you stand it?"

Dan smiled gently. "It doesn't feel hot to me. I'm gonna have to carry you, is that okay?"

I managed a nod. His skin pulsed hot against mine as he lifted me. He moved as quickly as he could, only slowing his steps on the stairs. As we descended, the feeling was instant, the air cooling around me and caressing my skin.

I curled up in my corner. "Thanks."

"Anytime, lil' bro, "Dan replied. "Want to tell me what happened?"

I looked from him to my niece. "She offered to help me heal and it made me desire, so I ran and found another human."

Dan threw her a frown, but it was gone when he looked back at me. "You just rest, lil' bro. Mackenzie, come on, your uncle needs to rest and we have to talk."

I didn't even nod, already drifting away.

The day flew by quickly and when the sun set, the energy that surged through me was a relief. I made my way up to the living room, pausing in the doorway. Dan and Rissa were on the couch, watching TV. He met my gaze, then glanced up the stairs. I continued my climb until I reached my niece's room. Desire stirred at her scent hanging in the air. I pushed it back, readied myself and knocked. The door creaked open, my niece peering around it, worry filling her face. There was only one word I knew that would let her know everything was all right.

"Acrobat."

****

My niece sat before the large mirror in her room. Make-up was spread before her as she debated which ones to use. She selected a thin, black pencil and began applying it around her eyes. "You should go back."

I perched on her bed, half afraid she was going to poke her eye out. "Why?"

She rolled her eyes. "In case Jamie comes back – when she comes back."

I dropped my gaze to the floor. "She won't come back, she's afraid of me."

My niece nudged my chin up, making me meet her smiling gaze. "How can you be so sure?"

I hated the answer. "Because she doesn't remember how I saved her." I fiddled with a tube of makeup, switching the subject. "Do you have to go?"

She accepted the change of subject, but the smile lingered on her lips. Plucking the makeup from me, she applied the red to her lips. "No, but it's fun. Too bad you can't come."

"I don't know how to dance."

"Half the people who go to dances can't dance. Now let me finish getting ready." She ushered me out the door, pausing for once last request. "Go back, Uncle, she might surprise you."

I headed downstairs and took a seat next to Dan. He raised an eyebrow at my seated figure, then turned his attention back to the TV. A sitcom wound down, one last joke squeezed in as the end credits rolled. I used to ask what the jokes meant, trying to get a grasp on humor. Eventually I grew tired of never understanding and gave up.

Once the last credit disappeared, the news started. "Our top story tonight: Vampire Forces captured and destroyed five vampires. Footage of the torching to come. Brian has this weekend's forecast of sunny, but cool weather and Andy has the late–" A commercial replaced the newscaster, a happy and cheerful tune playing.

"Don't!" I cried. "Put it back."

Dan flipped the channel back. "Why?"

I leaned in, staring at the screen. "I have to see if I know any of them."

"You know other vampires?"

"There's not many of us left. We banded together, keeping our eyes open for others."

Dan lifted an eyebrow at me. "A band of vampires?"

"Shh, it's on."

The newscaster shuffled some papers and gazed at the camera. It felt like he was speaking to me, this story meant only for me. "Our top story, Vampire Forces captured and destroyed five vampires. Nine years ago, Vampire Forces was granted unprecedented power by Congress and the Senate to exterminate the vampire threat. With captures and torchings at an all-time low, it is believed vampires are nearly extinct. Please be warned, the video we are about to show is graphic."

The screen changed to show five figures spaced across a platform, gagged and tied to posts. The crowd watched as five Vampire Forces officers ascended the platform with torches in hand. They touched the flames to the vampires and fire leapt to life. Muffled wails crackled through the speakers as four of the vampires struggled against the flames crawling over them. The fifth one remained silent, eyes staring defiantly as the fire crawled up her legs.

She was looking at me.

My throat felt tight, an invisible hand gripping it as sorrow welled inside me. I wanted to yell at the TV, "That's my friend; you could at least show a little remorse."

But it was pointless. Even if they heard me, they wouldn't care.

"Tommy." Dan's voice was sympathetic, knowing how I felt.

"She was my friend." My voice felt strangled, choked by emotions. "She wanted humans to understand us, to see we aren't soulless monsters and none of us wanted to murder our families. She said she always envied me for being strong enough not to kill you, but she was wrong. She was the strong one. She gathered us, kept us together and made sure we didn't kill each other. She didn't even have to do it to survive. Now she's gone."

"I'm sorry, lil' bro."

"It's not fair," I snapped. "Why can't the humans see there's more to vampires? I try to be more human, I rarely kill now, try to understand and do the right thing, but none of that matters, does it?" I pulled in a breath of air for the sake of it. "Why are the only *people* who see past the vampire are my family?"

All my vampire life Dan had been there for me, answering my countless questions the best he could. Most the time, I didn't understand and when I did, it was barely. Now I needed an answer more than ever, but he didn't speak. Instead, he placed an arm around my neck and hugged me.

"I know it doesn't feel like it, but trust me, it will be all right," he finally said.

I wanted – needed – to believe him, but I wasn't sure I could.

A car horn blasted through the silence and my niece jumped. "That's Mandy." She rushed to me and planted a kiss on my cheek. "I'm sorry about your friend, Uncle. Bye Mom, bye Dad." Then she was out the door, joining the human world.

I stood. "I'm going to rest in my cellar today."

Dan looked like he wanted to argue, but instead gave me his cell phone. "If you need anything, press one and hit call."

I nodded, then headed out the door and away from the human world.

Despite the night being young, I headed for my cellar. Amy's death filled my thoughts. I never told her my real name and I didn't know her real name either. The one time I asked, she shrugged and said, "Maybe Amy is my real name."

I stopped at the edge of the clearing, Amy's death pushed from my mind. The door to my cellar was lifted, a rope tied around the base of a tree, disappearing through the hole. Nearby, a bike leaned against a tree.

Someone had found my resting spot!

I took a cautious step forward, drawing a deep breath. Shock jolted through me, my mind filling with questions. What was she doing here? Why wasn't she at the dance with the other humans?

I jumped down, landing with a silent puff of dust. A voice gasped in fear and a bright light washed over me. I threw my arm up, instinctively shying from the warmth. "Can you turn that off? I don't like the heat."

She lowered the light with trembling hands. Black covered her, making her almost invisible against the wall except for the ivory skin of her face. Her voice was timid, a whisper as she stammered. "I-I-I'm sorry. You scared me. I-I didn't expect you to appear like that." She looked away, red staining her cheeks and fumbling with the light.

I moved closer, taking extra slow steps. I wanted to reach out and touch her, see how the red in her cheeks felt. But I remembered the way she shied from my touch, terrified of me. "You scared me."

Her eyes darted nervously to me, quickly looking away. "I-I-I..."

"You came back."

"Yeah," she breathed. "I thought that... I wanted to... I mean, you said..."

My grin grew by the second, happiness filling every inch. "My niece was right."

"Ma-Mackenzie, right?" she asked. "That was her dad that took me home the other morning. And she always talked about her uncle, said he was the coolest in the world."

"I don't like heat."

Her wide eyes looked up, locking with mine. She quickly looked away, more red coloring her cheeks. "Um, I don't think that's what she meant."

"Oh." I brushed my confusion aside. I carefully placed my hands on her red cheeks, lifting her face to look at me. "You're here now and I won't ever let anyone hurt you. You don't have to be afraid anymore."

****

She was here! Every time I looked at her, heard her speak, I realized it was true. I felt like I couldn't believe it, like it was a daydream. But I didn't waste time on daydreaming.

The blanket, from the last time she was here, was wrapped around her shoulders. A chilled wind blew above us, cold swirling in the cellar. She pulled the blanket closer, her teeth softly chattering as a shiver racked her body.

"I can get you another," I suggested.

Red stained her cheeks. "This is fine, thank you."

"Okay," I agreed, but wondered if I should insist. That meant leaving her. What if she left before I returned? The rope she brought to get down still dangled against the cellar wall. Maybe I should take it down so she couldn't leave.

No, I scolded myself. I couldn't keep her against her will. If I wanted her to stay, I had to leave the rope so she didn't feel imprisoned.

Silence filled the space between us as I watched her, unable to tear my gaze away. Her eyes constantly slid up to look at me, quickly looking away when she saw me watching. Red repeatedly stained her cheeks, sometimes lightly, other times filling her whole face.

"Why do humans blush?" I asked, wanting to listen to her voice. It was pretty and musical, like the chiming bells of the clock in the living room at home. It made me realize why humans liked music. It was pleasant.

Red colored her cheeks even brighter. "Well, sometimes when someone says something nice to you – gives you a compliment – it makes you happy and you blush."

"But how?" I asked, inching closer. "How does being happy make you blush? How does it turn your face red?"

She hesitated before answering, her voice a timid whisper and fear filled her scent. "It's umm… blood. Blood pools under the surface and turns your cheeks red."

"Blood?" I was next to her now. The red drained from her cheeks. Her body tensed and she pulled the blanket tighter around her trembling body. She stilled when I touched her cheeks to feel the blood and life pulse underneath her skin. "I don't have blood so I can't blush."

"Oh," she whispered.

I pressed my hands to her cheeks, noticing how still she was. Something had frightened her and I wanted to ease her fear. "You feel warm and I like it."

Heat flared under my fingers, red instantly rising in her cheeks.

"Did I make you happy?"

She pulled her head from my hands. "Maybe. Sometimes people blush because they are embarrassed by something someone says too."

I frowned. "I don't understand. How can you blush for happiness and embarrassment?"

"It's not something I can control," she replied. "It just happens, like blinking."

"My brother says I blink weird."

"You do blink slowly," she said in a small voice.

"Do you feel better now?" I asked. "Something scared you and I could smell it, but now you don't smell afraid."

"I thought maybe I shouldn't mention blood," she replied. "I didn't want to make you hungry."

"Why would the word blood make me hungry?"

She shrugged and her gaze dropped to the floor. "I thought since you're a-a-a vampire I shouldn't say that word."

"You can talk about blood, I don't mind," I assured her. "Humans are wrong about us, we aren't bloodthirsty monsters. We're just trying to survive and to do that we need blood. But you can talk about it. Blood, blood, blood. See, it doesn't bother me."

A tiny smile lifted her lips and I felt a bubble of happiness burst in my chest. I had made her smile.

Her smile disappeared and she lifted her gaze to me. "Can I ask you something?"

I nodded.

"Ten years ago when he..." Tears pooled in her eyes and she gulped down a breath of air. "Why did you rescue me?"

I moved closer, wanting to touch and console her, but afraid she'd shy away. I settled with her blanket-covered body pressed against my side. "What the monster did scared my family. My brother and his wife were terrified my niece would be taken. Every night I'd watch them and smelled their fear. I didn't want to see them like that and I wanted to help protect my niece, so I hunted the monster. I found your scent and followed. When I opened the door in the wall, I saw my niece, scared, and I finally understood why my family was afraid."

"But you took me with you," she whispered. "I remember now. The wind blowing through my hair, being invited in and you giving me a sandwich. I remember feeling safe with you."

"You are safe with me; I won't let any monsters get you again."

Her voice was hushed, like she was afraid to speak any louder. "I know."

"Why didn't you go to the dance at the school?" I asked. "My niece told me about it, she said most humans that go can't dance. Why go if you can't dance?"

She shrugged and some of her weight disappeared from me as she leaned away. "I don't have any friends to go to dances with."

"My niece said after I rescued you that you were different. She said you looked like you were afraid of letting the other humans close."

Her gaze snapped to me and anger filled her face. "Mackenzie doesn't know me and I don't need her or anyone else's pity!" As quickly as the anger flared, it disappeared. "I'm sorry; I didn't mean to snap at you. It's frustrating. Everyone knows what happened and they stare like I'm a freak. I wish they'd forget. I want to forget."

"If you forgot what happened, then you'd forget me. I don't want that." I touched her cheek and turned her face back to me. "Please don't be sad, I don't like it."

Warmth filled my chest as she smiled and leaned against my hand. Happiness shone in her eyes and spilled down her cheeks. She freed one hand from the blanket and curled her fingers around mine. Red filled her cheeks again. "I... It's kinda hard to talk to you when I don't know your name."

I hesitated.

"You don't have to tell me if you don't want to," she said quickly. "I understand if it's hard for you to trust humans."

I met her gaze, curious. "Humans?"

Her gaze turned curious as well. "What about humans?"

"Most humans refer to each other as people. That's odd to me that you don't."

Shame filled her face and she looked away.

I didn't like the look so I swallowed my nerves. "My name is Tommy."

"Tommy."

The sound of her saying my name sent an unusual bolt of happiness through me. I wanted her to say my name again and again.

She looked down, staring at her hands. "Tommy, can we go for a walk?"

I glanced at the moonlight shining through the cellar door. It caused heat to prickle against my skin, the light a reflection from the sun and trying to drain me of my energy despite the night. It was something I avoided when possible. "Of course."

A thrill jolted through me when she placed her arms around my neck. In a few quick moves, we were above, a startled shriek muffled into my shoulder. She clung to me for a second longer before carefully sliding off my back. Her cheeks turned red and I knew I'd never tire of the action.

"Where do you want to walk?" I asked while wondering why she wanted to walk. I knew humans liked to walk and sometimes I understood it. Like when it was for exercise and the human wanted to be healthy to survive. But when it was for pleasure, I couldn't wrap my head around it.

"Can we walk along the road?"

"Yes."

Her smile glowed as she took my hand, leading me down the road.

I stared at our connected hands as we walked. "Why are we holding hands?"

She dropped my hand, clasping her own together. "Sorry, I thought you wouldn't mind."

I took her hand back, curling my fingers around hers. "I don't, I just wanted to know why."

A relieved smile filled her face. "Haven't you ever done something for the sake of doing it?"

"No." I paused, thinking. "Yes."

She covered her mouth with her hand as she laughed. I pulled it away, wanting to see her smile. She swung our intertwined hands as her smile grew. "Which one is it?"

"Yes," I informed her. "But I never understood why." I tilted my head, forgetting there was a ruse I should keep up. "Why do you do something just to do it?"

Her smile turned shy and her cheeks redder. "Because it makes me happy. Sometimes I stare at the stars and imagine I have wings and can fly."

I couldn't imagine where her wings would be. "And you do that just to do it?"

She nodded. "I can spend hours daydreaming, it makes the real world easier to deal with when I can escape."

I frowned. "I don't understand."

The shame was back, quickly replacing her cheer. She dropped my hand, wrapping her arms around herself and hurried ahead of me. Her scent turned bitter as she put distance between us.

I quickly caught up and grabbed her hand. "Don't be mad, I'm trying to understand what you mean."

Her bottom lip trembled as pain filled her eyes. She sniffed loudly and wiped at the tears that were falling. Panic filled me and my hands fumbled uselessly in the air as I tried to console her.

"Please don't do that, don't cry. I'm sorry."

To my surprise, she turned to me and wrapped her arms around my neck. Her crying increased as she clung to me and her heart vibrated against my chest, racking me with her rhythm. Carefully, I wrapped my arms around her, uncertain if I was doing the right thing.

Moments passed as she cried, her tears dampening my shirt. Slowly, her trembling body stilled and her breathing evened out. She continued to cling to my neck until the tears completely stopped. She wiped at her eyes as she pulled away. "I'm sorry, I didn't mean to break down on you like that. Your tone... well, there wasn't a tone and I thought you were mocking me."

I took both her hands and pressed them to my chest. "I would never mock you. I love you."

I thought it was the right thing to say, something humans liked to hear. But fear filled my nose, her eyes widening as she pulled away. I took a cautious step forward, placing a hand on her shoulder. "I shouldn't have said that, tell me why."

She trembled under my touch. "It's... It's... It's..." Her voice stuck on that word. She paused and drew in deep breaths, her arms wrapped around herself. When she looked at me, I saw the little girl I had rescued ten years ago, terrified and alone. "Do you know what he did to me?"

"He took you and scared you. He was going to kill you."

She blinked to force the tears back. "He didn't just take me, he destroyed me."

"How?"

Her lips moved, words even I couldn't hear, whispered to herself. She looked into my eyes and started talking. "When he'd take me from the wall, he'd say it was time to play the love game. Then he'd tie me on the bed so I couldn't move and kiss me. Each time he kissed me, he'd say, *A kiss means I love you*. And he'd kiss lower and lower. When I'd start to cry, he'd put tape over my mouth and tell me a grown-up never cries."

"But you weren't a grown-up, you were a child. Why would he think you were a grown-up?" Her words confused and angered me. Everything I thought I understood about the monster was changing. If I could kill him again, I knew I would. I'd kill him a thousand times if that's what it took to break his power over her.

"He knew I wasn't a grown-up and that's why he took me," she whispered. She hugged me again as fresh tears fell. I held her tight against me, remembering how she fit in my arms all those years ago and that she still did.

"Everything is all right," I whispered in her ear.

She stilled against me. "You told me that ten years ago and I remember how I believed you."

"Do you believe me now?"

"Yes," she whispered and looked up at me. "I've never told anyone any of that, not even the police or my therapist. I was too afraid of what people would say."

I wrapped my arms back around her, holding her tightly. She tensed when I moved my lips to her ear and whispered, "I will never let anyone hurt my Sunlight."

She pulled away, eyes wide. As we stared at each other, the scared girl of ten years ago started to fade away. It was the most beautiful thing I had ever seen. She took my hands, gripping them tightly. "I know."

****

Usually when the sun rose, I hated every moment that slowly passed as I sat powerless. I was still powerless, energy sapped with the rising of the sun, but this time I was happy. Even when Sunlight left too soon, the happiness didn't fade. It stayed with me and helped me through the otherwise long day.

The smile was still on my face when I arrived home.

"Hey, lil' bro." Dan set his newspaper aside, face tight with worry. "How ya feeling?"

I tilted my head at him and my smile faded into confusion. "What?"

"I kept getting weird bursts of emotions, happiness, panic and confusion. Are you okay? I wanted to call, but Rissa convinced me to let you mourn your friend."

"Friend?" I paused to think, remembering Amy. "Oh, I got over it."

Disbelief was thick in Dan's voice. "You got over it?"

"She couldn't survive anymore."

He sighed as if he wanted to argue, but thought better of it and disappeared behind his newspaper.

"Danny." I paused.

He peered over the top of his newspaper. "Spit it out. If you're using my name, then it's serious."

"I love you. I love your wife and my niece too. You're my family and I understand that means we need to love each other," I started. "But your wife wasn't always family. How did you know to love her?"

He set his newspaper down. "This is about Jamie, isn't it?"

How did he always know?

I nodded. "I love her, but she's not family."

"I think we need a couple beers for this." He disappeared into the kitchen and returned with the brown bottles. I wrinkled my nose, but took one and sat at his beckoning. After a few sips and a long, thoughtful look, he spoke. "I know you like simple things, easily connected to survival, so I'll try my best. Love isn't simple. It's complex with many layers. Sometimes what you think is love isn't, other times what you think isn't love is. There are many different kinds of love as well."

Already I was confused. Another thing I thought I understood had changed on me. Why was nothing in the human world simple?

"For me, there are three kinds of love," Dan continued. "Love for my wife. I'm not afraid to share my deepest secrets with her. Love for my daughter. I'd do anything to ensure her safety. And love for my brother. I know I can always trust you to be here for me and I can feel that in our bond. They're different kinds of love, but each one is important and it doesn't matter if the person has any relation to me. I still feel that love."

"I can love someone who's not family?" I clarified.

"Yes," Dan replied. Worry flicked in his eyes, an unvoiced concern.

"I didn't take her. She came back."

Dan downed his beer and fixed me with a stern look usually reserved for my niece. "Okay, but be careful."

"I will."

"Are you still confused?"

"Yes."

"Did I help any?"

"Yes."

"Okay. Anything else?"

I shook my head and he resumed reading his newspaper. I wandered into the kitchen where Rissa sat at the table. I peered over her shoulder at the papers for my niece's school scattered before her.

"What are these for?"

Rissa jumped, her hand flying to her chest. "You startled me, Tommy." She turned back to the papers. "A fundraiser for Mackenzie's volleyball team. They want to sell little stuffed bears and, as their coach, I have to decide whether it's worth it."

"And the money helps the team survive?"

Rissa laughed lightly. "Yes, the team will survive if we raise enough money."

I left her and headed up the stairs. My niece lay on her bed, legs kicking the air as she chatted on the phone. She smiled and waved at me, then focused back on her conversation. Knowing better than to listen to a one-sided conversation I had no chance of understanding, I headed back downstairs and out the door.

Normally, I'd find Amy if my family was occupied, but she was gone now. A flash of sorrow bolted through me.

There were other vampires, the ones gathered in the woods. I had talked to a few and managed not to kill them. In my opinion that made us friends, but I wasn't in the mood to deal with other vampires.

Plenty of hours left in the night, I wound up at my cellar. I walked around the small space, feeling restless. Sunlight's scent hung in the air and filled every corner. If I closed my eyes, I could pretend she was still here with me. I didn't, but the thought crossed my mind.

I froze when the ground around me vibrated from footsteps. My eyes locked on the cellar door I had thoughtlessly left open. As the footsteps neared, a soft, snuffing sound floated through the door. Every part of me tensed when a pair of legs flopped over the side.

Sunlight fell into my arms as she struggled down the broken ladder. Her eyes and nose were red and leaking, and her chest shook as she gasped for breath between sobs. She flung her arms around my neck, her crying increasing.

"Tommy!"

I remained motionless, uncertain what to do or what caused her tears. When her tears stopped, she didn't move from me. Her arms continued to cling to my neck as her heartbeat slowed to a steady pace and the muscles in her body relaxed against me. Finally, she pulled away, wiping at her eyes.

"You look panicked."

"I don't know why you were crying and I don't like it," I replied.

"Sorry," she said and looked away. "I didn't know where else to go or who to turn to." Anger filled her voice. "My parents don't get it."

My stomach dropped to my feet. She told her parents about me! My gaze snapped to the still open cellar door. Time stopped as I waited and listened for the sound of sirens and Vampire Forces to rain down on me.

"Tommy, what's wrong?"

I turned to her, hating how accusing my voice sounded. "You told your parents about me?"

Her eyes widened. "No, I wouldn't do that. They'd panic and call VF. I meant they don't get me. They think that because I told them I did two things they think normal kids do means I'm better and it's about time." Tears filled her eyes again. "They act like I'm overreacting, that I had been visiting an uncle and nothing serious happened. That's not what happened. He took me, touched me and terrified me. I was only four and I couldn't fight back. I've been terrified ever since. Of life! Of humans! I hate it, I hate him and I hate them!"

She collapsed against me and I lowered us to the floor. Her sobs grated against my ears, the worst sound in the world. I tried to think of something to say and ease the tears and pain she felt. There was only one word. It popped in my mind and out my mouth without a thought.

"Safe."

Her face glistened with moisture when she looked at me. Through the tears, a sliver of happiness pushed passed the sorrow and fear and started to grow. She leaned back against me, her cheek resting against my chest. "Safe."

Time stopped and calmness filled the air around us with a soothing lullaby. I held her against me as the feeling seeped into me. I knew, after tonight, more things were changing on me. I didn't mind for once, in fact, I welcomed it.

Sunlight sighed. "Thank you."

"You're welcome," I replied, then laughed. "I've never said that."

She laughed with me and wiped lingering moisture away. "Why not?"

"I thought it was pointless, but I think I understand now. You're saying you're happy to make another happy."

She laughed again, the sound mixed with a sniff.

"Are you done crying?"

Her cheeks glowed red. "Yeah, I think so." More red filled her face. "You're the first person I've felt comfortable touching since he took me. I couldn't even manage a handshake at times."

"I don't get handshakes."

A burst of laughter escaped her. "Sorry, I guess vampires don't shake hands much."

"No, we try to kill each other."

Her eyes widened in shock.

"I shouldn't have said that. My brother says I don't think before I speak," I apologized.

"At least you always speak the truth."

I wiped a lock of damp hair out of her face, being truthful. "I don't like you crying. I feel helpless when you do."

"I'm sorry."

"I don't like you saying that either."

She leaned back against me and I looped my arms around her. A smile followed the hug. I had never hugged or smiled so much in my life. I leaned closer to her ear.

"How do you get me to do so many pointless, human actions?"

She pulled away, worry filling her face. "Is that bad?"

"No, why would it be bad?"

She shrugged. "You said pointless, so I thought maybe you didn't like…"

Her voice trailed off as I pressed my nose to her ear. She laughed and squirmed, trying to escape. I didn't let her get away, blowing soft breaths and grazing my nose along her skin until her bell-like voice rang with laughter.

"This is very pointless," I said. "And so much *fun*! I never understood fun before. Never knew it was so fun."

She laughed louder, still struggling to escape my pursuit of her ear. "Of course, silly. That's why it's called fun."

"Silly? How am I silly?"

She giggled more, voice singing. "Silly, silly vampire, he has no clue. Whatever can he do?"

"What?"

She laughed louder, filling the night with her beautiful sound. Eventually she quieted and the smile on her lips faded. She stared at the dark cellar with a faraway look in her eyes.

Worry wiggled in my mind. "Are you all right?"

A smile returned to her face as she sighed. "Yeah, I think I am... finally."

****

The photo albums were spread out before me, memories from my life displayed. There were images of me as a human, smiling and full of life, and accompanied by my brother and parents. In others, there was no sign of me, just my family who loved me as a vampire.

I leafed through the pages, my mind drifting to Sunlight. Did she have a baby book full of images? Was her life normal and happy before the monster took her? What would have happened if he hadn't taken her? That question made my stomach clench. If the monster hadn't taken her, she wouldn't have needed me to rescue her. She wouldn't know me.

Maybe she'd be friends with my niece and I could see her that way.

I dismissed the thought. I had to hide from my niece's friends. They thought I was nothing more than a vicious, bloodthirsty monster. If the monster hadn't taken Sunlight, she would believe the same.

Growling, I slammed the book shut and shoved the albums away. I thought of how happy I made Sunlight, how she trusted me to keep her safe. She knew me, the real me, the vampire me. Nothing would change that and it didn't matter that if I hadn't saved her she would hate me.

"Tommy, what's wrong?" Dan shuffled to me, a mixture of sleep and worry on his face as he rubbed at his chest and sat next to me. My pain woke him.

"I feel… guilty."

"About what?"

I licked my lips and tried to sort through the pain filling me. It covered my whole body, throbbing deep at the center of my chest and worse than any injury I had ever received. "She knows me as a vampire and it doesn't bother her. It makes her feel safe and she trusts me. But if I hadn't rescued her from the monster, she wouldn't feel that way with me. I'm glad he took her." I glanced at him. "Does that make me bad?"

A smile tugged at Dan's lips. He placed his arm around my shoulder and gave me a squeeze. "You're not a bad person… vampire. You're just feeling human."

I sighed. "I get tired of doing human things. Humans are too complex."

"I know," Dan said. "But you can't help it any more than you can help drinking blood. As much as you deny it, you are still human. It was just buried deep inside you when you were turned and it's slowly grown over the years, nurtured by me, Rissa and Mackenzie. And now Jamie."

"I can't stop it?"

"It's who you are and trying to stop it would change you. I don't know about Jamie, but I know I don't want that." A knowing look filled his face, one that told me he had the perfect answer for me, one I'd understand. "Think of it this way, if you hadn't changed, you might have never rescued Jamie and you'd never know who she was."

****

"I'm sorry!" I blurted out as soon as Sunlight pushed her window open.

Her face turned confused. "About what?"

I hissed at myself. I said I wasn't going to apologize without explaining first, had everything I wanted to tell her prepared. But, as usual, my vampire instinct got in the way and I said the only thing that really made sense to me: I'm sorry. I licked my lips and tried again. "I wanted to say I'm sorry because I realized if the monster hadn't…" My voice died and for the first time in my life, I struggled with words. "If the monster hadn't taken you, I wouldn't…"

"You wouldn't have had to save me," she finished.

I looked away and nodded. "I'm sorry."

Her fingers brushed my chin and turned my face back to her. A warm smile filled her face. "I have my life because you saved me. Thank you."

My guilt dissolved into a smile.

Sunlight's gaze dropped and her cheeks flushed red. "Do you want to come in or hang outside my window all night?"

Energy hummed and faded as I crawled into her bright and colorful bedroom. Toys filled a rocking chair near her bed and a computer sat on a desk by a bookshelf that overflowed with books. Clothing hung neatly in a closet – a stark contrast from my niece's overflowing closet. Everything looked neat and in its place. Except for one thing. It hung invisible to human eyes, but filled every inch of the room with its smell.

Fear.

I was by her side in an instant, searching for whatever scared her and ready to kill it. "What's wrong? Where's the monster?"

"There's no monster."

"Yes, there is, I can smell your fear. Don't worry, I won't let it get you."

She smiled sadly. "Nothing is going to get me. I just get jumpy easily. Before you showed up, I heard a noise that turned out to be a towel falling to the floor in the bathroom."

"You sure?" I insisted.

She smiled and pressed her palm against my cheek. "Promise." For a moment her gaze stayed on her hand and her cheer faded. "Is there something wrong with me?"

"Why?"

She shrugged. "Because after ten years the only connection I make with another is a vampire."

Her words cut deep. I rested my hand against her cheek. "Please don't say that. I don't want you to be ashamed you speak to me."

She placed her hand over mine and squeezed. "I'm not. It's just sometimes I feel like you should be human; that if you were, we'd be the same."

"If I was human, I'd look like my brother."

She dropped her gaze from mine. "I guess."

I lifted her chin and gave her a prolonged smile. "My niece says since I was a teenager when I was turned, I'll always be one. Besides, if I wasn't a vampire, then I wouldn't have been able to rescue you."

"You wouldn't be you either," she said with a smile.

A warm feeling filled my chest at her words. Sunlight understood. Even my brother didn't always understand me.

My gaze wandered down to her arm, noticing a mark stretched across her skin. Carefully, I touched the mark. "What is this?"

She pulled her arm away and tugged her sleeves to cover the mark. Head tilted down, she moved to her bed and sat. The change in her scent accompanied her withdraw and happiness faded into shame. "It's nothing."

I joined her on the bed, knowing her words were a lie, but feeling no anger towards her. I caught her chin in my fingers and showed her my confusion. "You did those to yourself, why?"

She shrugged, her eyes flickering to and from mine. I didn't try to catch her thoughts, but I couldn't stop the words from sneaking into my head. Words like, *So ashamed* and *I needed to feel alive.*

"I can hear your thoughts and they don't make sense to me. I want to understand."

She rubbed at the marks hidden by her shirt. "Sometimes I felt crushed by everything and everyone. There was so much pressure to get better and I tried, I really did, but I never felt better. Pretending wore me out, especially during holidays when visiting family. I'd have to smile like nothing was wrong when all I wanted to do was scream. It hurt so much and I needed to get the pain out and that felt like the only way. To physically feel pain was a relief from the pain crushing my heart."

Her explanation was complex, beyond what I knew of humans. Dan would know how to explain it, but I understood this was her secret she needed to keep.

"I'm trying to understand," I replied. "Did this help you to survive?"

"Yes," she whispered without a doubt.

I nodded, still not quite grasping her explanation. Hurting oneself felt counterproductive to survival, but if she said it helped her survive, I believed her.

Still, the marks were bad memories for her and I hated seeing the shame on her face. I wanted to do something that made her smile when she saw the marks. Replace the bad with something good.

She tensed when I bit the first mark. I moved onto the next, quickly popping my fangs through, but not giving her rhythm enough time to pulse blood into my mouth. I repeated the process down both her arms and forced myself to ignore her yelps of pain. Once each mark was bitten, I looked up and smiled. "Now when you look at them, you'll think of me and not the pain."

A puzzled look flashed across her face, and then she smiled. She held her arm out and happiness bubbled in my chest. As I drew on my bite, she leaned closed to my ear and whispered. "Now I'll be with you all day."

I hugged her tightly. "I think about you all day anyways."

Her cheeks flared red. "And what about me consumes your thoughts?"

"I think about hugging you, feeling your pulse, seeing you blush, hearing your voice and." I paused, wondering if my next confession would scare her. I peered at her, gauging her reaction. "I think about kissing you."

The red deepened and her eyes instantly looked away.

"I know you don't want me to because the monster tainted kissing for you, but I like thinking about it," I quickly explained.

She gave me a gentle smile. "You sound a little worried."

"I don't want you to be afraid I'll do something you won't like." I tilted my head. "That is odd, being afraid to do something because it will upset another."

"It's not odd," she assured me and placed a hand on my cheek. A thrill bolted through me as she leaned in. Was she going to kiss me? Slight disappointment flashed when she brushed her nose against my cheek instead. "After all you've done for me; I hope you can help me get over my fear of kissing."

"I'd like that."

"And..." She dropped her gaze, her voice turned more timid and red spread across her cheeks. "And you better know what you're doing too."

"I have kissed before. You pucker your lips and stick your tongue out," I replied.

Her embarrassment faded and uncertainty filled her eyes. "Who taught you that? Not Mackenzie?"

Blank eyes flashed before me and the guilt churned as hotly as it had the night I killed my friend. "I had to," I replied softly.

"Had to what? Tommy?"

I turned my eyes to Sunlight, seeing the life and trust burn in them. "I had a friend once and she helped me understand why humans made friends. She lied to me to make me her friend, but that doesn't bother me anymore."

"What happened to her?"

"She wanted me to make her a vampire and I refused. She found where I rested and spent the day with me. When night fell, I killed her because it hurts to be touched during the day and I get hungry faster." I pulled Sunlight close. Her nose grazed mine and I felt the heat from her lips. "My friendship with her ended badly, but I won't let anything ruin ours."

****

I paced my cellar, irritation rolling through me. With a growl, I slumped to the floor, then sprung to my feet and resumed pacing. Where was she? Sunlight said she would come visit me. Why wasn't she here yet? Maybe something happened to her...

Maybe another monster took her.

I bolted from the cellar, racing through the night, my thoughts flying. How much time did I have? The monster could have taken her anytime during the day.

A snarl escaped, anger glowing hotly. It shouldn't matter if the sun sapped me of my energy or having Sunlight near during the day would make me boil with need. All that should matter was protecting her, all the time. Day and night.

Lights glowed along the streets, in the windows of houses and everywhere else as I ran. Rhythms thumped around me as the humans moved in the early hours of the night. This wasn't a good place for me to be, the risk of getting spotted and caught high.

I didn't care if I was caught.

I reached Sunlight's house and scrambled to her closed and dark window. I knocked on the glass, but unsurprisingly, the other side remained dark. Dropping to the ground, I followed the trails her scent left. They led to and from her house, the freshest ending in the middle of the driveway. I tried to follow the trail of exhaust, but by the time I reached the street, I couldn't distinguish one car from the next.

Hurrying back to the house, I pounded on the door, not caring how stupid or reckless my actions were. I knocked until footsteps stopped outside the door and the knob slowly turned. A face peeked around the edge and I shoved everything I had against the human's will.

"Where is she?"

The human staggered as if struck, but answered in a flat voice. "Who?"

"Sh... Ja... Sunlight... Your daughter!" I struggled with Sunlight's name. Over the years I had become comfortable using nicknames, but I still feared the power names held.

"She was taken and I have to rescue her again," I finished with a hiss.

"Her friend Mackenzie came and picked her up," the human replied.

Confusion filled me. My niece took Sunlight? Why would she do that?

"Are you sure?"

"Yes, Jamie said she was going to spend the night."

Relief rolled through me. I focused my will on the human and gave one last push. "Forget I was here. When you opened the door, no one was here."

The human stared past me as if I wasn't there and shut the door.

I headed home, eager to see Sunlight. The house was dark and the door unlocked when I arrived. Rhythms beat behind the kitchen door as faint light glowed along the bottom. I had barely set one foot in the room when the lights flared to life, bodies jumped up and voices yelled.

"Surprise!"

My fangs shot out and I jumped back into the darkness of the living room. I hissed as I searched for the threat, but found only my family and Sunlight.

"I told you he wouldn't like that," Dan chuckled. He held his hands out and slowly moved towards me. "Easy, lil' bro. Do you know what day it is? What time?"

My eyes darted to the kitchen. A cake sat on the table near Sunlight and my niece. Rissa stood off to the side, camera in hand and trying hard not to smile. A small pile of presents sat on a chair and a banner above read, *Happy Birthday.*

I whirled around at a noise, hissing at the living room shadows. Warmth touched my shoulder. I jerked away and my teeth snapped inches from Dan's hand.

"Easy, Tommy," he ordered. "It's almost 12:32."

"It's my birthday?"

Dan nodded. "Yup, come on, the girls spent all day preparing."

I relaxed and climbed to my feet. "I don't like surprises."

"I know," Dan replied as he urged me into the kitchen. "And I warned them vampires are easily threatened."

My niece huffed at his words, then bounced to me and threw her arms around my neck. "Happy birthday, Uncle." She grabbed a present and pressed it into my hand. "This is from me."

I tore the colorful paper off to reveal a plain, black box. "Thanks."

"Open it," Dan whispered.

Finding the seam, I pried the box open and a thin, silver chain snaked onto my hand. Dangling from the chain was a tag with the world *Love* engraved on it. I looked at my niece. "What do I do with it?"

She grabbed the chain and secured it around my neck. "You wear it."

"Why?"

"Open Jamie's next." Rissa handed me another present before my niece could attempt to explain.

Sunlight's cheeks turned red as I opened her present. The box contained thick, woven threads in red, black, silver and gold. My niece sighed loudly at my confusion and tied the threads around my wrist.

"You're so clueless, Uncle. You wear this too."

Dan laughed as he handed me the largest present. "Here's one you'll know what to do with. It's the usual."

The usual meant clothes. I glanced at my own, hole-covered clothing, then set the present aside without opening it. "Thanks." I looked at the cake. Why was that here? We celebrated my birthday every year at my niece's insisting, but usually without a cake. That was done the day before when celebrating Dan's birthday. I caught his gaze when I looked up.

He grinned at me, a mischievous look in his eyes that reminded me of when we were young and looked identical – except that I looked dead. "You're not getting out of the birthday song this year."

****

Impatiently, I waited through the birthday song, as everyone ate cake and as I helped clean up. I felt like half the night had been wasted on birthday activities with my family. All I wanted was to have Sunlight to myself. I was tired of sharing her with them.

Finally, my family headed up to bed. I pulled Sunlight from the couch and headed for the basement.

"Where are we going?" she asked.

"To where I usually rest."

Her eyes roamed over the basement and stopped on my corner. Photos of my family were propped along the edge of a blanket that spread across the floor. She drew closer, eyes widening as she picked one up. "It's you as a human."

I leaned my chin on her shoulder. "Yes."

She traced her fingers over the image. "Do you remember being human?"

I shook my head.

"Why keep the picture then?"

I shrugged and placed the photo with the others. "I used to think photos were pointless, but then I learned I liked seeing my family when I wake. Would you like to see more?"

Her eyes brightened and she nodded. We settled on the blanket and she nestled against my side. I sifted through the photo albums and chose the one that had the most images of me.

She gasped at the first images, pulling the album from my grip and leaning in to look closer. Her laughter rang out as she turned the pages. At the end of the book, she lingered on the last image.

The one of me and my family on vacation.

"You look so different," she said as her fingers grazed over the image of my human self. "I can't even imagine you being human."

"I can't either." I tilted my head at her. "Do you think you would like me as a human?"

"I think so," she replied and blushed.

I brushed my fingertips along her cheek. "If I was human, I'd spend every day with you. I'm glad I'm not because I wouldn't be able to protect you as well."

Her blush deepened. "Did you like my present? I wanted it to be more personal so I made it myself."

I turned my wrist over and examined the woven threads. "It's beautiful, like you."

She hid her face against my chest and I felt her blush burn my skin. She didn't move and soon I felt her relax against me and her breathing slow. The door to the basement creaked overhead as I ran my fingers through her hair, Rissa coming down the stairs. She sat on the floor across from me, watching Sunlight sleep.

"I have to say I am not surprised," Rissa said. "Dan said you found someone new to obsess over. Should have known it would be Jamie; she really affected you ten years ago. Don't protest. I know how obsessive you get when you fixate on something. You were the exact same way with Mackenzie when she was little."

I closed my mouth and shrugged. "Is that bad?"

"Not necessarily, but you need to be careful."

"I trust her not to call Vampire Forces."

"I'm not worried about you, I'm worried about her," Rissa replied. "What happens if the wrong person finds out how much you care for her? Or how much she cares for you?"

I buried my face in Sunlight's hair and inhaled. "I won't let anything happen to her."

"You can't protect her from everything, Tommy."

"I won't let anything happen to her!"

Rissa, never afraid of me, pursed her lips, but didn't argue any more. "It's too cold for her to sleep down here, so the couch upstairs has been made up for her." She headed up the stairs, stopping and turning to me at the top. "Promise me you'll be careful. We'd be devastated if you were destroyed, Dan especially."

Careful not to disturb Sunlight, I carried her to the couch and tucked her in. I settled on the floor next to her, stoking her hair and watching her sleep. When the sun grew close to rising, I brushed my nose against her ear and retreated back to the basement.

When the sun set, Sunlight was sitting on the edge of the blanket. I pulled her close, grazing my nose along her neck and a smile on my lips. She tensed against me and fear started to fill her scent.

"Don't worry, I won't bite. Well, maybe a little nip. You're so irresistible," I teased.

She relaxed and laughed. "Irresistible?"

"I bet you taste delectable," I replied and pressed my nose to her ear.

She laughed and squirmed, trying to escape. "Is this how a vampire flirts?"

"I don't know, what is the point of flirting?" I asked, still pursuing her ear.

"It's what someone does to make another blush in happiness and embarrassment," she giggled.

"I like making you blush in happiness," I replied. "So yes, I am flirting."

Her cheeks blazed red.

I stopped flirting, but couldn't stop looking at her or keep my hands off her warm cheeks. Again, I wondered, what would a kiss be like?

As if she heard the question, she pulled away. "I need to go, I told my parents I forgot some clothes and needed to get them."

"You lied?"

She nodded. "Yeah, I wish I didn't have to, but they'd never let me out of their sight if they knew I was talking to a vampire."

I hugged her tightly. "I wish you didn't have to either."

With reluctance she pulled away, but kept ahold of my hands. She swallowed nervously. "Tommy... I..."

I pulled her back until our noses were barely touching. Somehow I knew she was searching for courage to say three words I wasn't afraid to speak, but terrified her. "I don't want you to say or do something if you're not ready."

Her body slumped in relief. She pulled out of my grip, keeping her eyes on me as she headed up the stairs. "I'll see you tomorrow night, right?"

"I'll always find you," I promised.

****

"Mackenzie," Rissa warned.

"In a minute, Mom," my niece sighed. "It just got dark."

"You have school tomorrow."

"A half day! Jeez, give me some space."

"Ten minutes, then get your butt upstairs and in bed," Rissa ordered, then marched into the kitchen. She stopped short at the sight of me with food. "Tommy, what are you doing?"

"Making a sandwich for her."

Lips twitching, Rissa wandered to my side and observed the sandwich I was assembling. "Ham and strawberry jam don't go together." She placed the food back in the refrigerator and pulled different items out. Once the sandwich was finished, she wrapped it in plastic and handed it to me. "This should taste better. Why are you making Jamie a sandwich?"

I shrugged, feeling reluctant to discuss the topic.

"Tommy." The warning was back in Rissa's voice.

"I want her to know I can care for her in case she decides to leave her family." I kept my eyes down.

Rissa didn't reply so I slipped out of the kitchen. Dan raised an eyebrow at me, but also stayed silent as I headed out the door and into the quiet night. I turned down Sunlight's street, clutching the sandwich and feeling slightly nervous. Would she like my gift?

She instantly appeared when I tapped on her window, smiling and stepping back to let me in.

I held the sandwich out. "I made a gift for you."

She took the sandwich with a giggle. "You made me a sandwich?"

"You said you don't like the food at school," I explained. "So I thought..."

She cut me off with a hug. "Thank you, I love it. I might not be able to wait until tomorrow, might have to eat it now."

I relaxed against her, closing my eyes and focusing on feeling her; her pulse, her rhythm and her life. "I should have never let you go," I whispered.

"I'm safe now," she replied and set the sandwich aside.

Her body pressed against me and again, I wondered what would it be like to kiss her? But she cringed whenever my lips neared her skin and I knew she wasn't ready. I wanted to do something though, something more intimate and there was only one thing I knew.

I tilted her head to the left, exposing her neck. Her pulse throbbed under the skin and the rhythm picked up as my lips neared. Hunger rumbled through me, her scent tickling my nose. A burst of blood hit my tongue as my fangs sliced through her skin. Instinctively, my grip tightened with a possessiveness that said this prey was mine.

But that's not what I wanted.

I pushed the hunger, need and desire to drink back and relaxed my grip. The blood pooled in my mouth as I stopped sucking, and with one last swallow, I let her go. Her skin was white, eyes as wide as the moon and a tremble rolled through her.

"I wasn't feeding on you," I assured her. "I wanted to be intimate with you and that's the only way I know how."

Her fingers touched her neck and came away stained with blood. Each breath she took shook her body. She moved to her bed, silent as she sank to it.

Worry filled me at her lack of expression. "Please speak."

"My neck feels numb."

"That's normal."

She didn't speak again and desperation curled through me.

"I thought it'd be all right. I'm sorry."

Her hand dropped from her neck and clutched a fistful of blanket. Determination flashed across her face like lightning. Slowly, she rose and faced me. She pressed her bloody fingers to my lips as the other hand curled around the back of my neck. She pulled me against her and pressed her forehead against mine. "I'm ready."

****

Sunlight lay across from me, our hands linked together. Wiggling, she moved closer and wrapped her arms around my neck. A blush colored her cheeks as she tugged the blanket back up.

I brushed my fingers through her hair. "I am never going to understand humans."

She laughed, then brushed her nose against mine. "I'll let you in on a little secret. We don't understand ourselves most of the time." Her blush deepened as her gaze dropped from mine. "How's this for intimate?"

"Very good."

"Probably not what you expected."

I tilted my head. "What was I supposed to expect?"

When she said she was ready, there hadn't been a trace of fear in her scent. Only nervousness. The nervousness grew as she pulled her clothing off, and then mine. Next, she pulled me to her bed, having me lay down before crawling in and facing me. Neither of us moved as time slipped by and slowly her nervousness disappeared.

Now it was back.

She chewed on her bottom lip. "Sex?"

I nodded. "I understand sex, but why do you think I would expect it?"

"I thought I was ready for sex, that I could do it if it was you, but..." She dropped her gaze, red creeping across her face. "I'm really glad nothing happened. I'm not ready."

She sat up and started dressing. I followed suit and dressed, pulling her close when finished. Together, we laid back down, Sunlight tucked tightly against me. She drifted to sleep, her face looking so peaceful. Around us, the smell of her fear faded into nothing. She finally felt safe in her home.

When I felt the sun approach, I gave her a shake. She blinked sleepily at me, then curled up against my chest. I shook her again. "I have to go."

"No, I don't want you to," she murmured.

"I don't want to either, but the day is too hot for me." My smile barely contained my happiness at her words. I pressed my lips to her ear and she squirmed against me. "We'll always be together," I whispered, then tore myself away and slid out the window.

****

Voices from the TV floated through the air and light spilled through the open basement door. I stared at it, confused. It should be closed, was always closed, especially if I was resting in the basement. I darted up and peered into the living room. Dan, as always, was hidden behind a newspaper while Rissa lounged next to him and watched the TV.

Downstairs normal, I headed upstairs and stopped outside my niece's door. Rhythms beat on the other side and two scents tugged at me. I tapped a few times, then pushed the door open.

Sunlight sat on my niece's bed, her smile glowing. She blushed as I sat next to her and tugged her close. "Did you rest well?"

I nodded. "I had happy thoughts about you."

"Aha!" My niece jumped to her feet, her finger aimed at me. "There is the proof Dad has been looking for to prove you're still human."

I looked between the two. "What?"

Sunlight giggled and turned her head against my shoulder. "She's saying you think about what every other teenage boy thinks about."

My niece fell back on her bed. "Sex!"

Downstairs, I heard Rissa. "Did she just yell what I think she did? Mackenzie, downstairs, NOW!"

"Ah crap," my niece sighed and stomped out the door. After a minute of arguing with Rissa, in which my niece declared she was fifteen and should no longer be treated like a child, she stormed back into her bedroom. "Mom drives me bonkers sometimes. I'm not encouraging you two to have sex. She also says to tell you Dad's ready to take you home, Jamie."

Sunlight's cheer died. "I was supposed to be home an hour ago. They won't mind. I'll just tell them we lost track of time." She rose and brushed her nose against mine. "See you tomorrow night. Bye, Mackenzie."

My niece grinned once we were alone. "You and Jamie are the cutest couple I have ever seen. I swear, if I met a guy as sweet as you, I'd die!"

I bit back a growl, thinking if a human ever made her want to die, I'd kill him first.

"Unfortunately, the guys in my class are immature losers," my niece sighed. "Of course," she continued and wrapped an arm around me. Her eyes glimmered mischievously. "I have the best uncle in the world. Use you to keep any boyfriend I have in line. Make him buy me gifts every day."

I looked at the woven threads around my wrist. "Am I Sunlight's boyfriend?"

She rolled her eyes. "Is Jamie special to you? All you can think about? All you want to think about?"

I nodded.

"Yup, you're her boyfriend."

"But I haven't given her a gift every day."

"You don't have to give her a gift every day, I was exaggerating," my niece laughed. She scooted closer to me. "You want to do something special for Jamie?"

I nodded.

"Then leave it to me."

****

A date was what my niece had in mind. She explained the concept to me. Three times. Then Dan tried explaining. I stared between the two, trying to understand. How would the date help me and Sunlight survive? Why was it important to our relationship? Nothing either of them said answered those questions.

Now, Sunlight sat across from me at the kitchen table, a plate of food before her. Her short hair was pinned back with pink and red flowers, silver sparkled around her eyes and her lips were ruby red. The dress she wore was black with a silver belt cinched at the waist. When she arrived, all I had been able to do was stare, only tearing my gaze away to look at Dan and silently ask, *Now what?*

Silence filled the space between us, awkward and heavy. She toyed with her food, eyes avoiding mine. I struggled for a way to break the silence, say something to make this moment special, a date.

"Do you like the flowers?" I finally asked.

Sunlight fingered the roses next to her. "They're beautiful."

"They're dying."

She touched the flowers again while her eyes studied the transformed kitchen. The usual knickknacks had disappeared into drawers, replaced by red hearts that dangled off edges and from the ceiling. A red cloth draped over the table with two candles burning in the middle.

"They're still beautiful, everything is."

"My niece did everything and told me I couldn't help. She said I'd get in the way and ask too many questions."

A small laugh escaped Sunlight before she fell back into silence. She took a bite of food. "Food is good."

I looked at her plate of noodles and sauce. "I don't know what it is."

She gathered another forkful and held it out to me. "Would you like to try a bite?"

I leaned forward and opened my mouth. The noodles were soft and warm, the sauce spicy on my tongue. I chewed, the pressure on my teeth uncomfortable, but not as uncomfortable as the taste. The taste coated my tongue and cheeks, lingering as I worked to gulp down the food.

Sunlight laughed. "Your face is priceless."

I coughed, wishing for blood to wash the horrid taste away. "I don't like human food, it's too complex tasting."

She laughed again and dabbed at my mouth with her napkin. She settled back in the chair and a sad sigh escaped her. "Tommy, this is…"

I rested my hand against her cheek. "Don't be sad, you're supposed to be happy and…" My voice died, my attention drawn to the flickering flames.

I had been trying hard to ignore the candles; my niece told me they would set the mood of the date. But it was hard to ignore the burning heat, the dancing flame that reached for me from the moment they were lit. To me, all I saw was danger.

Sunlight followed my gaze, her expression dark as she stared at the candles. Quietly, she rose and clicked the light over the stove on. With a huff, she blew the candles out. She sat back down with a satisfied look. "That's better."

I moved to her side. "My Sunlight, you're the only light I need."

Her blush burned against my skin. She tensed when I moved closer, my lips grazing across her forehead, but she didn't stop me or pull away. She trusted me. I moved to her ear and she squirmed as I whispered, "You look beautiful."

Awe filled her voice. "Really?"

I nodded, anger glowing in my chest. Every human alive should tell her she was beautiful.

A sliver of light glowed from the kitchen door as my niece poked her head in. "Uncle, hurry up, it's almost time for the movie. And don't forget the gift."

I fumbled in my pocket, fingers wrapping around the velvety box that contained a ring. It was the only part of the date my niece let me help with and I knew the instant I saw the words on the ring, *You are my love, my life, my sunlight*, it was my gift to Sunlight.

But I hesitated to present the gift. Something about the moment didn't feel right, something was missing, but I didn't know what. I left the box in my pocket and took Sunlight's hand. "Come on, I have to take you to a movie."

Her smile faltered. "You mean at a theater? Why aren't we watching something here? What if someone sees you and calls VF?"

I shrugged and led her into the living room. There, my niece watched with excitement. Dan stood next to her, his eyes catching mine and telling me his thoughts.

Should not do this, it's too dangerous. Should be the bad guy and put my foot down. Rissa will back me up; she agrees Mackenzie doesn't understand yet. Why can't I make her understand what I learned all those years ago? Don't make me do this, lil' bro.

"Tommy, you ready to go?" he asked softly instead.

I looked from him to my niece, then Sunlight. I wanted to make this date work, to give Sunlight a special night she'd always remember. But Dan's thoughts continued to echo through my mind, his plea repeating. *Don't make me do this, lil' bro. Don't make me do this...* I took a step back and shook my head.

"No."

I felt Dan's relief through our bond and saw Sunlight's tension drain away. My niece stared in confusion. I hated the look on her face, knowing I was crushing the hopes I glimpsed in her thoughts, the lie that my presence in her life encouraged. But Dan was right, she needed to understand the truth.

"I can't go, it's too dangerous for me," I said.

"Let it be," Dan cut my niece off before she could reply.

She stormed away in annoyance with Rissa on her heels.

Dan patted my shoulder. "Don't worry, lil' bro. It's time she accepted what I did back in college. People won't accept vampires, not even you."

"It felt fake, I didn't like it."

"That's why it was the right thing," he said. He lifted an eyebrow and I heard one thought loud and clear. *My little brother the vampire, all human and in love.*

Not a human, I thought and he grinned as if he heard me.

"Come on, I'll pick out a movie and you two can finish your date," he said.

Sunlight and I settled on the couch as Dan sifted through the movies. She took my hand, brushing it against her lips. "Getting there."

I curled my hand around the box in my pocket. "Yes, we are."

Dan climbed to his feet, giving us a stern, but mocking look. "Don't stay up too late, kids."

****

I stood in my niece's doorway, watching her. Her eyes were locked on the book before her and lips pressed into a tight light. The only sign she gave that she knew I was standing there was the pen in her hand had fallen still. Tense seconds passed, my voice struggling. I never wanted to use her name against her, never had to, but I needed her to listen to me, so I had to say her name.

"M-ma-mackenzie."

My niece's face was full of innocence when she looked up. "Yes, *Tommy*?"

I sighed. "Please don't be like that."

Anger flashed through her eyes and she threw her pen down. "Don't be like what? It was a movie, the theater would have been dark. All you would have had to do was sneak in through the exit. If anyone saw you, they…"

"Mackenzie!" I snapped, startling both her and myself. "I know what you want to believe would happen, but that's not what would have happened."

"You don't know that."

"Yes, I do. I know how humans feel about vampires and nothing you can say or hope will change that." I moved to her side. "When you were little, your mother told me once she wondered if letting you interact with me was a bad idea. I was hurt by it, but as you grew I started to understand why she worried. While you've always kept quiet about me, you don't see me like the other humans do."

"I see my uncle.

"Exactly, but the other humans don't. They see a vampire."

"If they gave you a chance..."

I shook my head. "I wouldn't treat other humans the same as I do my family. They're not wrong about me or vampires. They are the prey and I am the hunter."

"But Jamie, you don't want to hurt her."

"And I honestly don't understand why. I don't understand why I love her or what about her makes me love her. If I didn't love her, I would treat her like the rest of the humans. If you weren't family, you wouldn't be safe from me either." I took her hands. "I do wish humans didn't hate me the way they do, but there's nothing either of us can do. You have to accept that. For me."

"But it's not fair."

"I know," I told her. "But humans are just trying to survive and I can't argue against that. My life revolves around surviving."

"Dad does say that's the magic word for you." She turned silent for a moment before sighing. "Okay, I'll learn to accept that people won't see you the way I do." She poked my chest, a glimmer of defiance in her eyes determined to survive. "But I don't have to like it."

****

"Hey, Tommy?"

I tilted my head at Sunlight, waiting for her to continue. Instead, she buried her face against my chest. "Never mind."

I sighed and brushed my nose against her ear. "Why do you always do that to me? Sound like you want to talk, then say never mind."

Her blush burned my skin. "Maybe because I like hearing you talk, but I can't figure out what else to say so I say never mind."

"You like listening to me talk?"

She shrugged, twisting the ring I gave her on her finger. "You have a nice voice, with lots of depth."

"Most humans think my voice has no emotion."

"Your voice has emotion, it's just quiet and quick, but I always hear it," she replied. A shiver rolled through her and she curled tighter against me.

"Do you want to go upstairs? It can get pretty cold down here my brother says. I like it, but I don't want you to shiver all night," I offered.

"I like it down here," she replied and picked up the picture I took of myself. It was her favorite, always making her smile. "It's quiet down here."

"At least let me get you a blanket."

She nodded and I hurried up the stairs. I pulled a blanket off the couch, then skipped the last five steps on my way back down. She squeaked when I reappeared and wrapped it around her shoulders. Instantly, her shivering subsided.

"Tommy?"

"Do not say never mind," I warned.

She giggled then hid her face in the blanket. "Never mind."

She erupted into fits of laughter when I dragged her to me and pressed my nose to her ear. She fought to free herself, but the blanket pinned her arms. Finally, I stopped my assault and she panted to regain her breath.

"What were you going to say?" I asked once her breathing had slowed.

She shook her head. "Nothing, just a silly thought."

"Nothing you think is silly," I replied. "Tell me what you're thinking. I hate not knowing, makes me feel like I'm forgetting. Vampires don't like to forget."

"Fine, but I want you to know it's just a wish and can never happen." She took a deep breath. "There's a dance in two weeks, a Halloween dance, and since it's a costume dance, I thought it would be fun if you and I could go. Like I said, silly."

Something inside me clicked at the softness in her voice and suddenly, it didn't matter.

It didn't matter how dangerous it would be for me to go to this dance. All that mattered was what she wanted and how much I wanted to do this for her. With everything I had, I wanted to take her to the dance, see her glowing among the humans and know that when it came to love, hers was for me.

"Let's do it," I whispered. "Let's go to the dance. I want to take you."

Her eyes widened, then she laughed and threw her arms around me. She paused, uncertainty filling her eyes. "We'll need costumes, something that will cover your whole face. Maybe a mask. I dunno, I haven't done anything for Halloween in years."

"We can ask my niece, she'll know what to do." I frowned. "She might be mad I want to do this when I refused to go to the movies."

More doubt filled Sunlight's eyes. "Maybe we shouldn't do this. I mean, what makes it less dangerous than you taking me to a movie? Someone could see you and realize you're not human. What if I lose you?"

I pulled her close. "I want to do this for you."

"What about need? Don't you need to survive?"

"I can't argue against survival." I took her hands and looked into her eyes. "But I want you to be happy as much as I need to survive."

She curled her fingers around mine and squeezed. "I am happy."

We fell into silence and let the night slip by. Hunger murmured and grew, distracting me from the costume dance and Sunlight. Her scent tugged at my need, making my stomach rumble.

"I'm hungry." The words slipped out.

Sunlight didn't speak, she simply tilted her neck.

I grazed my nose against the rhythm beating under the skin. The few times I had bit her, the taste had been wonderful. Sweet and fulfilling, everything I needed to survive. I licked my lips once, tasting her scent on my tongue. "That is not a good idea."

"You're strong enough to never hurt me," she whispered.

"No, I love you too much to want to hurt you."

****

The noise was deafening, thundering and rattling the windows with a steady beat as the floor shook as if wracked by an earthquake. Bright lights flashed orange and purple, reflecting off the shaking windows. Thin smoke drifted along the floor, pouring from black pots placed around the room. Orange pumpkins with crude, smiling faces were piled in corners. A huge, silver orb hung from the ceiling, throwing light across the floor. In the middle of the room, humans filled the space, moving in time to the thundering music.

What was I doing?

I asked myself a hundred times. When I decided to take Sunlight to the costumed dance. When we asked my niece to help find a costume. The first time my niece dressed me up to make sure no one could tell I was a vampire. When we finally told Dan and he declared no, but eventually agreed when I told him I needed to do this.

What was I doing?

I was making Sunlight happy. Even as she fussed over the dangers, reminding me it was okay if I changed my mind, I knew she was happy. That alone made the risk to my survival worth it.

As I watched the humans, something vibrated against my leg. I pulled the cell phone out. A press of a few buttons and I smiled at the message.

Lil' bro, if you want to come home, CALL ME!

Then I frowned and realized I didn't know how to respond. He showed me how to use it to accept a call or message, but I forgot to ask how to do any of it.

"Humans are too complicated," I muttered and pocketed the phone.

"Hey." Two human males in tattered and dirty clothing approached. What I assumed was fake blood – since I couldn't smell any fresh – was painted on their skin like wounds. They nodded at me in approval. "Nice costume," one of them said.

Be human, I reminded myself. "Thanks, it's Frankenstein."

Both humans snickered. "We figured, the bolts on the neck kinda gave it away."

I nodded. "Oh. What are you supposed to be?"

They laughed again and one held out his arms and moaned, "Braiiins." He dropped his hands when I stared in confusion. "Come on, dude, zombies? Walking dead? Eat your brains? A menace to people?"

"I thought only vampires were a threat to humans," I replied.

Both scoffed. "Yeah, but who'd want to dress up like a sucker? That's disgusting."

I managed a smile. "Disgusting, right."

They quickly shuffled away to another group. Nerves churned in me as I watched. Did they suspect I wasn't human? Barely arrived and already I had blown it. But my costume was thorough; my niece picking it because she knew it would cover as much as me as possible. What wasn't covered by mask or fabric was covered with thick paint.

"Tommy, are you okay?" Sunlight walked up, her costume the other reason my niece picked mine. The dress she wore was flowing and white. It clung to her waist, billowing at her arms and legs. A tall black and white wig was perched precariously over her hair, held up only by a few pins.

I glanced at the two humans, seeing one look back at me and catching his thoughts.

Man, that guy has a creepy smile.

I turned back to Sunlight and took her hand. "I thought maybe those humans suspected me, but they just think I'm creepy."

Concern filled her painted face. "Maybe we should go."

"We just got here," I reminded her. "We stood outside in line for…"

"A half hour."

"A half hour," I repeated, then stopped. "I don't know what I'm saying. Time really doesn't have a lot of meaning to me. I find it more annoying than anything."

She laughed, the bell-like sound silencing the thundering music. She brushed her nose against mine. "Every second with you matters."

"I could stand for a little less noise."

She innocently shrugged. "You're the one that insisted."

I pulled her close, rocking her back and forth. "And you're happy I did. I can smell it."

Her laughter was muffled into my shoulder. I grazed my nose and lips against her neck, enjoying her sweet scent. Around us, the humans and music faded. I may not understand the costume dance or how our costumes matched, but when it came to her, I found it really hard to care. All I wanted was for her to be happy.

"Excuse me." A warm hand clasped my shoulder.

My fangs shot out and a growl vibrated in my throat. The only thing that kept me from ripping into the human, eliminating the threat I instantly felt at the touch of an unknown hand, was Sunlight gripping my face. She kept me looking at her, silently soothing me. Unwillingly, my fangs retracted and I reined my instincts in. I caught the human's gaze and shoved my will against his.

"Leave."

The human's eyes blanked out and he walked away. I turned my gaze back to Sunlight, her eyes wide with shock as two more hands grabbed me. I let myself get pulled into the brightly lit hall and to a bathroom where my niece slammed me against the wall.

"What were you thinking?" she hissed. "You can't press your will against a teacher. Mr. Williams was just going to tell you that PDA isn't allowed."

"What's PDA?"

"Public display of affection," my niece snapped.

I looked at Sunlight, then my niece. "Sorry."

My niece rubbed her eyes, smearing the sparkling makeup that was part of her witch costume. She paced back and forth, muttering. "Why didn't I listen to you the first time? You can't be human, even when you try to be human it's not the same. This was stupid, we should call it quits and leave before anyone realizes what you are. I hate it when Dad's right."

"But–" I started.

Sunlight placed a hand on my arm and silenced my protest. "It's okay. We came and I danced to a song, but Mackenzie's right. We should go before you do anything else that's not human."

I nodded.

She took my hand as we headed out of the bathroom. "I had lots of fun."

"That's good," I replied.

On the dance floor, the music had softened. A white light shone on the silver orb and reflected shimmering squares across the room. The humans had paired up, arms around each other and turning in tight circles.

"What are they doing?"

"Slow dancing," Sunlight replied with a wistful sigh.

I changed direction, leading her back to the room and stopping at the edge of the crowd. Her protest quickly fell silent when I placed her arms around my neck. A quick look told me where to put my hands. Then I started moving, turning her like the other humans were. Out of the corner of my eye, I saw my niece snap a picture with her cell phone, and then turned her attention to the human male who was pulling her towards the dance floor.

Sunlight melted against me, tears shimmering in her eyes as she rested her cheek on my shoulder. "Thank you."

"You're welcome," I whispered and grazed my nose down to her neck. A glance around showed every human occupied with another. She gave a small squeak when I popped my fangs through her skin, then relaxed against my bite.

"I love you," she whispered.

I let go, staring at her in wonder. How long had I quietly yearned to hear her whisper those words? My mouth felt strangely dry, despite her blood lingering on my tongue. "I love you too."

The silver orb reflected in her eyes, making them sparkle. Her thoughts whispered, telling me it was okay, she was finally ready. I tilted my head and closed the distance. Her eyes drifted shut and her lips puckered. I mimicked her, nerves boiling in me as everything prepared to change.

I couldn't wait.

The feeling slammed into me like a battering ram. My eyes snapped open, my instincts screaming to life. The music died, the hum of the equipment the only sound. Every human fell still, staring in shock. Sunlight's eyes fluttered open, hurt filling them as her thoughts wondered what she did wrong. She glanced around and gasped in shock at what the other humans saw.

A vampire.

But it wasn't me.

He was one of the vampires Amy gathered, the one that always got on my case about smelling human. His eyes were cold and accusing as he stared at me, his hands clenched into fists and his posture ready to fight.

I spoke, quietly enough so only he heard. "Are you insane? Do you want to get destroyed?"

The humans whimpered when he threw a glare around, his gaze lingering on Sunlight. I stepped in front of her and his gaze snapped to me. A twitching lip gave me a glimpse of fangs and I tensed, sensing the challenge behind the action. Long moments passed as I waited for him to make his move. Finally, he spoke one word, making it loud enough for the humans to hear.

"Traitor."

He looked into my eyes and I felt his will pushing, his thoughts forced into my mind. He let me know what he saw every time we crossed paths. A vampire living among humans and pretending to be one. A vampire whispering and smiling at a human, then biting her. A vampire speaking of love. He let me know he saw everything and hated me for it.

"Don't," I whispered, but knew it was too late.

He lunged, but I wasn't his target. Fangs bared, he headed straight for Sunlight as his snarl ripped through the air. I dropped the ruse, tugging the mask off so I could see better. When he reached me, I bared my fangs and slammed my palms against his chest, throwing him across the room. I turned to Sunlight, pushing her into a nearby chair and shoving it away. Then I turned back and met the vampire's next attack.

As he came at me again, the humans screamed in fear, stampeding across the room and veering wildly when they got to close to him or me. Over the commotion, I heard my niece yell for me, but I didn't have time to worry about her, my focus was on winning this fight.

We grappled with each other, fangs snapping and trying to tear flesh away. I wrapped my arms around his waist, slinging him into a display of trophies. Glass shattered and wood splintered from the force. But he didn't stay down long, lunging to his feet with a snarl. Pain bolted through me as he grabbed my arm, twisting it back and sinking his fangs into my skin. I yowled in pain, jerking him around and throwing him across the room.

My mind flashed to ten years ago and the monster I had turned into a pile of unrecognizable blood and flesh. This time there was no blood, only hard, stiff flesh. Vampire flesh. Flesh that tore as I pounced and ripped it apart. I sank my fangs into the vampire's neck and tore until his head fell to the floor.

Everything calmed in an instant and the red faded from my vision. Around me chairs and tables were overturned and pumpkins smashed. A light still flashed, illuminating the glass and trophies littering the floor. Not a single human was in sight.

"Uncle!" My niece held her dress as she raced to me. Her hand flew to her mouth and her skin turned white at the sight of the destroyed vampire at my feet. She grabbed my hand and started pulling me towards the exit. "We have to go! VF will be here any minute."

"Where is Sunlight?"

"Tommy!" Sunlight rushed to my side, a gasp escaping. "Your face…"

"I'm okay," I assured her.

"Come on." My niece pulled me across the room. "The gym doors should be clear if we hurry."

I stumbled as we ran down empty hallways, pain slicing through my leg with each step. Sunlight raced ahead, holding doors open and checking for humans. We made it safely to the gym, shoes squeaking on the shiny floor. My eyes locked on the doors across the wide space and the outside world where I could escape.

We burst through the door, red and blue lights flashing in our vision. Humans in black uniforms with silver VFs gleaming on their chests rushed forward. My niece was yanked away and Sunlight screamed as another grabbed her.

"Tommy, run!"

When the vampires had protested and I watched on TV, I never understood how the vampires could stand there and let Vampire Forces torch them. When the girl stood with her vampire mother, I was more confused. Vampire Forces had pulled the girl away and her mother attacked every human. How could she be so reckless?

Now I understood.

I lunged at the human, grabbing his arm and snapping it back to free Sunlight. I turned to the human holding my niece next and sank my teeth into his neck.

Pain jolted through me like a current and spots danced before my vision. My energy drained away and I crumpled to the ground. I weakly snapped my teeth, determined to keep fighting until my niece and Sunlight were freed. More jolts hit me as Vampire Forces surrounded me. Pain coursed through me, throwing me around like a rag doll and the spots grew bigger until they blacked my vision out. I fell into the blackness, no strength left to fight. The last thing I heard was Sunlight pleading for someone to stop.

Part Five: Hatred

The world faded in and out, from light to dark and back again. Noises came and went, whisper soft, then roaring loud. Throughout it all, pain was my constant companion. The tiniest movement caused pain, stillness caused pain. There were jolts of pain, prickles of pain, hot pain and searing pain. It was all there was and it would only get worse.

I had screwed up in a big way.

When Vampire Forces had pulled Sunlight and my niece away, I lost it. All thoughts of escaping and survival flew out the window. Humans were touching and hurting the ones I loved. The thought enraged me and I attacked.

Deep down, I knew there was no way to win. I was outnumbered, but I couldn't stop myself. Something had trumped my own survival. Surrounded, Vampire Forces shocked me into unconsciousness. When I woke, the room I was in had no windows, beds or chairs; the wall, floor and ceiling nothing but shiny silver. A single light bulb illuminated the room.

For the longest time I didn't move, resting and trying to regain energy I was incapable of restoring without blood. I didn't know if I was above ground or under, my injuries had me boiling hot. I waited in the silver room, knowing I was minutes away from being destroyed. When they came for me, my only thought was this was it.

Only it wasn't.

Instead of tying me to a stake and destroying me, the Vampire Forces officers took me to a large, white room. Machines and wires lined the walls and snaked along the floor. There, they bound me to a silver table and left. Other humans in long, white coats appeared. With hot hands, they examined me and used long, shiny instruments to pry open my injuries. When they finished, Vampire Forces came again and took me back to the silver room.

It became a routine, take me to the white room, examine and poke me, then put me back in the silver room. Each time, the pain coursing through me grew worse and my need for blood screamed.

"Is it alive?" a voice asked.

"Depends on your idea of alive," another answered.

I didn't try to move, trying to keep the pain to minimum by staying as still as possible. Carefully, I cracked an eye open, straining to see the scientists standing at a safe distance out of the corner of my eye. That one, tiny movement caused pain to pulsed through me. I bit my lip, fangs sliding into holes made from previous bites, to keep from making any sounds.

The scientists moved closer once they deemed I was secured to the table and incapable of moving. They sorted through their tools and quietly discussed what they hoped to learn today. Maybe why vampires turned to ash in the sun. Or what sort of energy kept a vampire out of a home unless welcomed. So many questions they had and they hoped I was their key to those answers.

I recalled Dan once telling me how scientists studied vampires. He said the official statement was they took the ashes and studied those, but every human assumed they had live specimens. Fear filled his scent and he was quick to change the subject. He had feared that happening to me.

I shouldn't think of my brother, I told myself. It would only make me worry about my family. Were they okay? Did he feel my pain? He probably felt mild discomfort if anything. The lie always comforted me.

The scientists leaned over me, one holding a long, jagged knife. Fear flooded me and pain rolled through me as I trembled. I scrambled for a way to prolong my suffering if only for a moment. "What are you doing?"

The knife froze above my skin. The scientists leaned closer, their eyes examining me. They never just looked at me, they *always* examined me. Then tortured me.

"It talked," one noted.

I dragged my dry tongue over my lips, hoping to keep them interested. The effort made my throat raw. "What are you going to do to me?"

They stepped back to the TV and camera recording each moment spent torturing me. One rewound the tape and my voice rasped through the speakers. Another made a note in a book. Then they turned back to me and the knife sank into me.

Spots popped in my vision as the pain flared hot. I ground my teeth together and swallowed the scream that was trying to force its way up my throat. I would not scream, I would not show pain or give any indication just how weak I was. I would survive!

After long moments of heat and pain, the scientists leaned back, a few swiping at their brows. They gathered around the TV to watch. As the video played, one noted today's findings.

"Specimen still shows no signs of healing. With no blood present, there is no clotting or scabbing. Heaviest injuries are to the neck. It looks like, when vampires fight, they go for the jugular to kill."

Vampires try to bit the head off when we want to kill, I thought.

"It's been a month, I think it's time to move to the next test," one suggested.

"I don't know, I think we should take more time to study the lack of healing," one disagreed after a long silence.

"There's nothing left to study," the first one replied. "It's time to move on and study how vampires survive on blood and how it heals them."

Hope spread through me at the mention of blood.

"We'll have to be quick, only one or two tests. Anymore is too dangerous," a third one said.

The scientists nodded in agreement.

"Excuse me, doctors." A Vampire Forces officer marched up. "You'll have to wrap it up; the vampire is due in court in fifteen minutes."

The scientists scoffed as the Vampire Forces officer marched away.

"Can't believe that it actually got a trial," one commented.

"It's only to appease the public," the second one replied and eyed me. "Reporters found some old VF reports on this one. Stalked family members and kidnapped a little girl to kill. The public would be in an uproar if this one quietly turned to ash. They want its blood… so to speak."

"At least it gives us time to study. VF always insists on torching them before we can find any real answers," the third one added.

The scientists disappeared and the Vampire Forces officer reappeared with two others. Strapping a mask over my face, they bound me to a wheelchair and began pushing it down the white corridor, bashing the chair against the wall repeatedly. Voices grew louder as we approached a door at the end of the hall.

One torture down and another on its way.

****

Bang! Bang! Bang!

The crack of the hammer echoed around the room, the sound reminding me of breaking bones and the ones the scientists broke. The cold eyes of the human sitting high above the rest glared at each human before turning to me. A whisper of a thought dared me to move and give the judge a reason to destroy me on the spot. When I didn't move, he tore his glare away with a scowl.

"There will be no fiascoes today."

The humans agreed with silence.

The judge turned his attention to his papers, sifting through them and choosing one to read from. I barely heard him over the sounds of hearts pounding around me and tormenting me with their rhythm. The smell of blood wafted through the air. My stomach twisted in hunger and need clawed at my mind. If I opened my mouth and drew a breath, I could taste a hint of blood.

It was hard to describe how much I hated each human in the room with me. The one next to me stank of fear and it was agonizing being inches away from a scent that sang to me. The ones behind me wore on me with their incessant talking and movement. The ones in front of me made me boil with anger at the unfair judgment in their eyes and thoughts. And the human I hated the worst was striding to the judge at his prompting, chest puffed out and voice full of confidence and lies.

"Your Honor," the lawyer said. "As I've stated many times since the start of this trial, this has gone on long enough. The evidence has been presented and there is no denying the monstrous acts this creature has done. Stalking a surviving family member and even following the poor man to college. How many students died while it was there? I shudder to think. And years later, it tormented his family. Again, I shudder thinking of the terror they felt. Then it snatched a young girl from the safety of her own bedroom with every intention on killing her. Probably raped her as well."

"Uncle wouldn't do that!" my niece's voice angrily interrupted. "You're not supposed to assume in a trial, you're supposed to present facts. Why isn't that damn lawyer asking for that comment to be dismissed? *Objection!*"

The judge banged his hammer. "I warned you, young lady, no more outbursts in my courtroom or you will be removed. Again."

"Well, maybe if you had appointed *my uncle* a decent defender, I wouldn't have to disturb anyone," my niece snapped. "Hey you, grow a pair and defend my uncle!"

"You better get your child under control," the judge growled as his gaze shifted.

"Mackenzie, you promised you wouldn't make a fuss, you said you wanted to be here for him," Dan spoke in a hushed, pain-filled tone.

Pain shot through me, skin stretching, wounds opening and broken bones shifting as I turned. My family sat three rows back, the rows between us and the seats around them empty. My niece was on her feet, anger written across her face as Dan tried to calm her. Rissa watched me with a mixture of sympathy and pain.

Tears filled my niece's eyes when she saw me watching. She jumped over the rows between us, struggling to reach me. Her skin boiled, her rhythm slamming against me and her scent burned my nose as she hugged me tightly. "I won't let them destroy you."

All I managed was a strangled noise, something between a snarl of hunger and cry of pain.

"Get her out of my courtroom," the judge ordered as my niece's commotion rippled across the courtroom.

Two Vampire Forces tore her away from me, kicking and screaming, her foot catching one in the chest. A third aimed a flame-thrower at me, eyes and thoughts daring me to try something. The two carried my niece out of the courtroom, Rissa following.

"Order!" the judge yelled as the doors slammed shut.

Once everyone in the courtroom calmed, the lawyer resumed his speech on how I was an inhumane monster. I closed my eyes and let myself drift half way as I listened. This was so pointless, no matter what the trial decided, the outcome would be the same. I was going to be destroyed.

****

It was a tiny spark, small and delicate. It coursed through me, struggling at injuries, pausing in attempt to knit skin together and mend broken bones. Finally it faded away, not strong enough to survive.

But, for a second, I had felt alive!

My lips no longer hurt, the holes I had bitten almost healed. Pain still covered the rest of my body, injuries and bones still unhealed. But the tiny drop of blood felt as if it had worked miracles and the pain had lessened.

The scientists stepped back to me and started their examination. Their awe filled the air like electricity. One lifted his hand as if he was going to touch me, but thought better and dropped it. They turned to the TV and rewound the video to seconds before they dripped the drop down my throat.

"What do you think?" one asked.

"Amazing!" the second one exclaimed. "Look how fast the blood worked, seconds and the injuries to its lips are almost healed. If we could figure out how."

After more discussion, they set the camera to record again and turned to me. One picked up a glass vial from the tray and unscrewed the lid. My eyes locked on the red, nostrils flaring at the smell drifting to me. I strained against my restraints, snapping my teeth and hissing.

The scientists backed away at my increased movements. I forced myself still and they cautiously stepped back to me. The one holding the vial held it out and a few drops fell. I caught each one.

"More!"

The scientist returned the vial to the tray and quickly stepped away. They waited a few minutes before moving back in to re-examine my injuries, and then watch the TV. They repeated the process and slowly I felt my injuries heal and a small trickle of energy wind through me. When the last bone mended, miraculously some blood left in the vial, the scientists motioned to Vampire Forces to take me back to the silver room.

There, I lay on the floor and carefully tested myself. The trickle of energy quickly faded, but my need for blood had eased with the healing of my injuries. The air around me wasn't as hot, the floor was refreshingly cool and the light not as blinding. With a sigh, I closed my eyes and let my mind drift to comforts beyond my reach.

I had grown used to daydreaming and understood now why humans did it. An escape from a harsh reality. For a few moments I could forget the pain, hunger and need. I pretended I was someplace better, home with my family. I'd listen to Rissa and my niece argue about her going to bed for school in the morning or watch Dan read his newspaper. I'd hold conversations with each of them and sit down at the table for dinner.

When I finally opened my eyes, the pain of reality threatened to consume me.

Too soon, Vampire Forces came back. They restrained me like usual and wheeled me back to the lab. Three times as many scientists were waiting, their excitement filling the air as they whispered to one another.

What were they planning?

Maybe this is it, a part of me whispered. *The trial is over and it's time to destroy the evil vampire.*

Was it wrong of me to hope that? My whole life had been about surviving and now all I desired was the end. Deep down, I knew I didn't want to be destroyed. I needed to survive, but the past few weeks had beat me down and I was tired. Tired of the pain, of waiting for what would come next and the confusion of it. If being destroyed meant I'd no longer worry or wonder, I welcomed it.

"Should we administer some anesthetic?" one scientist asked.

"I don't think it's necessary," another replied.

They moved closer, double checking my restraints and wheeled the tray of instruments closer. Next, they checked TV and camera, making sure it was ready to record. Each scientist held his or her breath as one closed in with a knife.

The first cut went deep, deeper than usual. I gritted my teeth and swallowed any sounds of pain. The next cut went even deeper and when the scientist reached bone, he set the knife aside and picked up a drill. The high-pitched noise grated against my ears as the blade spun to life. Bones cracked and snapped at a touch from the blade. The scientist grabbed other tools next, holding my skin open and prying more bones apart.

The rest were excited now, leaning in to examine. More joined the first, prodding into the wound they created and sending jolts of pain through me. I found myself gasping, unable to hold back any longer.

"Stop!"

The scientists ignored me and kept working. Maybe they hadn't heard.

I tried to raise my voice, wanting to scream, but unable. "Please, stop!"

I felt something snap in my chest and pain ripped through me. I arched off the table and a scream tore from my throat. Everything went dark.

****

It was a miracle when I woke in the silver room. When darkness washed over me, it felt as if permanent death had touched me. Black spots filled my vision as I stared at the silver walls. Pain throbbed through me, my skin on fire and burning down to my bones. My chest felt empty, the void terrifying me.

What had the scientist done?

Carefully, I crawled my hand up my stomach and along my chest. Torn skin met my fingers, the wound stretching down the middle. I could feel *inside* me, feel what was under the skin, the broken bones, torn muscles and tissue. Everything I shouldn't be able to feel. Except for one thing.

I pressed my hand over the wound and slumped, exhausted, to the floor. "Why can't I die?"

I slipped back into unconsciousness, falling completely unaware. I had never been unaware before, it wasn't possible for a vampire. We're constantly half awake, part of our survival demanding we know what's going on even if we're helpless to defend ourselves. When I rested, I couldn't imagine being unaware.

Now, I welcomed the moment. It meant I didn't have to think or feel pain or wait for what would come next. I didn't care because I was unaware. Was that what permanent death felt like?

When Vampire Forces came for me again, they didn't bother restraining me. They yanked a shirt over me and covered the wound in my chest. Next they dumped me into the wheelchair, enjoying each whimper of pain that escaped me as they wheeled me to the courtroom.

Humans filled the seats in the courtroom and more stood along the walls. Their excited whispers floated through the air and their energy filled the crowded room. I started hoping again, this had to mean the end for me.

All attention turned to my family when they entered. I twisted around in my seat, but too many humans crowded around them. I heard Rissa over the murmur of voices.

"Give us some space. Dan's not feeling well."

"Do you think the vampire did it?" a voice asked.

"Can vampires cause injuries from afar?" another chimed in.

More voices shouted questions until the words bled together into an unintelligible stew.

"Shut up!" Rissa snapped. "We went to the hospital because Dan felt ill, not because of Tommy. Now leave us alone. We won't answer any more of your ignorant questions."

The humans didn't back off until Vampire Forces pushed them back. My family broke free and took their usual seats. Dan slumped into his seat, his skin pale and face contorting in pain. His hand was clutching his chest. For once my niece didn't look angry, her eyes darting back and forth from me to Dan.

"Sympathizers," a voice yelled over the crowd.

More jeers rippled across the courtroom. My family ignored the jests – as they had the ones that came before. The jeers fell silent when the doors to the courtroom opened again. The crowd parted and Sunlight walked with her parents to a row near the front. The humans gathered around her, their voices sympathetic as they questioned her.

A human stood behind her, his hand on her shoulder as he answered. "Jamie is here to face the monster that terrorized her all summer. After today, she will finally put the nightmare behind her."

Confusion rolled through me. I killed the monster that terrorized her. Who was the human talking about? He didn't mean me, did he? But Sunlight didn't think of me that way, I wasn't a monster in her eyes. She loved me like I loved her. Why would she lie?

Why wouldn't she look at me?

A new pain filled my chest, burning hotter than fire. I felt myself burn up, the pain destroying me faster than the sun ever could. My body turned numb and my mind went blank. I fell back into my seat, nothing left of me. I was gone, destroyed without a lick of flame touching me.

I was nothing…

…Something touched my knees. The touch was soft and painfully hot. I blinked once, slowly becoming aware of my surroundings. Like the night I was turned, everything started to come back to me. I felt the ground beneath my feet, smelled scents in the air and heard noises. Only this time I felt like a zombie, an empty shell.

"Tommy, look at me."

A human girl stood before me, something so familiar about her. Wide, brown eyes stared into mine and soft whispers echoed in my head.

Oh God, what have they done to you? I'm sorry, Tommy, this is my fault. I shouldn't have let you go to the dance. Please forgive me. I'm sorry, I'm sorry!

A tear rolled down her cheek and fell to my hand. A flicker of anger grew as I stared at the moisture. Why did her crying anger me? The answer felt on the tip of my tongue and I struggled to speak. "Why… am I mad?"

"Don't try to speak," she whispered.

She knelt before me and lifted her hands from my knees. Her head tilted ever so slightly as her gaze shifted to something behind me. Gently, she lifted my shirt. Her eyes widened and her face turned white as snow. A scream ripped from her and humans rushed to pull her away.

"Let me go, I'm fine." She pulled from their grip and knelt back down. Her hands trembled as she lifted my shirt again and her voice shook. "What did they do to you?"

I glanced at the humans around us. They looked nervous and ready to pull her away again. I knew I didn't want that. The pain didn't hurt with her near and slowly, I felt my brain restarting and thoughts returning to me.

She was my Sunlight and I loved her with everything I had.

And she loved me too. I saw it in her eyes as her thoughts told me how they tried to keep her away and told her they knew what was best for her. She knew what was best for her, what she needed.

Me.

I gazed in her eyes, knowing I needed her too. I twitched my fingers and she curled hers around mine. "My heart," I whispered. "They took my heart."

****

The judge banged his hammer and demanded order in the court. The humans settled into their seats, a few continuing to murmur and earning a glare from the judge. Once the last of the voices died, he threw his glare to me.

"I understand the vampire wishes to change his plea."

"Yes, Your Honor," the human next to me, Mr. Anderson, sprung to his feet. "My client pleads innocent."

Everything had changed again, the trial, the torture and what it meant.

After Sunlight lied to get close to me and the discovery of what the scientist had done to me, she called to another human. He had strode forward without an ounce of fear in his scent and announced he was her lawyer and upon her request was taking me as his client. This fiasco of a trial had gone on long enough and it was time the court stop wasting tax payers' money.

I was whisked away, Vampire Forces hot on my heels and protesting any blood my lawyer insisted I needed. After a lot of arguing and insults, it was agreed I needed enough blood to heal. Not a drop more, to ensure I wouldn't be able to escape.

But before I got the blood to heal, I needed to get my heart back.

A piece of paper presented by Mr. Anderson quickly silenced the scientists and sent them scurrying to obey. I was placed back on the table and this time given something that pulled me into pain-free unconsciousness. When I woke, my heart was back where it belonged.

The trial was restarted and a new judge and jury selected. Evidence was resubmitted and some thrown out. Mr. Anderson worked hard, lecturing, preaching and fighting for me. Each day, more and more humans filled the courthouse to watch and the newspapers called the trial the biggest in history.

Every few days I was given a little blood and time with my family. Sunlight was with them too, showing her support for me. There was no more torture, the scientists not allowed near me. I was no longer bound to a chair and no one was to call me it, they had to use my name.

I didn't much care for that part.

"Your Honor," the other lawyer spoke up. "You can't seriously be considering it. He is a vampire, we know he has probably killed hundreds of people over the years."

"That's beside the point," Mr. Anderson replied. "It's an established fact that vampires kill to obtain blood. One cannot prosecute the lion for hunting the antelope."

The two lawyers started arguing, their voices growing louder as the judge started to yell. I closed my eyes and repressed a sigh. Anxiety festered in my chest, not my own, but Dan's. Every day I watched my family suffer as the other humans jeered or demanded to know why they supported me. They were being ridiculed and hurt. All because of me. I pushed to my feet and all attention turned to me.

"I need to talk to you."

Mr. Anderson rushed to my side. "What's wrong? We're doing well."

I glared at him and growled. "I don't need to talk to you, I need to talk to him." I jerked my head at the judge.

Mr. Anderson shrugged and headed to the judge to quietly talk.

The other lawyer quickly followed, his voice agitated. "Your Honor, you can't be alone with it, it will kill you."

"Please, my client is half starved to death," Mr. Anderson coolly replied.

"Your client is dead."

"Silence!" the judge ordered and dismissed both. "We will take a thirty minute recess while I talk with the vampire in my office."

Voices filled the air as the humans wondered what I could want. Vampire Forces jerked me up and did their best to drag me after the judge. The two lawyers followed.

The judge rounded the huge desk and fixed me with a glare as he sat. "Well, what do you want? You're wasting my time calling for breaks."

"I don't understand the trial," I replied.

Mr. Anderson sighed and moved to my side. "Tommy, if you're confused, I'll do my best to explain. You just have to ask."

"I'm not talking to you," I said with a flash of fangs. I looked back at the judge. "I don't understand why this trial is happening. I'll still be destroyed, so get it over with already."

"Tommy–" Mr. Anderson started.

"No!" I interrupted. "I'm tired of this. I'm tired of seeing my family suffer." I turned back to the judge. "What do I have to do or say? Yes, I'm a horrible monster that enjoys killing humans? Fine, I'll say anything you want, let you destroy me. All I ask is you keep my family safe, don't let the other humans hurt and shun them. I'd rather be permanently dead than see my family hurt every day."

The judge's face was blank as he listened to me. He rested his fingers together, but I heard his thoughts as he looked at me. They spoke of disbelief and shock that a creature as evil as a vampire – me – only concern was the four humans back in the courtroom who were insane enough to defend it.

He dropped his hands. "Fine."

"Your Honor, you can't–" Mr. Anderson protested.

"Quiet!" the judge snapped. "It's the defendant's choice. This trial is over and Vampire Forces will take the defendant into custody to do as they see fit. I'll place a gag order on the media, no paper is to report any story on the family."

"Sunlight too, she's family," I insisted.

For a moment the judge stared in confusion, and then nodded. "The girl too."

Relief filled me. It was finally over, I was over. My destruction was around the corner and I couldn't care less. My family would be protected from the other humans. That was all that mattered.

Vampire Forces grabbed me, eager to put the restraints back on. They marched me back to the courtroom and the humans fell silent. My family and Sunlight watched, each one silently asking me what was happening. I had no words for them, this was my last moment with them.

There was something I needed to do.

Summoning my last bit of energy, I snapped the cuffs and shoved Vampire Forces away. The distance between us felt like millions of miles, Sunlight impossible to reach. I put everything I had into crossing the room, to reaching her. And when I did, I spared a moment for my family.

"I'm sorry."

Dan locked eyes with me and the color drained from his face. "No."

Then I turned to Sunlight and everything disappeared. The humans, the courtroom and trial, the scientists and experiments. All I saw was our time together. The details sped by, every moment of every night spent with her crystal clear before me. It made me smile and laugh and want to cry. All those moments combined into one second in time, one moment that was only me and her, and for the first time nothing else mattered. Hunger and need didn't matter, my own survival was insignificant. As I gazed into her eyes, I finally understood what it meant to be human.

I kissed her.

She kissed me back.

Reality crashed back with a jolt. Pain raced through me, knocking what little strength I had left away. I crumpled as hot hands tore me away. My niece screamed, trying to reach me as Rissa and Dan pulled her back. They held her tight as she sagged to the floor, sobbing. Sunlight didn't move, her fingers on her lips and eyes staring into mine. I held onto the memory of the kiss as they dragged me away, wanting it to be the last one I had of her. Another jolt and blackness crashed down on me.

This was the end.

****

He called me his Sunlight and said he didn't hate the day because of me. When I was little, he stopped a monster from killing me. And when I was older and afraid of everything in the world and wishing for death, he saved me again. He made me feel safe, showed me that I wasn't alone in the world. There was someone else. There was him.

And he was a vampire.

Water dripped, a steady plinking that echoed in the blackness surrounding me. Somewhere, footsteps clomped down a hallway and voices talked with excitement. A steady drone rolled through the air and something shuffled nearby.

In the darkness, a pale face shone. It looked sick, skin slack, eyes hollow and dead. The vampire could barely lift her head from the floor. She licked her lips, finding the strength to talk. Even then, her voice was a weak whisper. "It won't be long before it's over."

We pulled in the parking lot that stretched around the domed building. Already, it was full, police directing traffic to remaining spots. As we crawled to an open space, people walked around us. They chatted and laughed, looking carefree and at ease. One would think it was a normal Friday night and everyone was heading to enjoy the football game.

Only it wasn't.

VF appeared to escort us once we were parked. They led us into the arena and onto the field. There was barely a space to stand and not a single seat available. News vans were parked along the edge and the reporters were already speaking to the camera and interviewing people. There would be no mention of myself or Mackenzie's family. Tommy's bargain had been he would allow himself to be destroyed as long as his family and I were protected.

The trial over, Mr. Anderson left, turned tail and ran back to the west coast. He had assured me he'd win and the course of history would be changed. I think what he wanted was a career making case. What he got was a career breaking case.

At one end of the field, underneath a goal post, a platform had been erected. Posts were spread evenly across with buckets of water and fire extinguishers ready. A fire truck was parked nearby. VF moved across the platform, rushing off the field and disappearing beneath the bleachers.

The VF officers escorting us took us to the front, mere feet from the platform where they left us. People around us backed away, murmuring as they stared. The only people not looking our way or whispering were my parents. My mom's eyes were averted and my dad's back completely turned. They had been dumbfounded when I requested emancipation, sputtering and asking what they had done wrong.

What had they done right?

From the moment Tommy rescued me when I was a little girl, my life had been one nightmare. I didn't feel safe, not at school or in my own home. I couldn't talk to people, waiting for someone to finish what the monster had started. I knew all too well of the horrors people were capable of.

It wasn't until Tommy found me again that I finally felt something besides fear. As I sat in that cold cellar, watching him attempt to take care of me, the fear had eased. He had done something my own parents had been unable to do. He made me feel safe. Around him, I wasn't jumping at shadows. I found myself relaxing, smiling and meaning it. I wasn't putting on a show or pretending I was fine. I had finally started to heal.

As the trial progressed, my parents kept me locked in the house. *It's for your own good*, they said. Therapists came and went, each one telling me I was confused. Yes, Tommy had rescued me, but my feelings weren't real. I was transferring my supposed-feelings on to him and once I accepted that, I'd understand Tommy didn't care about me, I was only food to him.

The humiliation I felt when the scars on my arms were exposed was unbearable.

The current therapist stated I had been trying to cut the bite marks off. No one listened when I said *I* made the cuts before Tommy, that he bit the scars to make me think of happier times with him. No one listened and no one cared. All they saw was an evil vampire taking advantage of a broken girl.

I didn't care how scared the other vampire sounded. This was the end and I was glad for it. My family would no longer suffer and I would be released from this torture. A slow smile filled my face. I think I understood irony now.

The quick smiles were my favorite, so fast I barely caught them, but I knew they were real. When Tommy prolonged his smiles, they didn't look right. Like waiting for someone to take a picture; you smile and smile and as the seconds pass the smile feels less real, losing its emotion as it turns fake. Now I'd never see those quick smiles again.

Rain started to fall, drops pattering softly to the ground, but quickly gaining momentum, hammering down and icy cold. Thick clouds covered the sky, stretching across the horizon, keeping the sun from making an appearance. No sun meant VF would resort to torches.

Silence fell over the restless crowd as a group of VF officers marched onto the platform. A limp figure was dragged between the two, a black bag covering the face. They quickly tied the vampire to one of the posts, and then pulled the black bag off.

They came and took the vampire. She didn't fight or struggle. As terrified as she was, she was relieved. I saw it in her eyes before they slipped the black bag over her head. For a moment, it was silent. I forced myself to my feet, stumbling to the door. I pressed my ear against it to listen. An awful scream filled the air as the smell of burning flesh tainted it. The vampire had been set afire. That meant the sun wasn't out.

"It's not him," Mackenzie's mom whispered, clutching Mackenzie, whose face was buried against her.

Mackenzie's dad raised his eyes. He looked at the platform, but I don't think he had seen anything since the end of the trial, too numbed by the fact he was losing his twin. I think that pain was worse than all of the shared pain he and Tommy felt during the trial.

The vampire screamed when VF lit her and the flames quickly spread despite the rain. The sound set my teeth on edge and goosebumps spread across my body. Sporadic applause trickled across the field. I kept my eyes on the platform, a desire to give the poor vampire a friendly face in the crowd. Her screams died into weak moans that faded as the flames consumed her. As the fire was doused, I blinked back tears, a bitter feeling filling my chest.

This was wrong. They weren't killing cold and emotionless monsters. They were killing people with feelings. Tommy had proven that!

Tommy who loved, laughed and *lived*! He understood what friendship and family meant and had been willing to risk everything for what he believed, for the people he cared about. He'd do anything if he thought it'd make me smile and nothing if he thought it'd upset me. He sacrificed himself because he thought it'd make a difference. In that moment, when he gave in, he was more human than every person gathered in this crowd.

The ashes were cleared away and the crowd resumed their chatter. VF moved across the platform, then disappeared beneath the bleachers again. I felt tears form in my eyes and a sick feeling fill my stomach. There was one other post. One more vampire to be torched. Instead of torching the vampires at once, they were doing it one by one and saving Tommy for last.

Footsteps approached and I knew. This was it, the end.

Mackenzie's dad doubled over as he cried out in pain. He clutched his mouth as we gathered around him. What did the sudden pain mean? Was Tommy being hurt? He was about to be destroyed, wasn't that enough?

"Dad?" Mackenzie's voice trembled.

"I'm all right," he whispered, his already pale face going even whiter. "It just felt like someone yanked on my tooth. Don't worry about it; I'm sure it's nothing."

I wasn't certain who he was trying to assure more: us or him.

I glanced at the platform. VF was back, but instead of tying Tommy to the post, they were hurrying down the steps and pushing through the crowd. They made their way towards us where they grouped around us.

One stepped forward, his voice low. "You need to come with us."

Something in Mackenzie's dad snapped. Maybe it was the torment of the trial and the torching being released at once. Or maybe it was the fact that his twin was going to be killed, the bond between them severed. His head whipped up and anger flared in his eyes. His hands turned into trembling fists. He met the VF officer's eyes and spoke one word that vibrated through the air. "No."

"Sir."

He jerked away from the VF officer, his body joining his shaking fists. "You're not taking the only friendly faces out of this mob. *My brother* needs to know we're here for him. We're not leaving."

The VF officer stepped closer, his voice so low I could barely hear him. "Where is it?"

His face faltered and his anger melted into confusion. "What?"

"Where is it? Where is the vampire?"

He lifted his chin, stepping closer until he was nose to nose with the VF officer. "If I knew anything, I wouldn't tell you."

"Come with us."

Hands grabbed us and VF pulled us through the crowds and towards the platform. Voices whispered and spread like wild fire.

"Did they say a vampire was missing?"

"Did the sympathizers free it?"

"Are we safe?"

Then I saw it.

No, I didn't just see it, I experienced it. I heard it, tasted it, smelled it, felt it. I was no longer being dragged towards the opening under the bleachers. I was somewhere else, someone else...

The smell of burnt flesh saturated the air with its putrid stench. I ran away from the smell, my legs shaking with fatigue. Ahead, a blinding light glowed like a beacon beckoning me. A figure appeared and the light shined like a halo. I forced myself to run faster and slammed into the figure. My teeth sliced through hot flesh and a burst of blood hit my tongue. More warm blood spurted on my face as I pulled away, forcing myself to leave the human behind. The brief taste ignited me, life coursing through me. I bit at the restraints around my wrists. A tooth tore free as well, but my hands were loose. I burst into the light, ignoring the burn of the daytime air. Row upon row of cars spread before me with trees looming in the distance. I raced past the cars, no destination in mind, only following my instincts, my need to survive. At last I broke free of the cars, the edge of the trees in sight. I put everything I had into reaching the trees, letting them swallow me up like fire.

One thought raced through my head. I, Tommy, would be no more.

The vision faded and I knew it was real. I felt it deep in my heart. A smile broke free and I lifted my face, feeling the cold rain pelt my skin. I laughed loudly, unable to stop myself. I laughed at the cold rain and the thick clouds hiding the sun. I laughed at the crowds that wanted Tommy dead and at the world that just saved him. I laughed until my sides ached, unable to contain the joy bursting in me.

"Thank you!" I cried at the sky. "Thank you!"

About the Author:

Patricia Lynne never set out to become a writer, and in fact, was never any good at it during high school and college. But some stories are meant to be told and this one chose her. Patricia lives with her husband in Michigan, hopes one day to have what will resemble a small petting zoo and has a fondness for dying her hair the colors of the rainbow.

Afterword:

Thank you for purchasing this book. If you enjoyed it, please consider leaving a review online.